Go Up, You Baldhead
and other short stories

D

First published in 2025 by

Walk in My Shoes Publications
36 Silverwood Close
Lowestoft
NR33 7LX

All rights reserved
Copyright David Porter 2025

The right of David Porter to be identified as author of this work has been asserted in accordance with Section 77 of the Copyright, Designs and Patents Act 1988

This book is sold subject to the condition that it shall not, by way of trade or otherwise, be lent, resold, hired out or otherwise circulated without the publisher's prior consent in any form of binding or cover other than that in which it is published and without a similar condition including this condition being imposed on the subsequent purchaser.

ISBN: 9780993489884

Also by David Porter:

Old Men's Dreams, a novel (2015)
Walk in My Shoes Publications
ISBN 9780993489808

A Rebel's Journey, my life and times (2017)
Walk in My Shoes Publications
ISBN 9780993489822

Wild Beasts and Plague, short stories (2018)
Walk in My Shoes Publications
ISBN 9780993489839

Scoffers Will Come, short stories (2019)
Walk in My Shoes Publications
ISBN 9780993489846

Detestable Things, a novel (2020)
Walk in My Shoes Publications
ISBN 9780244866228

The Scapegoat Keeper, short stories (2021)
Walk in My Shoes Publications
ISBN 9780993489860

No Lack of Madmen, a novel (2023)
Walk in My Shoes Publications
ISBN 9780993489877

Dedicated to Sarah, our four children and nine grandchildren we know and love.

And to their unborn children and children's children who we cannot know.

Introduction

I have written since I was very young. Stories, diaries, reviews, plays and novels. Communication has been my game all my life, and writing is part of that, big time.

The advent of self-publishing has been a boon to me. I've been able to get out to a fragment of the world three, now four, collections of my short stories and three novels.

I have also been able to publish on *TES Resources* and on *Drama and Theatre* magazine a variety of teaching resources on drama and theatre studies, using material I developed during my time as a drama teacher together with new ideas and guidance.

While I believe I have one more novel in me, I suspect that these short stories will be my last. Short stories are like mini-novels, capturing a mood, a theme, a character in a short time frame that shed some light on how we live and have our beings.

1. **Go Up, You Baldhead**, from the book of *2 Kings 2:33* about a crowd of boys who mocked the prophet Elisha and were punished by being mauled by a pair of she-bears. Written in 2021, inspired by one of my regular local walks to the sea in Pakefield.

2. **Everlasting Chains**, inspired by the trials and tribulations of trying to sell a house and buy another between 2021 and 2023.

3. Gibbering at the Oriel Window, from an idea originally developed as a piece of teenage-devised drama during 2006-7.

4. The Necropolis Gene is a story from the late 1960s, updated several times based on a real person in my own 6th Form at school.

5. The Full Experience, a tale first from the 1980s, then from the Covid pandemic of 2020-21, upgraded in 2022 from the pits of thinking, really.

6. Alexander the Coppersmith, mixing facts with fiction this is a memorial to the Wigg family of Kessingland and Don Rout, artist in Pakefield, revised in 2022.

7. Long Story Short, inspired by events and people late 2021, but not actually true.

8. We Should Have Built An Ark, brought on by incessant promotion of global warming in the 2020-22 period and experience of people never really listening to good advice.

9. Sallumus and Tolbanes, based on an event from the 1980s when I spoke at The Rider Haggard Society dinner in Kessingland which happily didn't end in the chaos of this tale!

10. Seven Henchmen, partly inspired by Prime Minister Boris Johnson and partly by changed versions of my own reality in my past, this piece is from 2022.

11. That Turpentine Tree, a story originally from the 1970s, my performing days, about the action offstage during a performance being more dramatic than what's being staged.

12. Person of Interest, originally from the 1970s, rehashed and updated in 2022 for this collection.

13. Tumbleweed Corner, written in 2023 from an idea originally sketched out in 2005 as a piece of teenage drama.

14. Several Slices of Slime Pie, rewritten in 2024 from a set of seafront ideas variously played with for twenty odd years.

15. Waiting for Idiots, a 2023 story written as I tried to work out how many hours of my life I'd spent waiting for others to arrive, leave, say/do something or just get on with it.

16. Hollow Gurning, a 2005/6 story rewritten in 2023 about a neighbour with a strange hobby, as many people have.

17. Life's a Bleach, from 2020-24, out of some older ideas and stories I gathered over the years. All things must pass. All things will pass.

18. Repairer of Broken Walls, 2010-23, off and on. This was intended as a book about church outreach in Kirkley, so when that was not going to happen, I rewrote it as a story.

19. Unclean Till Evening, an old idea regurgitated in 2023, partly inspired by my mother being in a care home and partly by some surreal thoughts about Artificial Intelligence.

20. Everyone Needs a Cause, written in 2023/24, as an attempt to be a little bit off the wall. More than usually so.

21. Liar Cesspit, 2024 story based on an older idea, probably from the 1990s, though I'm not sure now.

22. A Mere Laughing-Stock, 2024 and earlier, a tale written from the frequently dark sense of growing old and invisible in a world run by a ghastly government I do not understand and who do not care about oldies like me.

23. Three Punishments, from 2020, a story that was to be developed into a drama performance for publication as a scheme of work for teenagers and could still be.

24. Your Speech Shall Whisper, 2023/4, an idea from way back and wanting to write about the Lowestoft-Yarmouth rail line, together with fragments of the sometimes surrealism of generations of humans.

25. Last Man Standing Can't Bury Himself, a tale born in the coronavirus pandemic of 2020-22 and subsequent, inevitable ageing.

Contents

1. *Go Up, You Baldhead,* page 1

2. *Everlasting Chains,* page 16

3. *Gibbering at the Oriel Window,* page 42

4. *The Necropolis Gene,* page 55

5. *The Full Experience,* page 73

6. *Alexander the Coppersmith,* page 90

7. *Long Story Short,* page 127

8. *We Should Have Built An Ark,* page 141

9. *Sallumus and Tolbanes,* page 162

10. *Seven Henchmen,* page 174

11. *That Turpentine Tree,* page 192

12. *Person of Interest,* page 205

13. *Tumbleweed Corner,* page 218

14. *Several Slices of Slime Pie,* page 226

15. *Waiting for Idiots,* page 248

16. *Hollow Gurning,* page 262

17. *Life's a Bleach*, page 274

18. *Repairer of Broken Walls*, page 288

19. *Unclean Till Evening*, page 341

20. *Everyone Needs a Cause*, page 355

21. *Liar Cesspit*, page 364

22. *A Mere Laughing-Stock*, page 376

23. *Three Punishments*, page 389

24. *Your Speech Shall Whisper*, page 407

25. *Last Man Standing Can't Bury Himself*, page 421

1. Go Up, You Baldhead

It was a fair walk for an old man. From his two-bedroom, 1970s home at the top end of Anguish Street to the coast was a good half mile there and back.

But for little, old, bald-headed, stooped Silas Prendergast, with his crippled feet, ponderous gait and unreliable balance, it was a marathon.

Yet, he did it almost daily. Exercise, of course. Fresh air, yes, but when the wind howled, his lungs gulped more than enough of that. He just wanted to spend time with Sally.

An inner drive kept him sharing his thoughts, his plans, his troubles and his increasing aches and pains with her. Of course, she remained silent, completely indifferent to his shivering by her grave staring out across the churchyard to the grey-brown sea.

Occasionally he fancied he heard her passing comment or making that grunt she used when he mouthed bollocks. Or he saw that shrug she gave when he was determined to do something his way.

He never carried fresh flowers. No point, the neighbourhood kids loved scattering floral tributes to the wind. He carried a trowel in his shabby coat pocket to clear away the weeds encroaching on the resting place where his wife of over forty years lay.

1

A rickety, peeling varnish garden bench against the scrubby hedge afforded him a perch to enjoy some peace and quiet and absorb the sense of people lying alongside Sally. And those who'd lived in the houses he passed.

The familiar dwellings nearest to his home, at the 'modern' end of Anguish Street put up in the uniformity of the late 1970s, occasionally revealed a glimpse of events that had happened long before they were built.

In Number 29 he saw a dog beaten to death and nobody caring. Neighbours had complained so much about its whining that the owner had simply silenced the creature to get them off his back.

Once Silas crossed over the intersection with England's Lane he was in the older, mixed housing of the bottom of Anguish Street. Here he alternated walking down the odd and even sides, picking up the experiences, dreams and nightmares stored in the walls, soil and surrounding air.

He admired the traditional lines of Number 11 where an old soldier known only as Mr S had lived in his decaying house till he passed away watching the battle of Anguish Street, several years back now.

Billy Butcher, a mid-life-crisis biker in Number 16, had fallen foul of a hell's angel type gang from Norwich who'd come to wreak the wrath of God on everyone in the area.

People still spoke of it, but Silas got the full picture from his voices and visions as he passed.

Number 7 housed a young woman, Sarah Price, all sweetness on the outside but a killer within. She lived with the wife of the late Gerry Fletcher who'd disappeared after the battle.

Silas sensed Gerry was buried under the rockery. He'd been a hit-man, Silas was convinced. Something had hit him alright and the girl, probably related to him, and his wife had buried the secret.

Number 6 was one to be avoided, even with a covert glance. There resided one of the most miserable, angry old curmudgeons known to the human race, Ron Cody. Hating everyone, he shouted abuse and prejudice as often as he could get away with it. A regular on the police visiting list, he took pride in breaching hate laws. It was hard not to these days.

The bottom of Anguish led into Beach Avenue, a wider mix of mid to late 20th Century housing, with one old house that went back to the early 1800s. Every dwelling whispered to Silas. Women, children, girls, boys, men and animals locked in the eternal circles of their lives as they survived for a time, now poured out to passers-by who understood.

The only unsolved murder was of Gerry Fletcher. Silas saw adulteries, betrayals, robberies, lies and deceits galore. Many families existed in grinding poverty; several suffering injustices that were never put right.

He knew of good, honest men and women who did the right things for their times. And he watched the sorry mess of flawed human beings covering up their sins, being found out and dying in a wide mangle of states of distress.

Occasionally he wondered how people today could live in places which had seen such tragedy, but few had his gifts. To only a tiny minority are given insights into past lives and places.

Church Loke was the final leg of his walk, off Beach Avenue and down towards the sea. One side was the church graveyard that had escaped the floods of 1953, though the east part of the burial grounds hadn't. Bones and coffin bits had been seen floating as the surge tide of that January storm washed away most of what it encountered.

Today people stood on top of the sand cliff and looked at the curve left by the sea, the beach now dotted with marram grass clumps and the actual shore some way out. He'd heard that a builder proposed erecting luxury houses on the beach, totally without acknowledging the flood damage before he was born.

Opposite the little loke which used to run a quarter of a mile further to the east to what was then the actual beach, sat a line of tiny fishermen's cottages, most modernised and prettified. No-one from the 1700s would recognise them now. A couple were holiday homes; one was a guest house for gawping tourists to rent by the week.

In the rest, just clinging to life, existed an assortment of the old, dotty, neglected, ancient crones that modern life had passed by. While they awaited the grim reaper's knock at the door, they stared out at the graves, lost in old memories distorted by the passage of decades.

If Silas saw one or two living denizens out, he stopped for a word. Others he waved at though windows, conscious of hundreds who'd looked out of those windows in past times.

Walking slowly, awkwardly on his poor feet and weak legs, he navigated with pain and clumsiness the potholes, dents and misaligned paving. A frayed balaclava in winter covered his totally hairless skull that was always looking down for dangers, rarely up and ahead.

Even on strong windy days, Silas frequently heard footsteps behind him. Perhaps ten yards or so. They stopped when he turned to look behind. Some invisible phantom was playing Giant's Footsteps with him. Yet there was never any sight of another person there, living or departed.

In the past year or so he heard the footsteps of many feet from people who delighted themselves when he turned to look. They weren't ghosts; these were real, living kids, aged from about 15 down to six or seven, he guessed.

There were hundreds of them, almost always. Silas had counted them. They were local kids who'd torment the old, crippled baldhead. They appeared behind him or occasionally leapt out of an alley or a bushed garden on his route, shrieking banshee noises.

Why didn't their parents stop it? Did the parents even know? Hadn't the morons got anything more interesting to do, such as school homework or reading a good book? He recognised a couple of them, knew their parents and in one case, knew the ruffian's grandparents.

Unless the weather was extremely harsh, they'd be out most mornings at weekends and school holidays. Presumably they'd been chucked out of their homes to get air and healthy exercise and told not come home till dark or feeding time.

During terms, they were in their schools tormenting their teachers or each other. Silas heard and saw more in the houses he passed on those days. There'd been a car-bicycle accident in 1969 on the corner of Church Loke and Beach Avenue. Silas regularly watched it happen, unable to stop it or blot out the wails of the parents of the little boy dying in the gutter.

As often as not he was alone in the graveyard. More recent additions were often attended by relatives but after a decade he noticed people stopped coming; the headstones leaned a bit; the weeds took over.

There was one other regular. Retired vicar the Reverend Paul Samson would often be found mooching about, looking for the perfect spot for his own eternal resting place.

'Good morning, Mr Prendergast, Silas.'

'And a good morning to you, Reverend Samson, Paul.'

They'd exchange a few words about the weather, the time of year, their common aches and pains, the deplorable state of the churchyard and the mad clappy ideas the new vicar had imported while chucking out the traditional wooden pews to allow the 'creative Spirit to have free rein'.

Throughout his living at the church, old Samson had polished an enviable reputation as an English eccentric crank. He'd almost dined out on it.

Silas might share some titbit he'd picked up from passing one or two houses recently, as if the information was readily available. Certainly, the old vicar was knowledgeable about local history and recalled people and events with a batty logic that was lost on others, except Silas.

The old man would invariably leave Silas with a Bible quote, though lately Silas suspected they were from the pen of Shakespeare or Stephen Sondheim. Samson often swam in the waters of the Old Testament prophets, delighting in telling his listener all the sordid plagues on Egypt; he had a predilection for Jeremiah.

One day, Samson stood watching Silas hurrying as fast as his little legs would allow, his stick clumping angrily, ignoring the jaunts of the large crowd of youth up to no good. They greeted each other and Silas turned to see them sloping away, unwilling for some reason to mock the clergyman.

'My dear old fellow,' Samson said, taking him by the arm and leading him to the bench. 'An unpleasant experience. God sends his trials in many forms. I myself have been losing five-pound notes and finding penny pieces for some time now.'

'These kids, I don't know.'

'Well, I'm reminded of the book of *Kings, 2 Kings*, in fact. Chapter Two. Verse 33. '... and while he, Elisha, was on his way to Bethel, some small boys came out of the city and jeered at him saying, 'Go up, you baldhead! Go up, you baldhead!'

Silas looked closely at the man. Had he slipped off the edge, finally?

'Oh, I'm sorry, Silas, I meant no disrespect to your lack of hair. Mine is all too bush-like. Bats could nest in mine and I wouldn't know it.'

'Well, what happened to the boys?'

'He turned round and ... cursed them in the name of the Lord. And two she-bears came out of the woods and tore forty-two of them. There is no later mention, so we can assume they caused no further trouble.'

Silas nodded thoughtfully. 'What a good idea, a bloody good, brain busting, revenge is sweet, vengeance-is-mine-sayeth-the-Lord-idea. A stonker.'

'No, Silas, we can't have she-bears coming out of the woods and tearing up forty-two of our precious youth, now can we? There'd be a big fuss nowadays.'

They discussed it in the round as an idea, like someone might ponder how to get away with a perfect crime. She-bears? Where from? What about the noise from 42 kids being mauled? The blood? The shrieking terror? The police? The media? The health and safety issues?

The next day was a Sunday, but Silas had no trouble with his gang. Indeed, he noticed three emerging with their responsible adults looking smug and holy from the happy-clappy singalong that had replaced Sunday Morning Worship with Holy Communion and the Book of Common Prayer.

Silas enjoyed peaceful walks and fresh visions about some of the houses for five days before school ended for the autumn half term. It was a crisp, fresh morning, the sort that sees little kids relieved of their gloves, coats and phones by bigger specimens.

They heard their old victim approaching as he clumped into Church Loke. They circled him, moving with him, a seething mass of rats in a plague, almost tripping him, trying to take his stick away and slapping his bald head as he wasn't yet wearing his winter hat.

Each loud slap was rewarded with a chorus of cheers and jeers and a desire in each kid to be the next one to do better on the hapless man's pate. Silas heard their horrible adolescent voices – the oldest kid was just able to grow a straggly beard, the youngest was still in nappies – as the sound morphed into a chant.

'Go up, you baldhead! Go up, you baldhead! Go up, you baldhead!'

He didn't have to call up the pair of she-bears for they flew out of the tiny gap between cottages 17 and 19 opposite the churchyard, where a girl had been attacked by her brother in 1809 and sent away in disgrace as if she'd impregnated herself.

Music to his ears were their screams as they dashed all ways trying to escape the claws and jaws of the massive, pungent-breathed bears while they struck, slashed and threw the kids aside.

Not slowing to look, not helping anyone at all, Silas progressed to his wife's grave to tell her all about it. He looked around for his old vicar friend, but he was elsewhere. Nobody looked out of the cottage windows; there were no casual dog walkers in the vicinity.

The day was one of the most enjoyable he could remember on his walk. His return down the Loke involved carefully stepping over severed limbs, tattered clothing and heavy slicks of congealing blood.

He just knew there'd be no more trouble.

Sure enough, the next morning he encountered police tape across the Loke, officers and journalists going door to door hunting for locals to get a handle on what had happened to some of 'the most vulnerable and innocent young people in our society', as he heard one woman breathing down a hand-held microphone, fluttering into a camera.

When he was asked a million questions, he replied in gibberish, which was duly recorded and noted down and confirmed outsiders' views about the mental health of the entire community.

After several weeks, things quietened. Silas revelled in his walks without being accosted or followed. No marauding savages behind, around and in front. Visions and voices returned from many of the houses he passed. Footsteps sometimes followed him.

But there was never anybody there.

The only painful part was where the kids had been set upon by the bears. He replayed the scene over and over. No way free of it. All he could do was accept that the baldhead had been taken care of by a higher power.

He still couldn't help turning to see who was behind him when he heard footsteps. On this one day, his last on earth, he turned as usual to see nobody behind.

So, he turned to face front and noticed that he was walking silently a few steps behind a totally bald, little hunched old man with a stick who kept looking round at him but never saw him.

2. Everlasting Chains

People are regularly defined by their outward appearances. It's unfortunate, but there it is, thought Peeps. He'd made a note of this in his diary the other day. Take the pregnant woman or the black or Asian person who feeds on anger from the past when white people imperially ran his ancestors' world.

In fact, to go further, people rarely escape those everlasting chains that hold them to the past while struggling to prepare in the present for the future approaching with break-neck speed.

And to go even further, some people behave all along as if they are stuffed dummies, conforming to their own stereotypes without fail.

There seems to be not only a clock in everyone's head, but also an instruction manual. It tells us how to behave, even if it means to rebel or refuse to conform. And the members of the Lowerswamp Investment Club happily conformed to their stereotypes.

Peeps was a bit of a philosopher. So, of course, he didn't conform. He heard nothing back from his sweet lady wife as he called out to tell her he was off. His thoughts soon returned to this philosopher business as he made a right out of his gate to trudge through the village to The Bird in the Hand, the only local for miles around.

From the corner of his eye, he noticed at the Drage household almost opposite the flick of a curtain, a face moved away quickly.

Damn. Simon Drage. He'd applied last autumn to be a member, and it was now the March meeting. But Peeps was going to keep the man out as long as possible. Nobody would wear Peeps down. Over his dead body, and all that. He didn't want Drage at any price.

The man would probably have been an asset, but when Peep's daughters were little, they called Drage 'The Murderer' as he always walked out for an hour every evening and came back 'when he'd murdered somebody.' The girls never took hold of the fact that he walked a pair of tall dogs and there were no reports of murders locally.

No, it wasn't that. He was hardly going to form his views based on the opinions of two small children a decade or more ago. Peeps just didn't like the man's stooped tallness and lankiness, his spiky and lumpy skull, his staring eyes and his air of determination to stay fit despite advancing years.

For his part, Peeps embraced necessary exercise but never overdid it. He nursed a heart murmur so had to be careful. That's why he didn't take too much nonsense from people standing in his way. Especially as his way was invariably reasonable, sensible and logical.

He couldn't shake Drage from his head. Richard was in favour of Drage. But then, Richard would be. He'd probably be in favour of giving Hitler a second chance to behave. Richard refused to answer to Dick, though that would have suited him better. He was a former car salesman and lifelong student of the Bible. No meeting was complete without some quote accompanied by a mini sermon.

Besides Richard, there was his old dog. It was some sort of Labrador-collie cross Richard had picked up when helping a homeless man relocate from the street to a hostel. Why he had to bring it out every time remained a mystery. But then, God works in mysterious ways His miracles to perform.

And that was another line Peeps'd written in his diary, commenting on his fellow men and women. That's what diarists do. They observe; they comment. And they must be monumentally calm, patient and lucid to pull it off. Peeps knew he enjoyed those benefits in spades.

The canine lay at their feet, close to the hearth in winter and the door in summer. Panting; slurping water from an old metal cooking dish. Then suddenly, one month, Richard came without it and everyone knew it was gone. Just as old Percy or High Water would be gone soon enough.

But then, to confound and annoy Peeps, old Percy and High Water remained in their mortal coils, while so many others had passed on from the village and nearby communities. Meetings where they stood in silence for a few moments increased as ever more acquaintances called it a day.

He didn't think they'd be standing this month. No deaths reported; nobody murdered by old Drage.

Having smiled at that, Peeps forgot the man and his tiresome application.

Club members greeted each other, carrying their first drinks to their places at the reserved table in front of quaint windows, as yet uncurtained since the nights were pulling out nicely.

Peeps was a natural chair; the sort of guy juries chose to be their spokesperson. A crowd needing leading out of a burning building would look to Peeps for guidance and direction. He'd spent a career in the probation service, so he knew a thing or two about people, did old Peeps.

To Peeps' left always sat Roger Fry, invariably known as Small. He'd worked in house building and repairs with his company never more than two men and an apprentice. His inclination was always to invest in construction. A wiry little bugger, Small was of a fixed view on almost everything from the sort of loaf he ate to the way he kept his house in order. Peeps respected that.

Peeps was good with Small. He'd put some work his way over the years and the man was never any trouble in meetings or around the village. He provided stalls, benches and seating for every village function throughout the year. Peeps had often recorded the man's generosity and support to him in meetings when needed.

Kevin Sheldrake, a retired insurance expert was a musical theatre and poetry buff, called Percy after Shelley, who would, when in the right mood, spout long passages from obscure poems or mini operas he thought appropriate. He always sat last and would float about greeting people in the bar and elsewhere to the last minute before Peeps called the meeting to order.

As camp as a row of tents and happily so, Percy and his partner shared a ramshackle cottage that had not only seen better days but had hosted extraordinary crimes in times gone by: murder, immolation and unlawful burial of the dead, among others. Everybody was 'darling' and Percy cheered most wakes up with his absurd King's jester approach to life.

Peter Gates, a former financial wizard, was called Pearly, naturally, which some people thought was on account of his brilliant white teeth installed at great expense necessitating almost as much detail in recounting as Peeps' house buying/selling chains.

Pearly had been the group treasurer for decades, taking the job on at each annual meeting with the resignation of a man walking to the guillotine but showing stubborn unwillingness to relinquish it if anyone suggested he was getting past it.

Meticulous in his book-keeping and company research, he printed reams of information every month about stock prices, assets/liabilities, debt ratios and all they needed to decide whether to invest or disinvest. Sometimes Peeps just wanted to strangle the man; he was that pernickety.

The group's only surviving woman was High Water, Helen Birch, happy to designate herself an honorary man rejoicing in her label from 'Hell and

High Water', a yacht she'd once owned. She'd been a teacher and deputy Head in her day and still used her 'look' to bring naughty boys to order round the table.

Somewhere she'd lost a husband who'd finally had enough of the 'look' and made his escape one summer holiday when they drove in two cars back from a camping fortnight in Devon. She had the kids in one car; he carried the tents, luggage, food and all the toys in the other.

He just never returned home and, in the days before surveillance cameras were everywhere, police were unable to find him or the car. Ever.

Last Rites was invariably too ill, old, senile or full-scale barking to remember the dates of meetings much less get up, dress and attend one. He assumed he was still known as Off-Colour, his handle when he first started feeling under the weather.

He'd been some sort of civil servant and enjoyed a parsimonious lifestyle on a decent pension. He was paying 24-hour carers to his house in preference to paying 24-hour carers in some geriatric home.

And there was Samuel, of course. He kept copious diary notes on everybody, everything and every thought and had done since he was 15 years old. His name was actually run of the mill Michael, but the group preferred Samuel Pepys, the diarist. So he was Peeps or Samuel, the only member to enjoy two affectionate nicknames.

And Peeps, alone among the whole club, enjoyed the care and love of his enchanting wife of well over 40 years, the blessed Angela, his angel on high, who never criticised him or his ways, who understood exactly how he ticked.

This particular first Thursday evening in the month, he held forth on chains, everlasting chains of the selling and buying houses kind. 'Couple A bid for my house higher that Couple B which my long-suffering wife and I turned down. We found a house we liked that was barely downsizing, and outbid Couple B for it. Then Couple A pulled out of their purchase because they'd been let down by Couple C.'

Heads were nodding, eyes glazing, but Peeps pressed on. 'That meant they had to withdraw from their purchase and Couple D lost a house they'd bid on and been accepted for. We all returned to market simultaneously. They sold to Couple E who'd previously looked round ours. They changed their minds and came back to bid only to be pipped at the post by Couple F from 100 miles away, who had two houses to sell but were really keen.'

Peeps and his dear, patient missus liked Couple B's place so offered on it, only to find they'd upped their price and were not interested in Peeps as buyers. This was the climax of what had become a very long tale. But he couldn't settle to serious club business till he'd told it.

Richard felt it necessary to point him in the direction of *Jude 1:6* for reasons of his own.

'We are angels who did not keep to our proper domain. We abandoned our authorised dwelling place and have lived in everlasting chains, waiting. Waiting for that great day of judgement, of course.'

Trying to sell their grand five-bedroom executive house in a desirable village location and achieving enough to buy a reasonably modern two-bedroom executive bungalow in this or another acceptable area, was judgement already, Peeps thought.

It gave him fresh impetus to go off again about the injustices they'd suffered, the sheer hell when the chain broke or suddenly had more links added as people tried to shift their lives around.

'People are always marrying, having children, changing jobs, downsizing, upsizing. Or dying. So, the market for houses is almost always buoyant. Especially with a limited stock of houses and land available. So, it shouldn't be too difficult to sell and buy.'

Peeps warmed anew to his theme, now an expert in housing, a full-on victim of the plotting of others against him, unaware that last meeting he'd lectured High Water and Richard on using up rare stocks of his patience on some trivial tales of their own life travails.

What made Peeps spit teeth was why in a chain, as he repeated for clarity, people suddenly remembered they had two houses to sell or wanted to move an elderly relative in with them. Why didn't they think hard before their cold feet set in?

'Everlasting chains are constantly breaking and it isn't good enough.'

A few minutes later, the meeting under way, Peeps opened his phone surreptitiously in response to a ping and glanced at an email from Richard listing the slightly different variations of the wording of *Jude 1:6* from twenty or more Bible versions. Peeps assumed Richard had thought that would help somehow.

Versions included *New International, New Living Translation, English Standard* and *American Standards, Berean Study* and *Berean Literal Bibles, King James* and *The New King James, New American Standard, NASB 1977* and *1995, Amplified, Christian Standard, Holman Standard, Aramaic in Plain English, Contemporary English, Douay-Rheims, Good News Translation, International Standard* and *New Revised Standard, The NET, New Revised Standard, New Heart English, The Weymouth New Testament, World English* and *Young's Literal!*

Richard also recommended a Jewish edition he rated as 'thrilling.' Wading through that menu, Peeps felt like ordering the full English breakfast and seeing what came up. Nonetheless, politeness being one of many of the old school, gentlemanly traits of the Lowerswamp community in general, the investment club in particular, he thanked Richard and pocketed his phone.

The Club dated from back in the day when a few like-minded village folks of at least two years standing living in the curtilage of the ancient parish of

Lowerswamp, got together to launch a club initially to raise funds to renovate the village hall. Since then they'd paid for a new, large bus shelter, finished just as Lowerswamp lost its bus services.

The costs of a high-speed dedicated internet had also been covered by their judicious investing. Small regular payments were made to the local poor and needy - those decisions were delegated to a committee comprising Richard, Small and High Water, chaired by Pearly. Peeps had little time to waste on minute, faffing details.

How the mighty had fallen, Peeps looked around at the pathetic little group around him. For tonight's diary he planned: 'when we started, we hired the function room upstairs and almost filled it with 80 odd people. Now we've shrunk to this modest table in the corner of the public bar.'

He'd long thought they should rename themselves, The Grim Reaper Survival Club. So many had died off (five from Covid alone, two from cancer and one cardiac arrest when the ambulance couldn't find the house), moved away or become too far gone to cope with buying and selling shares or investing in projects. His remarkable spouse hadn't liked it.

He sometimes felt he was approaching that stage himself. Oh, those early days! They were all younger, of course, more energetic and comfortably enough placed to be able to pay the arrival fee of £1000 plus £750 a year to join the monthly meetings and watch profits doing good in the community.

They'd made a killing when big state companies were privatised; they did well from de-mutualising building societies. Less successful were some of their US, Japan and Indian equity purchases. However, the club kept a healthy bank balance of nearly fifty thousand pounds plus assets worth close to half a million.

At Peeps' insistence they'd invested in an embalming company that was promoting DIY embalming for financially hard-pressed families. The company sold fluid and instructions for animals and people. Strange how popular immortalising the dead had become, even if they still ended up buried.

Everyone knew Peeps was in favour – he'd been on about it for months. What they didn't know was that he'd started an online embalming-taxidermy course and was practising on as many wildlife as he could find or trap.

Ethical, socially responsible and environmental investments accounted for at least 50% of their assets. Pushed by Richard years back in the teeth of Peeps bored out of his skull by the justifications and arguments, this focus now reaped excellent returns from wind farms, recycling and alternative energy strategies.

Their rule book laid down a strict two drink policy from the outset. The treasurer pulled out enough cash to pay for everyone present to enjoy a drink followed by a second one, all covered by their fees. Any spare cash left over was re-deposited in their bank, scrupulously and rapidly. At least everybody trusted Pearly to do that small thing, though a visit to the bank was eleven miles drive each way.

This month it was Small's turn to elbow a way to the bar to order their second round of drinks. Naomi, the landlord's fluffy barmaid, had already poured and loaded them onto a large, curved metal tray. When she saw Small a little shaky in picking up the tray, she came round the bar and carried it for him, to a round of friendly banter about poor old Small being rather weak and frail.

As he waited for Naomi to go ahead of him, he spotted Simon Drage, that applicant loitering hopefully in the corner of the bar that turned at a right angel to the main stretch. He was waiting for them to consider his application to join them and now they were already on the second round.

So poor old Drage would be postponed yet again. 'Good evening,' Small smiled with a cheery wave as he moved away before Drage could ask him how it was all going. Drage sipped his glass, already empty but for a few bitter dregs in the bottom.

Simon Drage, former maths teacher, knew and talked knowledgeably about algorithms, irrational numbers, string theory and probabilities of guessing the stock market. In many ways he'd be ideal for the club. He'd been nominated by no less a worthy than Last Rites himself before he was too ill to care.

But Peeps was against him and what Peeps didn't want almost always never happened.

Drage's application was held over again. Buying and selling was agreed. Meeting's end was reached, confirmed by their second round of drinks being drained. These days, sessions always concluded, once broad agreement was reached on their stocks, with a light-hearted game of some sort.

Often a member would steal a word or association game from a newspaper or TV show. Occasionally they'd try a short quiz or medium-hard crossword, show card tricks or a play a single round of *Runs and Prials* or *Rummy*, as their numbers declined.

A game of darts had been disastrous with High Water needing first aid while a game of skittles caused a row that took three months to clear.

Two years ago Percy had brought in a 500-piece jigsaw to be completed in 19 minutes, Several cardboard pieces mopped up beer from the table and Last Rite's fingers had deteriorated so much, they sent half of it to the floor.

Peeps made a mental note to record in his diary that he expected Richard to turn up one month with a quiz asking everyone to list as many versions of the Bible as they could in 20 seconds.

While they had no real point, those games, they convinced some they'd had a good evening out in convivial company when decisions on investing in a favourite start-up had not gone their way. A little brain exercise before scurrying to their beds was good for everybody.

Catching sight of Drage moving down the bar nearer their table, even able to catch a word or two in the lulls in bar noises, Peeps was irritated. No, it was more than that. He was genuinely annoyed at the man's lack of manners and consideration. If they didn't want to consider his application, they just wouldn't.

Also, Peeps had a new game to introduce, one of his own devising. He and his dear, dear wife had already enjoyed hours of harmless fun while he explained it to her and she attempted to play it by his constantly evolving rules.

'Now then, gentlemen,' with a nod to High Water, 'You've all heard of *Pascal's Wager,* of course.'

Nobody had. '*Pascal's Wager* is the name given to an argument credited to Blaise Pascal in the 17th century for believing, or for at least taking steps to believe, in God. So, in turn we each must make up a truism, a formula or some such, and a very short explanatory clause with it.'

They looked around. Perhaps it would become clearer. Pearly said, 'I'm familiar with the concept. *Pascal's Wager* includes elements of **game theory** to show that **belief in the Christian religion** is rational. He argued that people can choose to believe in God or can choose to not believe in God, and that God either exists or he does not.'

'Of course He exists,' mouthed Richard, getting very excited.

'No, we're not treading into religion or politics, against the rules,' Peeps stated.

'This is just up old Drage's street,' High Water offered. She'd seconded Drage's application to join.

Further irritated, Peeps attempted to push on. 'So, if someone said, *Pascal's Wager,* an argument for belief in God and is not challenged, is not a repetition, is not offensive and is a first response and finally, is accepted by the Arbiter. Me. If it is, we move to the next player.'

'But what about if we don't know any mathematicians or philosophers?' Small wondered, while thinking perhaps Peeps shouldn't be judge *and* jury.

'We make them up! That's the whole point of the game,' Peeps reinforced his comment with thumps on the table as if everyone was an imbecile.

'I get it. *Ockham's Razor,* more assumptions, the less likely the truth.'

Nobody spoke. It was Drage who'd just called out from the bar. What a bloody cheek! Peeps seethed silently that he'd suggested a game that bloody Drage was good at.

Again, Drage spoke. 'There is also *Pascal's Triangle,* isn't there? Used to calculate probabilities, as you know.'

Drage took the liberty of coming closer to the table, to reduce the bar noises. 'In fact, *Ockham's*

Razor is the idea that, in trying to understand something, getting unnecessary information out of the way is the fastest way to the truth or to the best explanation.'

This was met with general approval from all, except Peeps, who gave him a curled lip and cold look followed by open-mouthed disbelief as the outsider had the effrontery to sit in the chair kept empty for Last Rites.

Pearly said, 'What about *Fermat's Theorem*? I studied it at university when being at university meant something. Fermat's last theorem, as I recall, states that no three positive integers, say, x, y, and z will satisfy the equation xn + yn = zn for any integer value of n greater than 2. Since ancient times, the equation for n=1 and n=2 has been well-known to hold infinitely many solutions.'

While blank faces stared back, Drage nodded warmly. 'I think that's spot on. The solution has been lost and over the years, people have claimed to have provided the proof. Sometimes, this theorem is also known as *Fermat's Conjecture.*'

Peeps spat out through gritted teeth, 'well, they don't have to be about mathematics or they must be made up names with a describer. Let all you creatives have a go.'

Somebody invited Drage to sit and join them, and Peeps distinctly heard the man ask if anybody would like another drink? He stood, poised to buy any requested, breaking the two-drink rule and making a complete charlie of Peeps, Peeps felt.

While Drage went to fill a tray with more drinks – only Peeps declined the offer – High water waded in, 'I'll go first. How about *Bison's Epitaph*, he grazed the fields of paradise lost?'

After several moments of thought, this received general approval. Richard, all smiles, beamed as Drage returned having ordered, 'You'll fit in here no problem, Simon Drage.'

Peeps replied, 'There has to be proper consideration and votes, first. Richard, you can't just say he's in. We ran out of time tonight ...'

'No, we didn't. The meeting is still in session,' Richard argued. Most seemed to agree with him. Peeps stood, 'I'll go next. Try, *Richard's Testament*, a version for tomorrow.'

While nobody could get the gist of that one, Richard was clearly upset, hurt even, and started to pack up his papers, to leave. Only the arrival of his third pint of Poacher's Rancid Blister of the evening kept him in his place.

Sensing an unpleasantness without understanding why, Small offered, '*Lepper's Hypothesis*, a broken pendulum is still a pendulum. Lepper, famous German grandfather clockmaker.'

Once it had sunk in, the company liked it. 'You shouldn't have to explain the obvious, it should be self-evident,' Peeps grumbled, petulantly.

Naomi arrived with the new drinks. Drage, gulping his beer as soon as it was in his hand, paused and suggested, '*Headroom's Intrusions*, Max Headroom on speed.'

Again, he secured general approbation for his cleverness and relevance, winning more friends. Peeps, with no idea who Max Headroom was, decided to stay silent – his evening was ruined anyway.

Then ideas flowed thick and fast, with Drage contributing most.

'*Several's Quantum*, one tiny leap for mankind.'

'*Brandon's Anomaly*, straight to the curved point.'

'*Urquart's Paradigm*, the uncopiable virtue.'

'*Glaston's Code*, unfathomable secrecy and deceit.'

'*Sarcophagi's Crypt*, underground, skeletal and quiet.'

'*Young's Game*, entertaining activity competition.'

As the game went on it picked up pace and became ever more distant form the land of common sense and rationality.

'*Pryke's Voyage*, a narrative yet to be explored.'

'*Bonnard's Skeleton*, held together by sinews.'

'*Smedley's Error*, one figure out and not to be confused with *Cornard's Fallacy*, full of mistakes.' This from Drage who was increasingly enjoying the camaraderie and acceptance.

'*Henderson' Formula*, a recipe for disaster if ever there was one.'

'*Sonderheim's Coincidence*, twin unexplained appearances.'

'*Apostles' Principle*, a firm rock on which to foundation a house.' Now even Richard was drawn into the game.

'*Law's Law*, a solicitor called Law lays down his own rules.'

'*Goodwill's Rationale*, a belief in something honest against all odds.'

'*Xenjing's Tangent*, going off on one to the side.'

'*Candalopoudis' Orbit*, staying on a circular track.'

When High Water and Percy began to show the folly of having that third drink, Peeps called time on his game and on the meeting before a vote could be forced on Drage's dream of joining them. 'April next agenda, items to Small, please, and it's Pearly's turn to get in the second round. Goodnight.'

He left as quickly as the crowded bar allowed. Striding home, he kicked leaves the spring wind had gathered against the pointless bus shelter and stumped indoors to persuade his sainted wife that they should drop the price on their house. They needed to move out of the village as soon as humanly possible, everlasting chains permitting.

Exactly as he'd left her, the serene Angela was slumped in front of the telly watching a rerun of *Midsomer Murders*. How very fitting, Peeps concluded, sinking next to her on the settee. He carefully adjusted her arm that had slipped a little and tucked in the blanket round her knees. She certainly felt the cold these days.

As he watched, he wondered which of the 300 plus grisly murders, dispatchings and suicides the series had shown over the decades he could copy and whether that would make a quiz one night.

Or if Simon Drage could be the next victim with Richard as the certain, cut and dried chief suspect.

What would his long-suffering wife have to say about that, if she could speak?

3. Gibbering at the Oriel Window

Good evening, and welcome. All you ladies, gentleman and non-identified others, as we have to say nowadays, welcome, all.

I've no idea if it's really evening or Friday, but people don't listen. They just want to get on with the tour.

Now, you may be potential buyers of this fine building, albeit one crying out for some updating and renovation. Or you're inspectors. Welcome, nonetheless. I have a feeling that last time we failed the test, whatever it was. Special measures, ever since, I do believe.

No matter. No brain refused here.

Or maybe you're among the curious, that tribe of people who must nose around what others are doing, thinking or eating. Maybe you're no more than that. You've heard noises. You've seen me gibbering at the oriel window twice a month, as in the Oscar Wilde story.

Oscar? A fine writer. Sad man, but extremely funny. They tell me humour is one of the best virtues a person possesses. I'll take their word for that. There's no choice for me.

So, whatever your motive for turning up today, if you'd like to follow me, try to keep together. Hey, we don't want anyone lost or with their legs caught in one of the spring bear traps we've strategically installed. These devices close themselves slowly, biting through whatever they've grabbed. Ho! Ho! Ho!

Now, mind how you go here! Step this way, please! Be careful to step over the Putrefaction. Anyone with club feet can come round this side. That's it! Now, we've left the Putrefaction behind. That's the hard part done; few get past the Putrefaction.

Here, as we go, please keep up and listen. This is a guided tour of suffering. A tour of the asylum, but I'm not sure if that's too fancy a word for this institution. Didn't someone say something witty once about marriage? Marriage is a fine asylum, but who wants to live in an asylum?

Perhaps it was our old mate, Oscar, again. Who knows?

To your left, no, no, your left. Alright, have it your way. To your right, there is a dark, tiny room. In it sits Sam, a person.

I hesitate to call Sam a male person, a Jew, a person of colour, non-white, of fluid gender traits, a migrant to these shores, an enemy or you. Yes, you, old chum. I hesitate to call Sam, you, though Sam is universal.

Sam will now stand, letting the ancient Merlin gown somebody left lying around for Sam to steal to flap around. It sports stars and other-worldly symbols. It means only that Sam will be warm at night. It gets sub-arctic in here some nights.

No, Sam, stop being silly behind that hanging carpet and come out and entertain us. Tell us about your dreams. The latest one. What did you dream last night?

Sam speaks after a pause to gather thoughts or ensure a more attentive audience. 'I had a nightmare. I was being chased, slipping and sliding down rock faces, an indeterminate black cloud inches behind me. I couldn't scream as my throat was being used by somebody who arrived before me, No, it was a nightmare.'

And what woke you?

'Fear, I suppose. I silent-screamed myself awake and found …'

Yes, Sam, what did you find when you woke from your nightmare?

Sam, looking at the filthy ground, says 'I dreamed I was in an even worse nightmare.'

So, as you can see, Sam is not responding well to treatment. Sam is scum. Sam is starving. Sam is afraid. Sam is unheard and unrepresented.

No, ladies and gentlemen, please don't look away. Oh, OK, as you like. Just dog-waddle on to the next display. Your choice, after all. Sorry Sam. Next time. Night, night Sam. Sweet dreams.

Down here. Steps. Some are uneven. Oh, you've discovered that. People with club feet can slide down this rail. That's the ticket. Now, here we have a room, or sometimes it's a suite of rooms. Let's become acquainted with Zoll, neither man nor beast, neither female nor neutral. Just something. Not unlike Sam, yet nothing the same.

Zoll dreams much, the dream merchant, dream pedlar, the dreamscape artist of all. And the hilarious thing is, it's never any good. Hey, you, stop doing that against the wall and turn to Zoll and listen.

Zoll replies, in a borrowed voice – they may be hired on entry – and informs the crowd, 'I dreamed of being chased by something I couldn't see, taste or smell, but it breathed close behind the back of my neck. It came round the front and seized me by the easy part of my throat.'

'And it strangled me, choked me, shook the life out of me. Well, it would have done. If I hadn't woken up.'

You see how close to Sam is Zoll? And what did you wake up to, dear Zoll?

'I woke up from being strangled to find I was being strangled.'

Enough, I cry, enough. Let's go. Now! I shall shepherd my party into a reasonable line and stalk ahead of them as they shuffle. Well, it does get quite gloomy in these parts of the house. We have a few minutes, so as we meander, let me explain that when I said I gibbered at the oriel window, I meant just that.

I gibber. Demonstration follows. I gibber till snot flies from my nose and drool escapes from the corner of my mouth. My eyes swivel!

Oriel windows like this one, open on rusty metal hinges and anyone outside can get the full sense of me and what I'm on about. Every home should have one. Oh, it does.

We're in a hospital ward, of sorts. Not that you'd want to be ill here. This is no place to arrive sick; it'll make you sick enough. Now here, folks, in this particular, angled bed lies young Jik. I say young which may startle you.

Jik has the body of an eighty-year-old. Jik has club feet, yes, but that's not proof of youth. Jik is in fact a teenager. Let Jik gasp at you in his, her, its own words, if any can be spared.

'I'm Jik and I'm fifteen years old. I live with my mum and stepdad on the estate over there. I would point it out, but my arms are strapped to the bed, as you see. That's in case I fall out of bed.'

'The trouble is that when I arrived here, I was tired having got up as early as noon, and I succumbed to a nap. 40 winks, a brief shutting of my eyes. I dreamed.'

Ah, yes, what did you dream, Jik?

'I dreamed I was being strapped down in a bed, and I was inside a body of an old person, an ancient dying person.'

And when you woke up, young Jik?

'I am inside a body of an old person. I'm dying.'

Now then, don't get upset. No crying in the corridors. What Jik says is true. A youngster is trapped inside this old frame. But where's the old soul? Inside the young Jik even now having fun with other young people? We don't ask those kinds of questions.

No, I said we don't ask questions. There are opportunities to speak later. If, that is, your tongue isn't glued inside your fat mouth. I beg your pardon; I didn't mean to be rude. Merely unpleasant.

We're going outside now before we come back in, waking upstairs before we go down in a variety of elevators and out the doors before we crawl back through windows, but not oriel windows.

Alright, I'll tell you. An oriel window is a form of bay window that protrudes from a wall but does not go down to the ground. It's like a balcony behind glass. A perfect stage for gibbering. Frightens the neighbours and the horses a treat.

For our next experience, you'll have to crouch to the floor, grovel down to hear what the cracked lips of our next exhibit are mouthing. Just let your cartouches and other neck ironmongery hang loose. That's it. Well done!

Lo, and behold, this is Tav. Tav's age or circumstances are irrelevant. All you need to know is that Tav didn't fit in, didn't conform or adopt the correct language and mindset for an establishment as advanced as this.

Tav is strapped by a chain manacle on both wrists to the arms of a weird wooden armchair, which is itself inside a purpose-built cage. An interesting grubby flannel coat adorns Tav's equally filthy body and limbs. Barefoot, Tav occasionally wiggles a toe through the leg casing that's secured to the foot of the chair legs.

Oh look, Tav is mouthing something, but it's unsolvable. Means nothing at all. Fifteen times a day, twice an hour, his performance in this part of the theme park is beginning to take a toll on poor Tav. Let me translate.

Tav dreamed of standing in front of a firing squad. Indeed, Tav *was* stood against a wall in the garden facing an amateur firing squad. The shock was enough to bring on a deep sleep or coma, if you prefer.

And I can sense you want to know. Yes, Tav was awakened from the coma by the sensation of being strapped into an electric chair. And as you see, Tav *is* in just such a chair. All wired up, hair shaved on the top and skull watered, ready to go. Anybody like to pull the lever and send Tav into... wherever?

Nobody? Oh well. Not fond of burning flesh, scorched muscles and twisted bodies, hey? I don't blame you. The stench lives in the nostrils for weeks. I remember once, when ... oh no, better not travel to that dark place. We have enough terribly grim nooks and crannies here as it is.

Now, please don't spread out too far. And if you're going to be sick, ask for a vomit bag, please. Have some manners.

Now, if we can all bunch forward, please. Hold your breath if the pungency from people so cramped together is too strong. Release it when I say.

Over here. Up this step and sloping ground to this glass case. It is, in fact, an oversize monitor, a bloody massive TV set. In fact.

Now, release the breath and peer in here. See, it's a child's story. Or rather a child's program. In this cartoon-like, two-dimensional world, a handful of odd, exaggerated and irrationally unlikely non-lifelike creatures 'live' out a gentle, totally artificial non-life.

The most they ever worry about is being late for school, going to the park or the shops, feeling a little under the ever-perfect sunshiny weather, helping a parent bake a cake or tidy the garage. It's a bland, wholesome life with no reality whatsoever. But it's stunningly popular among pre-school kids, so who are we to judge?

And you'd be surprised how many of our residents here crave just such a life.

Well, I did! Yes, I did.

The only baddies in this world in here are a bus making too much smoke out of its exhaust, a naughty dog who keeps running away, and an old person who shouts and points a lot but otherwise is totally harmless. And useless. And pointless. And witless and unreal.

It's a nightmare world only if you're inside it. Then it's absolutely surreal. Glance to your left and see... there I am! Yes, I am inside this game, this kiddies' entertainment programme in 10-minute story sized episodes. I dreamed I was in it and I actually am.

Though, I must admit that occasionally I do dream of guiding three-dimensional people around this installation.

Inside, I wake up beside a representation of a 'man' next to a jumbo-sized elephant who speaks and is kind. And a handful of little squiggles meant to be children, birds on the wing or sandwiches and potato crisps for a picnic.

And when some little snotty oik has the telly switched on while Mummy washes up the breakfast things or talks to a moron on her phone, I leap up on cue to do my bit.

Nobody has ever realised that I'm too big, too normal, too three-dimensional and too human reality to be in here, that something must be wrong.

Of course not! Everyone thinks gibbering at the oriel windows or the inside of the television screen is perfectly acceptable and is actually quite clever.

See yourselves out, to your right, please. Thank you, oh thank you.

Gratuities are not expected but gratefully received. I'll use any I get today to buy a fishing rod to go out with my lifelong chums, a panda on a string, a postman with one arm, a doll with no eyes, half a crocodile and a guillemot bigger than all of us.

4. The Necropolis Gene

1. There was a man who worked on the Necropolis Railway. Technically still a boy, toiling as a daily dogsbody on the train from London Necropolis Railway Station beside London Waterloo 23 miles to Brookwood Cemetery in Surrey, made him a man.

Every outward passage was mournful and heavy under the loss of dearly departed ones; the return to the city was usually joyful, a sense of relief and lightness. The human normally grieves only so long.

The line was established in 1854 to carry around 2000 dead a year on their final journey to eternity from the burgeoning, overcrowded capital where burial spaces had all but run out. It also solved the health problem of human body waste seeping into water courses.

Following the 1846-49 cholera epidemic a fine, spacious burial ground in the countryside offered the perfect solution. Brookwood covered 2268 acres of what'd been heathland and quickly became the world's biggest graveyard at that time.

Sections were allocated by London parishes and the whole was properly landscaped to create perpetual springtime. The south side served those of Anglican faith; the north took care of non-conformists.

To avoid reckless, criminal-minded lower masses mingling with the superior classes, both passenger and hearse carriages were provided into first, second and third compartments. However, the whole thing was relatively affordable. Ordinary travellers could sneak among funeral parties to buy cheap Necropolis tickets.

The platform at Brookwood was shaved at the edge to facilitate the transfer of coffins from the train. The station at the London end was relocated in 1902 but having suffered extensive bomb damage in WW2 it was demolished in 1941 when the line closed down.

The early parts of this fascinating history the young man knew. Most days he just kept his head down and did as expected in order to avoid a tongue-lashing from his boss, Thomas O'Rourke, an Irishman who'd come to England to find work building railways.

O'Rourke's task, besides carrying lists of the deceased, their class of travel and plot destinations, was to ensure trains ran smoothly and timely, that decorum was maintained and his staff looked and behaved in a suitably modest manner.

The young man's job was to ensure coffins were safely stowed and to demonstrate respect for loved ones on their final journeys. He was required to help lift the boxes on and off the train, onto the horse-drawn carts and to walk slowly alongside making certain no horse misbehaved.

During the committal services, he lingered respectfully on the fringes, ever ready to assist mourners, clergy or gravediggers as needed.

In reality, he drew strength from watching the solemn laying to rest of person after person, man after woman, child after child - all part of the rhythm of man's lot on this earth.

He read over and over the wealth of names and dates on headstones that were placed eight weeks after the earth had settled. Often lives were tragically short; sometimes a wealthy family spent lavishly on a resting place, be it a mausoleum, a monstrous statue or an angel.

'Looking for a likely place to lie, are you, lad?' O'Rourke demanded, having caught him in a trance staring across the cemetery.

'No, Mr O'Rourke, this isn't home for me.' He stood almost to attention in front of the small, wiry form of his boss and looked into his fist-fight battered face with its missing teeth.

'No, nor me.'

'Where will you lie, Mr O'Rourke?'

'Home is where the body lies, to be sure.'

Some days a little boy shadowed him. He looked familiar for no obvious reason. The little boy never spoke but took an interest in everything the young man did and said. And, it seemed to the man, everything he thought.

****

2. There is a man who sits for hours in the churchyard, still, barely breathing, thoughtful among the decay. He's young; but a man in many ways.

Sitting, long legs crossed, bony tall shoulders rising within touching distance of his ears, he makes himself comfortable. His thin hands, long and elegant fingers, already showing signs of nervous wastage, clutch an artists' sketchpad and a wire-spiralled notebook.

What does he feel today? Sometimes he sketches with pencil or charcoal. Graves; ornate decorations; simple messages, 'here lies....'; rotting vegetation; overhanging branches and the crazy uneven tilting of stones sinking into settling ground.

Other days he writes. Poems. Song lyrics. Thoughts. Rarely does he note the wildlife, birds and insects who regard the place as their own. It's people who pull him to the churchyard as if by silver threads.

It's always the same themes for sketching or writing, with occasional representations of the beings he sees from the past, their lives ended but leaving a trail of memory he tunes into.

Sunday, but the church is disused, so he shouldn't be disturbed. Rare visitors are invariably startled catching sight of his eyes and sallow face watching them. Some mistake him for a gargoyle or a ghost. It amuses him.

One grave particularly beckons. A simple slab, badly cracked by three fault lines and heavy with green lichen. A Celtic cross rising above the ground at the head, pointing skywards, marks the resting place of the mortal remains of Thomas O'Rourke.

Of wife and children there are no signs and in his roaming, he's never seen more O'Rourkes. What's a Celt doing buried in these eastern lands? It's a question he cannot answer; one day he'll research the parish records. Just out of interest.

He's no particular feel for Thomas O'Rourke that he can put a finger on. When the figures appear, dancing, sleeping, eating shadows or keening on their graves, he knows they're the dead, old and young, rotting and perfectly formed. He converses with them but never sees O'Rourke among them.

Like puppets, some dance awkwardly across slabs and pillars, footpaths and trees, their invisible strings tangle as if the puppeteer is losing the deft control needed to make them move in a lifelike fashion.

He suspects he alone can see them. His mother, a tall, greying woman in the last throes of elegance, never gives him a clue that she understands any of that.

Puppets appear demented. They're the tragic victims of plagues, diseases, poverty, accidents, murder, sanitation and dispensability. Pitiful, they cry for justice, a second chance or a little bit longer in their mortal coils.

Some thoughts lead to songs. Occasionally he carries his guitar slung across his back and sings his lyrics in a deep, sad voice. One of his 6th Form mates likens his songs to a cross between the recently discovered Leonard Cohen and The Incredible String Band.

His history teacher/form tutor is concerned for his well-being and tells him several times, 'no man is an island, entire of itself.'

The teacher watches him closely. This youth is a natural fit in his tutor group, composed of arty-farty, airy-fairy, creative, left-field types. 'We all need each other. I know you like your own company, but it's unhealthy not to spend at least some time with others.'

For his compulsory English class recitation of a favourite poem with at least three points of justification for his choice, he recites Boris Pasternak's *August*. Then he repeats the verse that speaks the most to him.

'In the churchyard, under the trees,
Death, a bit like some government official,
Stared at my pale face, trying to work out
How big a grave I'd need.

It confirms what most of his classmates think: he's weird, seriously weird. If asked, he confesses that he's generally shunned in the 6th form, despite forming 'The Gaping Graves' with three other oddballs, a soft-folk group who land occasional gigs at the local folk club, often trying out his own original compositions.

He's painfully shy yet burns with passion to perform. On any stage he hides behind the personas he creates, often flitting from one to another. This contradiction is widespread among the performing classes, but is rarely understood.

He's drawn to a tall, willowy girl, with long blonde hair tending towards curls as it cascades down across her shoulders. She speaks to everyone, exuding a relaxed, apparently warm friendship to all. Yet there lurks under that façade an icy cold, blue-eyed steely woman who weighs up the value of everyone she interacts with.

He sees in her that beneath the physical beauty there's a person he wants to control, to own. Yet he can't. He's already owned by her. He is her puppet; her clown in a mask; her own pocket freak.

One minute she's heads-touching close to him discussing his wilder imaginings; the next she's leading the herd as they laugh at him.

Never seeing the cruelty of her friendship, he pretends to let her introduce him to Bob Dylan; she refuses to lead him to anything else. Someone is going to steal her, for she will be stolen, he knows that.

There's a report of a girl attacked near the college. No name yet, but he fears the worst. He needs to know it's not her; needs to be sure he didn't do it.

Looking up the number in the phone book, he rings the police station from the phone box by the corner shop. He explains he wants to enquire about her health. His name, address and connection to her are demanded.

Shaking, he hangs up, still not knowing if she is well. Next day she returns to college, laughing as normal. Another girl is lying in a hospital bed.

Could it be some man that steals her? Or will it be death?

Single pulls on the old church bell, every twenty seconds the mournful note rings out. He looks up, across O'Rourke's tomb, crouching beside a giant yew. What is it about yew trees in churchyards? What is it about a single bell tolling?

A small funeral begins, shuffling through the gate and straight to a freshly dug grave. Still and quiet, he watches the grief, sadness and regrets, people at different levels.

The girl is being laid to rest.

The next week he returns to paint. Setting up an easel and oils he stands facing the church's west gable. With a rough basic outline done he begins carefully painting grey flint walls, the turrets, the gargoyles, the overgrown drainpipes and guttering.

Nearly finished, he adds a small black smudge in the middle.

As the puppets dance, the black smudge grows bigger till it almost fills the canvas. It's a bat, one of thousands that have occupied the church.

And she's dancing clumsily on the graves among the others. The puppeteer awkwardly works her limbs. She finds a place that feels right.

It's the gravestone of Thomas O'Rourke, her great, great grandfather.

****

3. There will be a man who'll enjoy limited small time recording and writing success. He will self-publish a work of poems and short stories illustrated with his own sketches of forgotten, peaceful and gently decaying churchyards.

One day the idea will grip him to collect and write about as many clichés for final departure as he can gather. He will write an acrostic poem, but the letters will not work out right.

Kicking the bucket, popping the clogs, giving up the ghost, slipping away, passing on, passing away, at rest, rest in peace, gone to his maker, in paradise, eternal rest, called home, slipping gently into that long goodnight, buying the farm and, harshest of all, dying.

The man will marry a dark-haired girl, completely different from the blonde – this one is caring and sensitive. She'll be unable to share his passion for old churchyards and abandoned cemeteries, partly because she'll find them spooky, cold, sinister places. But also because she'll understand the dangers of digging up the past.

She'll grasp that he has his visions but not what they mean, if anything. At home she'll play the piano to soothe him, to calm him. She will record herself so he can take her music on his device and listen while the puppets dance across the tombs.

She will give him two children who will show early signs of creativity.

****

4. There will be a man who after a bad case of twisted back from a fall over a tumbled grave angel hidden in long grass and brambles decides he must know more about his family.

There will be a time when the internet provides almost everything anybody wants to know. He will research the Necropolis Railway and his grandfather and when he brought his family to Suffolk.

He will ask why the old man moved from London. The man will find it harder to discover that. He will receive suggestions of poverty, disease, the eternal quest for work to feed a family or the escape from horror or crime.

He will unearth names, birth and death dates of relatives with blood lines right up to his. He will discover parish marriages, deaths from a range of illnesses. He will find gaol records for one and a local newspaper report of the suicide of another.

His figures and puppets will fade away. Unable to write poetry he will acknowledge he's more content as husband and father than at any time in his life. Sketchbooks will curl in the sun; one pulped in the rain.

When his children are fully grown and enter marriage and parenthood, the man will hear a solitary mournful note from the distant churchyard. With apologies to his wife who will hear nothing, he will stride to the ancient churchyard. She'll hope he's not seeing things again.

He will arrive at the tail end of a funeral procession following an elaborate coffin to a grave by the plague pit, between two gigantic yews. It will be the laying to rest of his grandfather.

Feeling someone close beside him, he will reach out and touch his granddaughter who followed him, concerned about his health.

She will be pregnant. He'll see the boy she'll be carrying.

He will see the young man who will sit, long legs crossed, bony tall shoulders rising within touching distance of his ears as he makes himself comfortable. His bony hands, long and elegant fingers, will already show signs of nervous wastage clutching an artists' sketchbook and a wire-spiralled notebook.

The young man will look familiar.

****

5. There was a man who one day, walking through the churchyard looking for his spot to sit and thinking backwards and forwards, agreed to hear the tale, again.

He stood almost to attention in front of the small, wiry form of Thomas O'Rourke, his boss, and looked into his fist-fight battered face with missing teeth. The story had to be told again.

It was a saga, long-winded and full of asides and anecdotes O'Rourke thought were either amusing or needed to be shared. The man had heard it enough times to finish it for him when O'Rourke was overtaken by the emotion of the love he found when he moved out of London to manage the new cemetery.

Normanston Cemetery was begun in 1885 as the municipal graveyard and later contained dead from both world wars, including 11 German war burials, their stories untold. How did the enemy come to be rubbing dead shoulders with town locals?

The man preferred walking in churchyards. There was something impersonal about civic burial grounds which evaporated in the calm of a churchyard. Here lay the bones of hundreds of faithful believers, their spouses and children. Their stories told tales miles long.

And in his favourite churchyard, there was one solitary grave, unmarked by headstone, slab or metal cross. Even the dead in asylums had an indicator of who was laid in a particular spot.

This hole in the ground contained the hastily dropped remains of a woman who'd committed suicide. The man knew she was Mrs Edna O'Rourke, a local girl who'd gone mad and married a foreigner.

When all the puppets had stopped dancing, only Edna O'Rourke sat on the spot, staring sadly at the silence around her, broken by the single tolling bell.

'Who is that for?' the man asked.

The puppets chanted the end of the poem the history teacher had advised him to read. 'Send not to know for whom the bell tolls, it tolls for thee.'

****

6. There is a man who must break the mould. He is tall, angular and awkward.

Sitting, long legs crossed, bony tall shoulders rising within touching distance of his ears, he makes himself comfortable. His bony hands, long and elegant fingers already show signs of nervous wastage clutching an artists' sketchpad and a wire-spiralled notebook.

But he's going to be different.

No poems, songs or sketches. No sitting in the churchyard speaking to dead puppets or figurines. No, he's not drawn to decaying human corpses.

He is puppet master, not observer. He is in control. He resists the voices from the past and the future.

This man is irresistibly drawn to dead dogs, instead.

This man is still going to die, breaking the mould of his family or not.

This man will be almost forgotten in time.

5. The Full Experience

A handful of film script hopefuls stared at me. Three seemed quite interested, including the lecturer. Simon was a retired gas fitter who knew every Disney film backwards. Fleur worked in a travel agency. Helen was big in environmental projects.

Goodwill was a student at the University of East Anglia desperate to gain credits but more concerned with his phone. Cynthia was, I think, a woman who worked 'in long term elderly management projects,' and looked as if she was away with the fairies.

Anyway, it was my turn to outline ideas for my proposed film script. I was going to enjoy it. I had a killer idea, and I felt the first stirrings of the dawning of hope that it would be hailed by my fellow evening class toilers.

We'd been meeting for four weeks so far and had been fed copious notes on plots, sub-plots, characters, points of view, how to write a script and pitch it and watched numerous film clips. Some illustrated a point; others were what the lecturer, Teddy, obviously enjoyed repeat watching.

Teddy was something of a mystery. Clearly a film buff, he'd been a roadie on some unheard-of singer's European tour and had once plugged cables in at a BBC outside broadcast but otherwise knew of film only what he'd read. His lecture status was perhaps a fluke.

I glanced at my scribbled notes. Here goes. 'It's called *The Full Experience*,' I began. 'Not so much a nod to *The Full Monty* as a wave in the direction of post-modern, post-masculine re-education, particularly in the way the females have to fight to be taken seriously.'

Some heads nodded; Teddy beamed. This sort of claptrap was a requirement of the course and our film scripts. We also had to make at least half of the characters black, Asian or mixed race. And genders? I was lost at the first lecture on that one.

My film plot was filled with characters I knew. To hell with the politically correct quotas.

'Given his nickname in his early teens, it had stuck. 'Donk' was truly hung like a donkey.' It was the opening line of the synopsis and of the voice-over narrator I was planning.

'Obvious in the communal school showers after sports, boys were decidedly envious. Girls soon got to hear about him and through the giggles and winks and nudges one or two braver, more adventurous, young women found out the truth of the rumours. He was certainly well-built.'

'Filling in a fun self-analysis quiz in a magazine, to the invitation to list his teenage hobbies, his response was, 'deflowering schoolgirls.' He kept a tally before he lost count.'

'Later, growing into early manhood, Donk would decide during his romancing process if he'd go easy on a girl – just half – or if she was to get the full experience,'

'He knew from the day he met Julia, that she fitted his type perfectly: petite and blonde. On their very first date she got the full experience and could barely walk for a week but assumed all men were that size, as she'd had no other.'

'In just three years they welcomed three kids into their family. She loved him unconditionally as her mother had taught her and was always caught by surprise when marriages they knew failed or went through rocky patches. Like George Washington, she could not tell a lie.'

'So, Donk sat on a bedrock of stability in his life which he put at risk by his behaviour and taking Julia absolutely for granted. A totally unconstructed male bastard,' I added to nods from those still awake.

'However, for Donk, old habits died hard. Even in his happy marriage, he continued his secret adult hobby. He sometimes used the services of women who plied their trade for money. Certain streets in Norwich and Ipswich provided them till police activity increased; cameras made it a dangerous game.'

'Then he found his blondes advertising in local papers or online. Again, some got the full works; others half measures. As time passed, they became older and their blonde hair was from a bottle, though several were greying brunettes and decidedly bigger-bodied than he'd first craved.'

'He became less fussy, less particular in his demands, seedy. His only rules were never to see the same woman more than twice and never to use a condom if he could get away with it.'

'My description of him in those terms speaks for itself.'

Teddy interjected, 'er no, Mikey. While the characters will speak for him, her or other selves, your synopsis, your pitch must speak for him, succinctly and directly.'

'Thanks, Teddy. Got it. The fact is that I hate Donk. He's a piece of lowlife detestable scum that should have been strangled at birth. I'd like to kill him, even now.' Puzzled faces showed I'd confused my audience. Was Donk real? Was this a murder story?

'Actually, I was planning to do it when things turned out rather well. For me. He became the prime target in a murder case. Yes, dear old lovable Donk was the police's favourite for the horrific murder of a young woman.'

'I suppose all murders are horrific. This one carried Donk's trademarks, including that she'd had the full experience.'

Even if I hadn't known him as a real person who inspired my character, Donk was to my mind guilty as hell. My film would treat him as he deserved.

'She, a single mother just coping on a council estate about a mile from him; he, doing well at his import/export business. I mean, nobody really knows what import/export actually is, but it's his front, its success opens doors to Rotary, the Masons, good restaurants and business deals others can only dream about.'

'Brash when it suits; he's menacingly quiet when he wants people to incriminate themselves or reveal their business hand.' I dropped into present tense as I remembered that was needed.

'On the other hand, I'm quite ordinary. I have no difficulty merging in a crowd. I've been called nondescript, an insult I've accepted. I'm that five and half inches sort of guy, a writer of stories and teller of tales demonstrating how to live with a huge inferiority complex.'

'At least I'm not lugging around a massive chip on the shoulder ...'

'So, are you the narrator? Is this your story rather than Donk's?' Helen of the environment projects asked, on the ball, really.

'Just bear with me a moment, it'll be clear, that it is my story,' I told her, a bit annoyed at being interrupted mid-flow.

Teddy told me, 'the agent you're pitching at will have put this on the slush pile and turned to the next *Star Wars* meets *Jurassic Park*.'

'Oh, and I have a soft spot for animals. I donate to every creature cause I come across, however ridiculous. I pay £5 a month each to five charities to preserve penguins, polar bears, lynx, Spanish donkeys and red squirrels.'

'Now the day I decided to kill Donk was when I came out of the local Hedgehog Sanctuary having become devoted to a cute little specimen we called Prune on account of his funny little face, to watch his launch back into the wild having spent weeks and several hundred pounds on restoring him from terrible injuries.'

Helen beamed at me as she pictured all sorts of wildlife, surviving and flourishing, while Goodwill, a person who'd done time for GBH according to his/her film idea, pictured them dismembered on the butcher's block.

'A small crowd of volunteers gathered at the rear of the building which led on to a former wheat field the farmer had given over to re-wilding, so it was ideal for returning them to nature. And it meant after waving them off, staff and volunteers could get back quickly to the mission.'

'Prune headed off into the mass of trees, brambles and ferns. After applause, most people returned to the building. I took a last look at Prune and to my surprise he turned back along the path towards the sanctuary.'

'I was about to call others out to see but didn't. Instead, I stared as Prune continued past the doors at a steady two miles per hour heading for the front. With horror I watched as he reached the corner of the building and carried on under the front garden gate, across the little car park.'

'Dashing back inside the sanctuary, I found nobody who wasn't up to his or her neck preserving hedgehogs. By the time I got back outside and towards the road I was too late to intervene.'

'Prune was crushed under the wheels of a brand new, gleaming, bright yellow Zenvo TS1 GT, retailing at just over two million pounds and stopped up the road so the driver could climb out, walk back to stare at Prune's flattened remains before inspecting his tyres for blood or damage.'

'It was Donk. He'd just butchered Prune after we'd done so much to keep him alive. 'Oops,' he said as we stood staring at the mess.'

'How are things?'

'Oh, you know, Donk, things carry on. We can put so much into saving the life of a hedgehog only to see him crushed by a driver, moments later.'

'Well, it wanted to commit suicide. I didn't see it. There should be a sign of warning.'

'Oh, but there is. Ah, no, there was till someone drove a car into it,' I told him.

'That'd be me. That's why I upgraded my wheels. What do you think?'

'Plot twist coming now. The thing is that Donk and I were cousins. Still are, I suppose. That's how I know so much about him.'

'No, that should have come earlier!'

'Too contrived!'

'Why?'

My fellow scribes were adamant that was a step too far on the corn road.

I ploughed on. 'We must go to a night a year later, when I was in a pub with a group of people after a rehearsal for a play I was directing. I had no agenda in mind; I was simply enjoying the spontaneous socialising.'

'After my half of bitter, I started my excuses to leave. My bladder couldn't hold more and besides it was getting late.'

'Her name was Rae. Short for whatever, I didn't know. She was petite, with long blondish-brown hair to her shoulders and a set of alluring blue eyes. She'd attached herself to me as soon as we crowded into the pub and kept gazing at me as we talked and joked with the boisterous am dram crowd.'

'When I stood and announced I had to get on, away, things to do, messages to return, calls to make and my beauty sleep, she grabbed her coat and asked if I'd give her a lift, it was only a little out of my way.'

'I could hardly say no in front of everybody, so I agreed, and we made our way out to my car parked in the street. A familiar figure emerged from the shadows, 'Hello, Mikey, how's it hanging?'

'Oh, hi Donk. It's hanging well, I think.' Donk employed his trademark pseudo hippie clichés as he spoke to me while giving Rae the eye.'

'Rae for her part offered her hand and I could see that before long she'd be offering him any other part he fancied. They smiled, chatted like old friends and I found the thought creeping into my mind that she was to get the full experience.'

'This is way beyond a synopsis, now, Mikey.'

'Gratuitous sex scene, is it, from a man's point of view?' Cynthia who'd yet to contribute piped up. At least I think Cynthia was a woman, hard to tell with the asexual clothes, hair and attitude and she might have introduced herself as Synth which I misheard.

'Something about Donk's smirking confidence, his easy charm and his careless use of women angered me a little but strangely interested me.'

'Typical male reaction!' Fleur spluttered, righteously.

'Listen, I'd not thought of going further with her; I wasn't addicted to Donk's hobby. I just didn't want him to use her, not this time. Not now.'

'Donk gave me a wink as if he knew what I was thinking. 'Hey, Mikey, could you give me a lift? My car is waiting for roadside rescue and it'll be at least a couple of hours… Just time enough!'

'Rae smiled as if she knew what was in his mind, too. Before I could think of a reason to refuse, I was behind the wheel while Rae took the passenger seat; Donk behind her.'

'Later I could barely recall the conversation, but I know Donk suggested a little drive for a laugh and pointed out a layby good for a pee off the main road about a ten-minute journey away. Rae chirped away happily and though I switched off a bit, wondering if I was supposed to sit and watch them or wait outside the car, I seem to think she informed us that she was on the pill.'

My audience groaned as one.

'Who wants to go first?' Rae brought me back to reality as I stopped in the deserted layby, well off the road and switched off the headlights.'

'Oh, Mikey must go first. You're his bird, Rae, after all.'

'Well, not really, not yet,' she replied turning to look at him behind.'

'Anyway, I like sloppy seconds,' Donk informed her seriously, as he stepped out of the car to pee against the back number plate.'

'Now, I was unsure if I wanted her as she was so easy, yet the idea that Donk was going next turned me on. I went along as she kissed me, found the lever to lower her seat, discovered my pathetic length and allowed me to slide her knickers down.'

'I'd barely started when Donk's distorted face appeared at her window, pushed against the glass. It didn't put me off my stroke because true to my form, I'd already finished.'

'The door flung open and Donk practically pulled me out of the car with one hand as his other undid his belt. It was my turn to pee, but away from the heartily rocking car; it was his turn to give her the full experience.'

'I know he did because of the loud gasp she gave in the car and the way she later walked into her house to the loving embrace of her husband.'

'Now at this point, I thought we need details about the killing, the local reactions, the funeral, to flesh out the background to Donk's arrest for killing her, so I think …'

Cynthia asked, 'does the girl fight back at all?'

Fleur wanted to confirm, 'it's just a male sexual turn on story?'

'I think it's actually a post male domination tale, which will see him castrated and brought down to average size.' This from Goodwill.

Simon unwound a boiled sweet as he proclaimed, 'I think it's actually a comedy.' The others disagreed.

It was then open house, the group making free with their comments. They stirred Teddy out of a coma to think I'd finished and to praise me, critique the lack of coherent plot and sustainable characters and too many asides and prior knowledge before finishing with more faint praise.

Simon suggested that I 'summarise the rest in two minutes flat?'

At that, they all looked expectantly at me as I flipped through my notes.

'Well, Rae was found dead a week later in that same layby. Strangled. There was no DNA evidence of any sort – the perfect crime, you might say. So, she hadn't just had the full or any experience, but the cops still pulled in Donk. I was questioned and on account of my rock-solid alibi of being seen at the dance show at my daughter's school, I was off the hook.'

'They had her husband in for hours of questions and discovered that he knew all about her activities but was quite incapable of harming her as he had verifiable weakness in his hands.'

'Julia, honest as ever, did a great job of telling the truth, that she knew all along about his games and that no, Donk was not at home all evening on the day in question. So, he was picked up, questioned, held his hand up to all sorts of things but not murder.'

'So, it was Donk and could only be Donk.'

'You've slipped into the past tense, so is this a true story?' Helen frowned.

'Where's the twist? Where's the character development?' Teddy was disappointed that that was the best I could come up with. Had I learned nothing from his lectures?'

'What about the narrator? You?' Simon demanded.

'Oh, I got to write about the experience in my novel that none would touch and my narrative poem that died a death and my ballad about it that lacked musicality and a catchy riff. But now I'll see it as a film script after your helpful comments.'

The group looked at each other.

'We just have time before the coffee break, Mikey. How does it end?'

'It doesn't.'

Rae would have agreed with that ending if she'd lived. And Julia would have loved it if she'd lived. And Donk would have been impressed by it if he'd been real. And Teddy, Cynthia, Goodwill, Fleur and Simon would have approved it if they'd been let out of their cells for treatment.

6. Alexander the Coppersmith

Happy days they were, looking back. At least, they were for some.

When he found God at a terrifying moment in the trenches of the First World War, Caleb Wright also discovered his gift for itinerant preaching. Already established as a local 'colourful character', a walking eccentric, from then on, he spouted several reasons a day to confirm the view that he was a bit odd.

Clever; yet decidedly odd.

There was even talk of how a period in the asylum would help Caleb to adjust to modern life better. He wore a faded professor look when his hair was trimmed and his second-hand glasses firmly placed on his nose. But just as often he had the look of a madman hoping nobody'd noticed he'd tiptoed from the circus where he was in charge.

There was a lean and hungry look about him, too, which may have been due to his religious fervour, but equally could have been accounted for by his dreaming up some new invention, a wild scheme to confound his critics.

He was outstandingly good at problem solving. As a boy he fiddled with old machinery and broken clocks. He rigged up the bell to ring at the front door and the kitchen simultaneously. He mended things. He was given a corner of a shed on his family site to store things and rig up a bench of timber scraps.

Early in that war, Caleb found himself laughed out of his senior officer's tent when he'd suggested improvements to facilities and told to 'stick with looking after the horses. You're good with them, whispering in their ears.'

He thus applied his inventive mind to the trenches. Unable to rely on him to go over the top, the powers decided to keep him back from the actual front line and busy inventing ways to make trench life less horrific.

Caleb came up with a backside-wiping device that kept both hands free to fire a rifle while crouched. He devised better ways to brew and serve tea to the men down any line. And he secured a box of surplus tin helmets to create a contraption to store drying underwear off the ground.

Volunteering before he was enlisted in the 2nd Battalion, Suffolk Regiment, he was part of the British Expeditionary Force sent across the channel to support France. Dismissed by The German Kaiser in August 1914 as 'the treacherous English… in a contemptible little army,' the fact is that they suffered many casualties.

Despite surprising the Germans at Mons with their fight, the French Fifth Army was withdrawn which exposed the BEF's right flank. They were forced to engage in a 200-mile fighting retreat over ten days. Holding actions at seven positions cost thousands of British lives.

Caleb Wright survived outwardly and returned to Suffolk at the end of hostilities. It was a long four-year void from his life that he was never known to talk about with anybody. Not even his wife, the devoted Elsie, nor his own two children, joined nine months later by a third.

Elsie sensed without being told that it was the horrors of war that had changed him from a patriot to a turn-the-other-cheek man and she loved him for it, but never told him. People of their generation rarely did.

As men returned to their jobs and women to their kitchens by and large, life in the village found the equilibrium of a patient suffering from a long trauma and slowly trying to live as before. The Wrights made their living from selling vegetables, hauling produce and fish in their carts. Their beloved lorry had been requisitioned and never arrived back.

Post-war, his trademark invention was what he called his Fundrome, a large hall, a ramshackle concoction of old doors, salvaged wood, corrugated iron sheets, ornamental carvings and bizarre, mismatching colours. In the early 1920s, during the heyday of silent film, it offered affordable seating to village families, fisherfolk and the handful of local middle classes.

After a couple of years, it boasted a stout wooden floor made of old found planks on which sat the greatest assortment of chairs outside a furniture mart. If there was word of a theatre, cinema, pub, dance hall, shop or stately home closing or renovating, Caleb was there buying bits and bobs.

So, suddenly, *Balcony, Book Here* and *Ice-cream* signs appeared on the walls among the carvings and treasures. In line with his ahead-of-his-time inventions, he devised walls that collapsed in the event of a fire, a perennial hazard in all places of public entertainment.

People watched the great comedic and dramatic stars of the day on his screen made of a stretched, thin white sheet. The projector often seized up mid-showing and twice the film melted as the device caught fire. The crowd were generally tolerant of these mishaps, joshing Caleb for his inability to invent a projector immune to fire.

Because he'd met God, he also used the building for occasional services of rusty hymn singing accompanied on an old foot pedal organ he found in a congregational chapel being demolished in Great Yarmouth and had it carried to Clottingham by horse and cart.

Every session ended with a few of his choice words, stood on a wooden fish box that had found its way from the Lowestoft Fish Market, now thriving while Clottingham's declined. Most of his audience slipped out as quietly as they could through the back doors, leaving a few polite people to hear him out.

The first man he sought to enlist once he'd returned home was the local Church of England vicar, the Reverend George Potts-Dawlish, a pompous stuffed shirt who'd been an officer, blowing his whistle with pride to send dozens of men to their deaths. He refused Caleb's offer to preach one

Sunday morning saying that only God-fearing and trained parsons were called to that. He said it in the manner of a senior officer, weary with talking to the lowest ranks.

Caleb simply shrugged and pointed a long bony finger at the man. 'It's a mistake that's yours for the making, Brother Potts-Dawlish. Repent while ye may.' When he wanted to be, the dark-eyed Caleb was all heavenly trumpets, angels of God and avenger of blood, Ten Commandments and last chances to get back on the straight and narrow.

He developed a particular fascination for the more obscure Biblical people and what may or may not have happened to them. Lot's wife, the wives of the sons of Noah, Jonathan's armour-bearer, the children of Jesus' disciples, Judas Iscariot's family, Rahab the prostitute and Lazarus' friends featured large. He often talked of Joseph who had to accept Mary's virgin birth; Alexander the Coppersmith was a particular favourite.

Also referred to as 'the metalworker' Alexander was strongly damned by Paul in his second letter to Timothy as someone to be aware of as he 'strongly opposed the message' and did Paul 'great harm.'

There's no further information about the man; two other Alexanders are mentioned. One had made 'a shipwreck of his faith' and blasphemed. A second, a metalworker who fashioned idols to the false god, Artemis, and made a brisk trade of it, stirred up a crowd against Paul and his message.

While it was a common name at the time, it's by no means certain whether there were three Alexanders or simply the one troublesome piece of work. The fact was that locals who followed Caleb's sermons over a few days heard much about the infernal evil on legs that was Alexander the coppersmith and perhaps imagined a big, strong armed devil with fangs and a forked tail.

Any image left in listeners' minds suited Caleb just fine. He seemed to know instinctively that if a message was to work its magic on people for more than a few moments, it needed to shock, startle or shake their idleness and complacency.

Time to repent was short. Pitifully short.

His own family was not Jewish, as far as they knew, but Caleb warned his flexible, mobile congregations that Alexander *was* Jewish, one who clung to his cultural traditions. He could have defended Paul as a true worshipper of God, instead he chose to distance himself from Paul in apparent support of the polytheistic pagans of Ephesus.

Paul never sought personal revenge against Alexander; he merely warned people not to trust the man. Caleb equally cautioned against personal revenge and refused to allow himself to indulge in hatred and anger. Instead, he preached 'the Lord will repay him according to his deeds.'

Leave retribution to the Almighty, 'never avenge yourselves, but leave it to the wrath of God, for it is written, 'Vengeance is mine, I will repay, says the Lord.'

That didn't mean, Caleb pointed out, that you should suffer an Alexander in silence while the harm he caused swirled around like a strong easterly wind.

A familiar sight around the area, Caleb wobbled his trusty old boneshaker bicycle around the alleys, streets and pathways. Trouser bottoms tucked into socks to avoid touching the greasy chain – nothing as modern as a bicycle clip for Caleb – he was welcomed as a source of amusement as he shared Bible verses or wise thoughts. Parents let their kids near him, talk to him, play alongside him on his site. People did in those days.

****

By the late 1960s, Caleb was in his eighties. He occasionally found his mind reaching back through the mists of faulty memory to dwell on past mistakes, those errors of judgement and twists of life that had caused the most upset.

He reflected on how his parents and grandparents had been when he was young. And their family home, a sprawling area of partially developed industrial land. Centred in a disused mill near Beccles with outbuildings and workshops, they added new structures as Caleb's father Ernest and brother William grew up. Once adult, both boys found wives and decisions were needed about where everybody would live and work.

His father and uncle were brought up by parents who themselves were raised in the Victorian era of thrift, hard work, virtue and well-meaning philanthropy towards some. When their old patriarch died, the brothers felt able to modernise, to some degree. They installed tanks and pumps and sold petrol, with a little rickety counter by the till offering cakes, biscuits and pies made by Elsie and her mother-in-law.

Keeping apart most of the time, each brother chased different parts of the business to be busy in. However, the family came together on a Saturday evening to count the cash takings, setting aside in jars what was needed for wages, food and fresh supplies.

Founded in the late 1950s, Green Shield stamps were a British sales promotion, loyalty and reward scheme where shoppers used stamps to buy goods from a catalogue or member retailers. By the early 1960s, most petrol stations became self-serving and competed by offering double, treble or quadruple stamps.

The Wrights grudgingly gave double, arguing that the nearest petrol station offering more was a mile away and if people only put a couple of gallons in their car every week, they couldn't drive that far before running out.

One day, as the brothers walked together towards the cash kiosk they both spotted a dropped, single Green Shield stamp, half the size of a postage stamp and bent to pick it up. They grazed knuckles rescuing a stamp with a cash value of 0.001 of an old penny. It said a lot about them, as they were talking less and less to each other.

Rumour had it that on the toss of a coin, Ernest's family lost and moved to Clottingham where the Wrights held an option on a field on the clifftop. It housed a farmhouse that was nearly derelict when the Wrights moved in and Ernest began intermittent repairs with materials he found or bought, but never stole, from all over the area.

There his three children, Caleb, Lydia and Harry were born and raised. Gradually the wider family drifted apart as Ernest and William saw eye to eye on fewer things, even at Christmas and special days. Beccles was a fair distance from Clottingham, after all.

It was clear from early on that Caleb would take over from his father when the time came. William stayed on the Beccles site which in the 2020s was developed as housing with the name, 'Wrights Acres' without an apostrophe.

Lydia launched herself on an adventure with a group of others sailing round the world and was never heard of again. Harry moved to Lowestoft to set up as a scrap metal merchant and did well during hard times and easier periods.

Elsie, Caleb's wife, was from travelling stock but seemed to settle on the land without hankering overmuch after the open road. Any spare moment she had, particularly when hanging out washing on a line of old knotted rope by the cliff edge, she gazed out to sea, dreaming of nobody knew what.

Elsie and Caleb themselves produced four children, one still-born and named Rodney, Rosemary, a living Rodney and Dennis, who grew up with all the freedom of the site and the nearby village. They learned how to scrounge, sell, mend and make do, scrimp and save in their hybrid Victorian-20th Century upbringing.

Half a lorry with solid wheels that was illegal to drive on the road and seven incomplete, pre-1930s cars gathered rust and hosted weeds beneath and around – 'all weeds are flowers; all flowers are weeds', Caleb pontificated if anyone mentioned them. All his machines were destined for the transport museum as their children expressed no interest in them once they'd outgrown playing on and around them.

Clottingham, dubbed the richest large village in England five centuries ago, housed whole families with fixed, old fashioned or plain dotty views. The joke in the nearby town, Lowestoft, was that it was home to a number of interbred generations who produced offspring with two heads who only came out at night.

Since its glory days, sea erosion, the silting of the harbour and changing fashions and tastes left Clottingham on the fringe of life, deep in the outer reaches of people's consciousness during their daily lives. Until they came across someone with a pair of heads.

****

Caleb never blamed the Germans for what was done but as nobody was privy to any of his inner views, everyone assumed he loathed and mistrusted that whole nation as much as they did.

By the time the second war came, too old for the front line, Caleb offered his inventions to the war effort – a new type of rotor/planting plough, a gramophone that sung to chickens and a car that parked sideways.

While he waited to be called to join other inventing boffins in a secret location or for men from the ministry to remove all his scrap metal lying about, Caleb grew potatoes and kept chickens to do his bit for King and country.

In the end, he was never asked to do more than accommodate three sailors for a week as the Lowestoft billets were full. After a single night, the unhappy seamen chose to sleep in the open air, under the stars, away from eccentrics.

Much of Lowestoft was rebuilt after the war, because the Germans had dropped so many bombs on the five ship repair installations and any planes flying back with left over bombs from the Midlands dropped them on the town. Clottingham remained largely untouched.

Rain or shine, North Sea wind or those rare calm days of little activity except from the birds and the racket of little kids playing, Caleb biked his daily tour of the area, preaching at and talking to anyone he encountered, young and old, sane and barking.

The thwack of willow against cricket balls was never part of Clottingham tradition. Yes, it was an English backwater, but not entirely cut off from the world with televisions, fridges, new homes, smart cars and pop music arriving regularly.

One element of life from the late 1960s that surprisingly refused to ignore Clottingham was the hippie movement at its height in the UK during the 'Summer of Love,' 1967. This was the manifestation of a life view among late teens and early twenties who'd escaped national service, grew up under the NHS in a war-free country with all life's advantages and education that their parents and grandparents had missed.

Opposing tradition and convention, disdaining the normal working lives of most, they wanted to chill, let it all hang out, do their own thing, take drugs and have sex on demand with the contraceptive pill and abortion freely available. Heady days, indeed. For some.

The Wright kids were right in there, in a manner of speaking. The baby, Dennis, still at school, chafed against the uniform, tie, jacket and petty rules. Rosemary was married to a man from the traveller community and had no time for anything but raising the five children of her own and three from his deceased wife that her husband gave her.

Rodney, a chip off his father's and grandfather's block, worked as odd jobber, fetching, carrying, mending and lending a hand for a few quid here and there. He looked out the most for his old Dad and

Mum and Caleb had high hopes that the boy would either invent something to make them all rich or take on and develop the Fundrome for the modern age.

It was a late summer weekend when the Wrights encountered the modern hippie theatricals on a site less than a quarter of a mile from their own.

Of course, while most free love and hippiedom was rampant in London and other big cities, smaller communities produced their own home-grown participants.

Villagers had seen and laughed at the first motor scooters in Clottingham, put-putting, mirror-laden Lambrettas or Vespas, usually driven by boys with hair as long as girls. People heard of the first arrest for peddling dope and were bombarded by the music from tinny, transistor radios, much of it broadcast from pirate ships in the North Sea.

That Sunday afternoon brought an unexpected and, in the event, totally unwanted encounter with hippies. They called it a 'Happening', when what was actually going on was much lolling about, dancing to over-loud music, drug taking on an industrial scale, pawing and canoodling and a lot of naked dancing and frolicking.

Those dressed looked like native American Indians, like tramps, like mannequins for a jumble sale and like kids dressed up for a madcap garden party for somebody's 14th birthday.

A man old enough to be the father if not grandfather of most of them led a Tai Chi demonstration. Unhealthy looking, about five foot six tall, quite rotund, wearing long culottes, a leather jerkin decorated with stars and rainbows and sporting a tie-dye neckerchief round his forehead he spotted Caleb among the audience.

And Caleb knew him. After years without crossing paths, Caleb was watching his cousin, Gabriel Wright.

A lull in the demonstration allowed about twenty young people to relax, smoke something, break into small groups and do their own thing for a moment. Gabriel stood in front of Caleb.

'Hello, cousin.'

'Hello to you, cousin.'

The men shook hands formally and slowly.

'This is Rodney, my son. Rod, this is Gabriel Wright, my cousin. So, is that your second cousin or cousin once removed?'

Rodney shook hands with the cousin. 'I don't know, Dad. But you share the same grandfather, Ernest, then?'

'No, it was Ernest's brother William who was my granddad.' Gabriel continued, 'there's a scabby sheep in every flock.'

'Are you referring to me, Gabriel?'

'Well, as they say, a ground-sweat cures all disorders.'

Caleb noticed that Rodney was puzzled, so told him, 'it means that you don't suffer when you're dead and buried. But I'd say those who have done the Devil's work for nothing will suffer for their sins in a big way.'

Silence, while the men looked at each other. None felt it necessary nor polite to ask about the close relatives of the others. Some hippies gathered for part two of the Tai Chi show.

'My baby, Dennis, is about here, somewhere...' Caleb offered, at the limit of his information sharing. Caleb and Rodney spotted Dennis happily smoking something in the company of two girls dressed in long gipsy skirts, see-through blouses, their shoulder-length hair parted in the middle.

They also sported montbretia, trumpet flowers in shades of red and yellow, tucked behind their ears. Seeing Caleb and Rodney looking, both girls waved and plumped their breasts up, making them roar with laughter.

While Rodney kept his eye on the girls around Dennis, wondering if he'd be welcome to amble over, Caleb shrugged his shoulders at Gabriel. He suddenly remembered when he'd last given this cousin of his any thought.

A couple of years back, he'd been challenged mid street sermon by a fisherman who'd oiled his throat a little too liberally and asked just *how* Alexander the coppersmith actually looked. Caleb, with little thought, had described the physical appearance of his cousin Gabriel who lived in Lowestoft with his ancient mother, 'he looks like this ...'

The mother'd long since dipped more than a toe into the twilight world inside her crumbling mind. Gabriel, almost a generation younger than Caleb, was well on his way to joining her, and if they'd both lived in Clottingham it would have been a perpetual competition to be the more eccentric, Caleb or Gabriel. But their paths rarely crossed.

In his early heyday, Gabriel had worked on the fisheries research vessel and sailed to the Arctic on exploratory visits to measure fish stocks, breeding grounds and pollution. He'd been a scientist.

Gradually, after being pensioned off early, a victim of mental turbulence doctors had no proper name for, he embraced esoteric, mystical, occult and obscure writings and people.

The dawn of the hippies was a boon, allowing him licence to roam, spout rubbish and behave as if he was eighteen again. He painted on scraps of wood, bits of glass, some roof tiles and even the round surface of a coffee table. The advent of luminous quick-drying paint was a great help.

He rented an apartment in the southern area of Lowestoft with his mother who kept imaginary cats. They only ever ate properly if invited out, otherwise they grazed when the mood took them at dishes of bits of meat, fish, vegetables and fruit left lying in all weathers on a long table, propped with a pile of house-bricks.

He called on many locals, exchanging words and ideas. He was invariably invited in to relate to the youngsters living within; or engage in arguments about God, truth and light with their parents.

Most of his artworks were parked at houses he visited. Often, he'd add a bit more while he talked to them. Many hung on to the works, praying that one day they'd be valuable.

The site of this Happening was a former army firing range and some of the youngsters created a Hare Krishna style chant and dance around 'to cleanse the vibes of guns and killing.'

After the awkward conversation, Gabriel set to on the Tai Chi, leaving Rodney to wander off in search of whatever he could find. Caleb recovered his pushbike from a hawthorn hedge and did a rove around warning everybody to be ready for the second coming of Christ.

As the afternoon wore on, a beer tent was freshly supplied by a hippie entrepreneur with barrels of his homebrew that was as welcome as the dope being passed around. The money man held out his hand for coins for his beer, and despite some criticism that it should be 'free, man, free,' did well.

Finding no customers for his tales of Alexander the Coppersmith or Rahab the prostitute, Caleb was ready to call it a day. He found Gabriel, having finished the Tai Chi, eating oatcakes stuffed with something to make the day seem even better.

In a spirit of goodwill that came from somewhere in his mind, Caleb offered his cousin a job barking in his events in the Fundrome grounds. At least, that's what Rodney thought his Dad said. For some reason, this offended Gabriel who said he didn't want a charity job and he'd manage very well, thank you.

Whatever the cause, as Caleb started pointing fingers at Gabriel and others around and calling them 'whores of Baal', several hippies joined in and tried to get him to 'chill, man, chill, stay cool.' For his part, Gabriel contributed, 'one crow on a tree, two crows on a tree, three crows on a tree that looks dead to me,' which a pair of hippies knew must be profound if meaningless.

Gabriel, a natural showman and Caleb, a natural preacher sold out for Christianity, were well matched. It was what could be called an eristic argument. From the ancient Greek goddess for strife, discord and chaos, this was argument for victory, not truth.

Whether it was the beer, the oatcakes, the smokes or tiredness some of the peace-loving hippies felt that they'd like to smash Caleb's face in, so he stopped being a twat and embraced love and harmony.

This was the loudly-voiced view of a shoulder-length hairy hippie called Dappled who'd taken an instant dislike to Caleb; he wasn't over-fond of Gabriel, either. A few followers agreed and together

Caleb was bodily placed on his bike facing backwards and invited to fuck off.

Rodney released a girl who'd he'd become attached to and followed his dad off the site. 'You are Alexander the Coppersmith, Gabriel, you're doing these people harm instead of warning them and nurturing them.'

By the time he'd shouted that, everyone had turned back to having fun, just as three police cars turned up and out stepped six of the local constabulary, noses twitching, truncheon hands trembling.

It had been an interesting afternoon, and a report with photos of it made the local news rag, second page. Apparently, there'd been complaints about trespass, noise, nakedness, playing music without a licence, drug taking, selling beer without consent, under-age sex and misuse of a hedgerow for unauthorised public urination.

****

The following Friday evening, start of the weekend, Caleb having thought little more about his cousin's strange friends and behaviour, was caught unawares when Gabriel arrived on foot at the head of about thirty of the same hippies.

Gabriel shouted from a distance that he was ready to take up Caleb's offer of a job and had brought a few friends along to help him get over joining the bourgeoisie. Within an hour, a camp had been set up of random tents and coverings on sticks and poles, a fire lit and water taken from the tap Caleb had installed for his chickens.

Elsie wondered if any of them were from the travelling community, while Rodney likened Gabriel to Moses leading the Israelites in the desert. That didn't go down well with his father. Dennis was delighted to see some of his new friends so soon, leading his mother to take him aside to whisper in his ear the perils and damnation of pre-marital sex.

That weekend Caleb had scheduled a dance for boy scouts and girl guides on the Saturday evening, a service on the Sunday morning and a film show in the afternoon. The family quickly discussed the advisability of pushing ahead with their plans before abandoning them.

Caleb rode through the village to the police house with its front room designated 'The Station.' Asleep at a desk was Sergeant Catchpole, their local bobby who'd seen it all. When he was awake, that was.

Catchpole roused suddenly when Caleb clattered through the door to tell him of the invasion of his land. He warned the officer of the imminent trespass, noise, nakedness, playing music without a licence, drug taking, selling beer without consent, under-age sex and misuse of a hedgerow for unauthorised public urination on his land.

The officer pondered a moment, watching a fly against the window, before telling Caleb, 'We'll keep an eye out. But, if there's no law breaking, we can do nothing and that's a fact.'

Caleb's protest about last week (that was Army land), about undesirables on his land (he hadn't put up a notice forbidding them entry), about drugs (Catchpole would come along and sniff the air) and sex (ah, it's a different world, these days, Caleb.') achieved nothing.

Caleb's big line that it was contrary to God's law brought on a fit of coughing forcing poor old Sergeant Catchpole to seek a glass of water from inside his house. He never returned to the office.

By the time Caleb reached the Fundrome, the hippies had truly taken over. They'd scrounged every bit of food from Elsie, used the toilet till the cesspit overflowed and Gabriel had set up a painting studio in the Fundrome itself. He repeated what the law had told him and they decided to make the best of it. It would only be for a weekend.

Gabriel resumed the argument with Caleb almost at the point they'd left it last week. Whether they were briefed or not, several hippies decided to form a ring round Gabriel and aimed sarcasm, insults and bad jokes at the Wright family, goaded by Dappled now dressed like a prisoner in striped pyjamas.

Dennis mingled; nobody knew he was a Wright. Caught in the middle, Rodney fell foul of some real-life threats: 'if you don't embrace peace, harmony and love, we'll smash your fucking brains out.' The same as Caleb had received and from the same loudmouth, Dappled.

Caleb made a thing of turning his other cheek, forgiving them and inviting them to his service on Sunday forgetting it was cancelled and to enjoy his site till then. This opened the can on more offensive, critical and poisonous worms.

Seeing her husband stumbling to a chair on the floor of the Fundrome, looking very white, Elsie took charge and ordered Rodney to go to the village and phone an ambulance from the call box.

When he reached it, out of breath, it was filled with two hippies entwined while four more painted the outside in lurid colours, an early form of street art. He rushed on to the next one, past the King's Arms where the landlord was ejecting a trio of happy hippies. This box was as yet undiscovered by the intruders.

The arrival of the ambulance with lurid blue flashing lights was part of a trip for many. One applauded Elsie for laying on such 'groovy' entertainment. Gabriel stopped the men carrying Caleb on the stretcher and told him, 'We love it here, cousin man, we'll buy it from you if you live and from Elsie if you don't. Yeah, right on?'

After examination, the doctor advised Caleb to rest, undergo tests on his heart, blood and eyes and after a couple of days in Lowestoft Hospital he'd be good to return to the Fundrome.

Only Elsie visited him, as Rodney was holding the fort and Dennis was busy discovering the joys of such wonderful people. His wife listened to his version of the doctor's view before finding a doctor to ask for herself.

She sat back at his bedside. 'Caleb, they think you're unlikely to recover properly, to be what you were before. You're over 80, remember. Promise me we can move back to the rest of the family near Beccles. The children are grown up. Sell the Fundrome to Gabriel, let Rodney manage the other bits of business and Dennis go to London as he dreams of doing.'

Caleb was more stunned by that than anything that the hippies and their unlikely leader had thrown at him. He heard himself mutter a promise.

****

Over the next two weeks, Gabriel became fascinated by all the junk and inventions on the site. He especially liked the quirky placing of a handle on the main door to the Fundrome. It was on the same side as the hinges. Opening was always an amusing exhibition of gymnastics and contortions.

While he didn't exactly feel the bond of blood or any guilt about how Caleb was regarded by his young mates, Gabriel couldn't help but be aware that several of the hippies appeared out of control.

Unable to express himself clearly and relying on the jargon of 'peace and love, man' that he'd steeped himself in, Gabriel had 'a chat' with Dappled who had hidden when Sergeant Catchpole made a visit to sniff the air. Many of the hippies had gone into town to collect their benefits, go through the motions of looking for work or to beg in the shopping area.

Smelling nothing, seeing nothing, the law never spotted Dappled, who was actually wanted for a number of police enquiries across East Anglia. And as soon as he'd driven off, Gabriel was seen to talk to Dappled in more earnest tones, surrounded by an ever-enlarging crowd of hippies as the groups who'd gone to town returned

Caleb, Elsie and Rodney watched the meeting outside through their window. It was pantomime, a mime show, though as voices rose, words were heard through the glass. They appeared to be rejecting Gabriel's leadership; he was too old, too uncool and too old-fashioned...

They thought they heard something about setting fire to the Fundrome and watching it 'burn, man, burn' with the Wrights inside. Dappled's voice was shrieking; spit flew from his mouth as his rage spilled out and his face darkened with hatred.

Caleb said he should go outside and try and calm Dappled with soothing words from *Psalms*. The family rapidly dissuaded him. Rodney said he had an idea and would be gone an hour. Ask no questions, leave it to him. Trust him.

****

Two days later at the next weekend, hippie numbers had increased by all sorts of waifs and strays looking for a free meal and music. New arrivals filled the land around the Fundrome and within it when it rained.

Meal times were the hardest for the Wrights, for if they cooked anything the smell would draw in many of them to beg, pleading imminent starvation and 'share, man, share.'

This Saturday, late morning, the sound of the hippies was drowned by a flood of scooters entering the site. Perhaps twenty of them, kids with shorter hair, many wearing parka coats against the early autumn sea breeze. No crash helmets, some bikes carrying two people.

Somehow Rodney had whistled up a mods' cell from Yarmouth and they were no friends of hippies. The bikes were parked in a semi-circle and the mods strode over en masse to the hippies who were already squaring up.

Caleb and Elsie were alarmed. A full-on battle seemed inevitable, despite the protestations of peace and love. Two brave girl hippies approached the mods to give them flowers. Dennis decided it was time to join his parents rather than be part of a battle.

Rodney arrived, pleased with himself. This would sort everyone out. He'd called at the police station, too. What he hadn't realised was that word would spread on the grapevine. And if a bunch of mods were due at a given point, it was provocation to the Hells Angels, the Rockers from Yarmouth who saw it as their mission to bury every mod in Britain.

A deafening roar filled the air, motorbikes shook the ground. The chapter swept onto the site, big motorbikes and smaller ones, mounted by leather- and studded jacketed youngsters, no crash helmets, girls and boys up for a scramble.

Their front wheels knocked over most scooters. The rockers parked up, ready to crush pansies and sissy dressers, the mods. And if a few hippies went down too, then it was a good day for rockers everywhere.

Rodney had not expected that, and muttered apologies as his parents looked at him in horror and Dennis slipped indoors and said, 'it's gonna be world war three out there.'

And so it would have been but for the arrival of two police cars and two vans, a police motorcyclist and some local villagers who'd also thought they were up for a good scrap.

While neither mods nor rockers were afraid of police intervention and the hippies were caught in the middle suddenly lying down passively singing about peace and love, the police set about individuals. They soon ran out of handcuffs, the vans were full, but the battle was done.

Reinforcements arrived and made short work of lingering aggression, taking in five hippies including Dappled who was recognised by his foul-mouthed language, six rockers and nine mods.

The battle of the Fundrome was history. All that remained was for the police to fill in their paperwork, take endless statements including from the Wrights, the local reporter and regional television to arrive and villagers ordered home.

****

Three years later, the Battle was still talked about, but Gabriel was in charge of his Fundrome now. Caleb and Elsie had moved to a caravan on the Beccles family site where they prepared to survive old age. Elise looked after him and he rode his pushbike around preaching, just as he did for years.

Rodney became a salesman for the Wright family and found he enjoyed motoring around selling and looking for new family business opportunities. Dennis finished school and went to London as a student. Somehow he just never came back to the area at all.

Gabriel had no head for business and as the world moved on, he found hippies were out of season and nobody wanted a ramshackle picture house. A few stalwart hippies found their way to Beccles to see what fun was to be had at the Wrights' expense. There wasn't much.

One trip when he'd injected and swallowed more than advisable, Gabriel thought he was Alexander and waited for Caleb to come back to visit so he could cause him trouble.

But Caleb never returned to Clottingham.

The site grew more neglected. Gabriel tried a re-launch as a hippie friendly outpost of the 'real' world, films, events, just like the glory days.

But no hippies turned up. The local reporter was busy. The hippie period was gone. Many became pillars of the community, occasionally a little embarrassed by what they'd done in their youth. Times moved on.

A housing development company offered Gabriel money for the site of the collapsed Fundrome. And there was talk of time in an asylum and how it would help Gabriel adjust to modern life.

Shortly after signing the sale agreement, the men in white coats in a van with green wheels were seen coming for him. Rumour had it that he was taken to a special home in Norwich where he encountered his very ancient mother. She didn't recognise him.

Happy days, they were. For some.

7. Long Story Short

Bumping into old Carmichael made an unpromising start to Jon's evening as he walked to his near neighbours. A pair of dogs strained at their leashes. Why on earth did the man need two greyhounds?

He didn't say, instead he regaled Jon with a tale about the price of private dentistry (£1500, in fact) he'd been forced to pay for his wife. He'd had his own mouth inspected for £80 and was told he needed major bridge repairs for about £2800.

Carmichael was having none of that, but did Jon know that when he got home from his dog walk last night, he sat down and his whole front row of well-repaired teeth fell into his lap? Jon made sympathetic noises and moved to leave, but Carmichael said, 'I can see you're in a hurry, Jon, so long story short ...'

After ten minutes of that, before he got into his neighbour's bungalow he was obliged to stand with other arrivals in the front garden and admire a tree they'd festooned with lights to the point of childish absurdity, though they'd put no monstrous ornaments out nor draped the house with flashing lights.

Jon was allergic to Christmas, season of humbug. Yet he attended the annual neighbours' get together that the Pratt-Thompsons insisted on hosting. Every year he wondered why the moment he crossed the threshold and was offered drink, plate and seasonal delicacies he couldn't take with both hands full.

At once he was being bored with mind-numbing tales ranging from derring-do to sheer survival, from expensive holidays to house maintenance. While he'd been allowed to ignore almost everybody since last year, some were determined that he should catch up on their news.

Whenever anybody mid-tale drops in the immortal lines 'long story short', you know you're in for an extensive haul of smiling, nodding, frowning, shaking/nodding your head and gurgling, 'ahh,' 'no!' and 'really?'

He'd worked with victims of crime and abuse, with refugees and people suffering debilitating diseases that affected their speech and the mantra was always, 'don't interrupt them, don't make them think you have neither time nor patience to hear them out. Don't truncate their stories so they feel unimportant.'

So, really, he should've been better able to cope with the excessive narratives of people who regularly buttonholed him. That was why he rarely went out except for work. He'd occasionally checked in a mirror that MUG or LISTENER wasn't tattooed across his forehead.

But he had more than enough piled on his own plate. His woes included constant imposter syndrome, being found out, a sense of inadequacy and needing to prove himself. By the time he'd reached his mid-sixties, that ought to have worn off.

Pleading an inability to stand longer on account of his war wounds was a ruse he'd used previously at these gatherings. Nobody ever picked up 'war wounds' when he was clearly the wrong generation and too unfit to have served in any war.

Besides, nobody listened – everyone was wrapped up in making their own voices heard above the background chatter and muzak somebody else had decided was the right fare for this crowd of neighbours at the Christmas bash.

Well-fed, well-shod and well-dressed Barry was in full flow about the good works he and his missus carried out on behalf of the little people, the down and outs on the fringe of society, the voiceless. Mr and Mrs Scott from across the street were gamely hiding their boredom when Jon realised he himself was losing the will to live.

He pretended to stumble on one leg, rub it furiously while muttering his line about war wounds before hobbling away from the cluster. Both Scotts made to move with him, the wife feigning anxiety about the leg. Jon waved them away, knowing that given half a chance they'd tell him more than he needed to know about running and paying for a vintage car.

He found a small settee in a nice corner of the second reception room the Pratt-Thompsons were blessed with and sank gratefully into it. Barry squeezed in close, the settee groaning under them. It was designed for two bantam weights, rather than the ample bulk of Barry and the medium loading of Jon, his unwilling listener.

Cursing to himself that he'd actually brought Barry with him and rescued the Scotts, he pondered his next escape route. Barry gulped from his beer can that was hopefully near empty, so perhaps Jon wouldn't have to sit too long.

'Did I ever tell you about when I was in London, just before we moved here? It was Camden Town, or was it East Barnet? A good friend, Robert, passed away from a terrible cancer. He'd made me and his sister co-executors of his rather complicated will ...'

Jon had heard the gist previously; it wasn't interesting then. Barry twisted his body round better to half-face Jon. He'd have preferred a seat directly opposite the man, but still, this would do.

'Robert owned a house in France which was rented, a studio flat in Barnet, or was it Finchley? Anyway, it was nice if you know what I mean and worth a bit. Robert left sums of wealth to 15 relatives and had specified that a house in Surrey and one in Essex were to be rented so the income paid his beneficiaries. Anyway, to cut a long story short ...'

There it was. Jon prayed for somebody to crash in and talk rubbish about football, petrol prices or the sands of time, anything to shut Barry up and release Jon.

But nobody came. Nobody saved Jon from a convoluted saga of death certificates, selling property in France, finding tenants of the right calibre and a history of all 15 of the late Robert's greedy, grasping, impatient relatives.

By the time Barry finally finished with a promise to tell him about the Japanese knotweed problem in

Surrey gardens another time, Jon was all but asleep. It was the arrival of Leopold, an ex-pat German who lived opposite Jon, that woke him and drove Barry away.

Deciding not to plead his war wounds – everybody was sensitive to poor old Leopold's ancestry – he instead pleaded his weak bladder and his medication to stop Leopold taking Barry's place on the settee.

'Ach, I know what you mean. I'm on so many kinds of medication I lose count, must keep them in little trays like seeds, you know.'

He reached out an arm and helped Jon up and walked with him to the toilet by the front door. He kept up a patter about drugs, illnesses, hospitals, private health care and the cost of staff healthcare in his factory.

Leopold ran a manufacturing and export business of souvenirs and trinkets from any part of the world you could name. Wherever it was, he made and exported tat for sale to tourists as if locally made. He was an expert in exports, customs, red tape, transport planes, lorry problems and insurance for decent healthcare.

It was all Jon could do to stop Leopold going into the toilet with him. He stood peeing, listening to the drivel being spoken outside. The window was too tiny to crawl through; the shower rail wouldn't take his weight if he made a noose of hand towels from the cupboard.

He spun it out, but eventually, Leopold pounded on the door, shouting, 'Hey, Jon, don't overdose in there. Think of the paperwork! People are here waiting for the toilet, you know.'

When he emerged, it was to a one-man round of applause that Leopold staged before he put his arm round his shoulders and led him to the conservatory. He was like a scavenger who'd found a delicious morsel and was scurrying away from others to keep it for himself.

The morsel was Jon, who noted the absence of other guests in the conservatory with dismay. Leopold somehow managed to grab two cans of pale ale from the dining room table as he passed and handed one to Jon while opening the other, all smoothly.

Settling himself on the arm of John's lounger, Leopold drained a good half of his can. Jon marvelled as it poured down his long gullet like water down a drain.

'Yes, the art of business is not dead, my friend, yah. You employ people and nowadays they want every benefit they think of and want to work from home as if my business can be made in the house! And you can't sack them. I do better than zero hours and minimal wage, yah? But I tell you, with all the inspections now and the insurance against the inspections, I must work longer than before to earn less than before. Jon, long story short ...'

And there it was again. Old Leopold was off, relishing the attention, loving sharing details with a man he genuinely thought cared and was interested. He droned on for a good ten minutes Jon knew he'd never get back on the perils of being an employer, the incompetence of Her Majesty's Customs and Revenue, employees and the inequities of Value Added Tax.

The torture only ended when a herd of neighbours led by the Pratt-Thompsons, a charming couple who wouldn't hurt a fly, everybody said, swarmed in as fast as their average age of 69 would allow.

'The Victorian photo is here!'

And everyone clustered round a framed sepia photo of the town's high street in 1899 showing upper floors of shops still present. As everyone rejoiced and whoever had suggested otherwise was put in his or her place, Jon heaved himself from the chair, joined the cluster before sidling out to the hall.

Safety by the front door, he thought. But he'd forgotten Marian Gray; she'd not forgotten him.

'Ah there you are, Jon, where've you been lurking?'

He wanted to tell her he hadn't been lurking but had been listening to umpteen selfish, pointless stories from people who should be licensed and kept under lock and key.

Recalling that resistance was futile, he meekly acquiesced as she parked him by the hall wall, beside a lovely painting of seven golden daffodils floating in a breeze and imparted important information he really didn't need to know.

'Jon, you may have heard that my younger son, Will, has been having trouble with the constabulary. And I have been so distraught.' Jon remembered the youngster only too well; he'd been a royal pain in the backside for five years at secondary school.

'He's a lovely boy, such a kind heart. But he got in with the wrong crowd. I mean, you were a teacher, you know what a bunch of wrong 'uns looks like. Well, my baby boy agreed to help some of these ruffians out, well you would if you're overflowing with the milk of human kindness, and he carried some bags to and fro to help. He even stored a few in his wardrobe because one of them was desperate…'

'That's terrible, Marian, you need a solicitor, but my old war wound in my knee is playing up, it's the time of year that does it, I'm allergic to Christmas and I need to relieve my bladder and my daughter is coming for me in case it's icy outside.'

He should have saved his breath. Marian ploughed on, blocking the hallway as she told him everything she'd discovered about bail, visiting inmates, the remand system, search warrants and how individual officers took against certain innocents.

After what felt like an hour, a couple had to get home afraid of leaving their sick dog too long, Jon took himself out with them, omitting to say goodbye to the Pratt-Thompsons or grabbing his winter coat from the bedroom.

Marian followed but gave up when he put his head close as they walked to hear all about sick dogs, the cuteness of their little Bonzo and the inhumane fees that vets charged. His mind stored away the sick dog excuse as a good one for next time he needed an escape.

The couple clearly had no idea who Jon was but bid him goodnight and a Merry Christmas as he reached his gate and they pressed on to the end of the lane. Jon watched them, shivering and wondering about going back for his coat. Tomorrow would do. Then he noticed a toddler's doll sat on his wall, obviously fallen from a pram and left to help the child's parents who'd lost it.

He'd call round and apologize to the Pratt-Thompsons and explain that he he'd left his pain killers at home. They'd surely give him a long story short, but after a night's sleep he might be able to cope.

Of course, he had a little planning to do first.

What nobody ever wondered out loud was how Jon managed to live in that locality on a teacher's pension. And they never asked him about his side interest, his little hobby that was a nice little earner.

His late wife had told him people wouldn't ask because they had no clue what he did, apart from not being interested in him. Who would suspect that Jon, an ordinary, late middle-aged gone-to-seed PE teacher, was available for hire to carry out assassinations?

They'd pay attention if they knew. They'd be fascinated.

Next morning, the entire area was sealed off with police cordons and vehicles. When he went out in an old coat of his wife's to fetch his, he heard the news.

Marian Grey had been found dead while her automatic garage door kept trying to close on her body. Barry was head down in his bath, fully dressed. Leopold was discovered on the golf course half a mile away, his intimate body parts stuffed down Holes 14 and 15.

The sick dog had decided to commit suicide by cutting its own throat and the Pratt-Thompsons had apparently been adjusting their massive Christmas tree when it fell and electrocuted them simultaneously.

Jon's coat would definitely keep till another day. When it was his turn to talk to the door-to-door cops about last night's event, he played the dotty old man role, launching into an extended, garbled tale and offered to make it 'a long story short.'

The officer, suspicious of Jon from the moment he spied a child's doll hanging by the neck from the washing line, said, 'No, sir, I'd like the long story long, if you please.'

8. We Should Have Built An Ark

Fed up with everyone on his back, the young man finally decided to knuckle down and look for a job. Just to spite them, as much as anything else.

His grandparents, biological mum, pathetic stepdad Pedro, and even his real, loathsome dad who'd just completed a three year stretch for robbery and was celebrating like someone who'd walked the entire coastline of Britain for charity, were all on about it.

Everybody wanted Drake to stop wasting his life pissing up walls and being misled by undesirables who seemed to have taken a shine to him. The trouble was, he had almost all he needed at home. His mother waited hand and foot on him; food, laundry and company were on demand.

Tall and lean, sporting a shaved head and face, a massive hole in each ear lobe held open by bright purple bungs, he was a walking bovver boy, an eastern European gangster looking like the great grandson of a Nazi escapee. With knuckles perpetually red raw, strong, wiry, fast-footed he was distinguished by enough ugly tattoos to scare old ladies.

He had a brain, as his teachers had told him and his mum over years and years, but he chose not to use it. Or rather he used it in what might be termed 'alternative' ways. Drake made few friends. He had a smidgeon of loyalty to family and a loathing for his real dad who'd left them so his mum hooked to that nonce, Pedro.

He'd decided in his own time and way to surprise everyone. He'd find a job and really go for it. He didn't have to take it. Just go for it.

Online searches produced a shortlist of three jobs he thought suited his skills, his temperament and were interesting enough to keep him constructively engaged for a month or two.

At the Sunday family barbecue while the delicious non-meat and meat-substitute burgers and sausages were slowly incinerating, his Mum started off, prompted by seeing him swill a can of beer, squash it and drop kick it over the garden fence.

'Stop that, Drake, think of the neighbours for a change. Drink properly.'

Ignoring her, he rose with no support from his arms in one clean move and walked across the garden like he was on a dance floor. He stood at the table - a door on breeze blocks - grabbed a bottle and downed the high-strength brew in four seconds. He rounded the feat off with a ground-breaking belch, which amused the children, at least.

She watched, aghast, shaking her head. Where had her parenting gone wrong? Was it because with her second husband she might as well have been a lone parent?

If only Drake was more like his contemporaries who held down proper jobs, sensible relationships and some were even now parents and pillars of society. If only he'd turned out half as good as younger brother Raymond and big sister Chloe and his cousins with names she couldn't recall.

'Hey, Morgan, catch!' Drake yelled at the cousin turning burgers as he hurled the empty bottle over to him. Morgan dropped a spatula from one hand and a barbecue fork from the other, but the bottle slipped through his fingers and shattered across the patio.

Shocked, horrified expressions took hold of every face turned towards him. He took a bow. What a loss he was to the entertainment business.

Drake hadn't expected Morgan to take it so moodily, shrugged and sat down on a garden chair while the grown-ups led by a tight-lipped Pedro flapped about with cloths and a brush and dustpan. It was just a laugh.

His mother shared her desperation that he'd not even looked for a job with the entire family spread across the garden, which featured as its centrepiece a Ford Poplar with no wheels on a pile of bricks, a lopsided stack of roof tiles that might come in handy and a wooden shed stuffed with flammable detritus.

'In fact, I've got a shortlist of three, Mum, so stuff it. Three jobs I mean, not women to poke!' He yelled his triumph for the broader neighbourhood to appreciate.

'Nice one, Drake, let's hear what you've chosen...' his stepdad, Pedro, invited him, pulling up a garden chair. Others gathered closer. This would be worth hearing.

Milking the moment, Drake made a pantomime of searching through his jeans pockets and down his backside for a piece of paper. He almost lost his audience's focus, everyone ready to believe Drake was playing about again.

Then he took off his third best trainer and removed a piece of folded paper that must have made walking uncomfortable. He'd got his audience back again. Pedro recognised the paper as coming from his briefcase, a work matter that the boy had stolen when looking for something to write on. But he kept quiet.

Drake grinned, unable to stop himself. He showed it to a couple; there was nothing on the paper. It was all on his phone! He waved that proudly.

'Right, come and get it, make a proper queue, you animals,' Morgan shouted. And be careful of the glass here that Drake hasn't cleared up.' Drake raised an eyebrow; Morgan was pushing his luck.

The family did queue in a more or less orderly manner to collect paper plates and refresh their drinks. Drake spent a few moments sending the three job ads to everyone. Family sat where they could, eating from one hand and scrolling their phones with the other.

In that short, blissful silence, next door looked hopeful when he peered through the fence. Six houses away a child howled as it was hit by a sibling. Or a guardian.

Job 1: Scammers Wanted
Work from home,
must have reliable internet connection and
be willing to have our blocking, identifying and
nosey parker programs installed.

Work your own hours, scam in any country.
Variety of scams available:
false NHS, business invoice, Amazon and other delivery company scams.
Remote scanning available by planting viruses in selected people's inboxes
Or calling them.

You can advance to making physical calls in person in an area not too far away,
but far enough.
We're looking for a special team of grifters
to carry out the greatest scam in history.
Take your pick.
Call us today.

Job 2: Chamber of Horrors
Could you be a lookalike for a real baddie?

If you have the right skin colour, hair, facial expressions, bone structures
and are of the requisite height, you have a future
in our unique hire-a-lookalike service.
From real villains to fictional psychopaths,

people love to liven up adult and children's parties, dinners or
   just walk down the street beside you.
   You'll certainly draw a crowd.

People pay good money to have Adolf Hitler show up at their Christmas party. Or for Jack the Ripper to first foot them on New Years' day.
   Or to be the first to have Vladimir Putin appear at their kids' birthday events. They pay to have Dr Harold Shipman make a house call on an elderly friend or relative.
   Peter Sutcliffe is a guide on a scary night tour of Yorkshire.

We even run a couples service.
   Fred and Rose West will call on your friends to see if they fancy a weekend in Gloucester.
   Ian Brady and Myra Hindley will do a spot of child-minding for a fee.

If you look like anyone who did or who might spread terror or go on a killing spree, get in touch.

Job 3: Go Places with Replicar
We're a bespoke company making replicas of wooden things,
   or real things in wood.

   Bats, clubs and battering rams? Yes, we turn them out.

   Historical implements for collectors and the curious alike?
   Of course.

The French Revolution guillotine is our top seller, with the short drop gallows or the long or measured drop version a close second.

We make garrottes and electric chairs without the metal parts.
We've made a number of crosses capable of crucifying an adult.
We created two triremes and three Viking longships
but we also build boats, junks, barges and wherries
of all kinds to sail anywhere.

Decorated coffins are popular nowadays and we do a special service for customers to choose
and reserve their own casket in advance.
Some pay more to decorate their boxes to their own tastes.

Whatever the customer wants in wood,
we'll make.
So, if you can saw, measure, design, love making things in wood
or are keen to learn how to,
we have work for you.

The sky darkened, heavy clouds blotting the sunshine out. Before they finished reading, Granddad said he hadn't got his glasses, so one of the kids read to him. Drake, having given them long enough and they'd had a second reading, demanded their opinions.

Voices shot at him from all over the garden, his family sharing opinions. But there was no consensus.

'I'm going for them all!' Drake cried in triumph. He really was full of surprises. His mother thought he was taking the piss; his siblings thanked God silently for bringing a change in their dear brother.

And then the first raindrops fell.

Big rain dollops, like bullets from the sky, hit the ground and them. Gradually, the drops built, the family made for cover. Now it was a sheet of rain; then a wall of wet.

The Sunday of their barbecue and Drake's surprising behaviour would be set in their minds forever. It turned out to be the one that the rains caused by global warming began and never stopped.

Making their way indoors, Raymond, Chloe and three of the cousins with forgotten names, decided to go to their own homes as it wasn't going to improve. Thanks, Mum, for the lunch. Bye Granddad. Good luck, Drake.

Their real Dad, the loathsome man, was outside loitering, drenched as his two oldest made a dash for their cars. He was hoping to touch his family for a few quid to tide him over. But nobody stopped to listen or to subsidise his new beginning.

Despite the weather, over the next two days, Drake attended three interviews. He wore the same clothes and made no effort to look smart. Why would he? He'd never been to an interview before. His attitude as he entered each office in turn was that the world owed Drake a living. No more; no less.

For the scammer job he was directed with a dozen or so other hopefuls to a room with headphones and computers and told to make calls following a script with several variants. He stumbled through one before saying 'fuck this' and leaving.

Besides the actual interview, he missed the other simulations they'd set up – door-stepping, online virus spreading and gaining confidence of suspicious people. He wasn't surprised to receive a message later that morning telling him he looked 'too honest' for a scammer. But if had an accident and came out with 100% burns, come back and see them.

He killed time in town making faces at people huddling in shop doorways against the incessant rain and jumping in puddles like he was a kid. Why wasn't there a job doing that? He'd be great.

Then he splashed to the Chamber of Horrors HQ, a small house made up to look like a fairground sideshow decorated with plastic skeletons and distorted face masks. Water poured out of grass-blocked gutters, so he slid sideways to get inside.

A girl behind a desk, only a little older than him, spoke pleasantly to Drake and told him what was to happen. He wondered when would be a good moment to ask her out as he fancied her instantly and imagined her spread across the desk.

Pictures were taken of him by a bored photographer who answered to 'Dad' from the girl. They snapped him full on, sideways, from the back, made him walk and stand, sit, perform everyday tasks and speak into a recording machine. He had to smile, grin, laugh and make out he was sad.

He was given a meatless sandwich and a glass of vegetable puree while the girl took two bookings for interviews and one for the cancellation of a Josef Stalin appearance at a summer fete because of the rain. Her Dad set his computer to work analysing Drake's vital statistics.

He'd only taken one bite of the sandwich before looking round for a bin to spit it into, when Dad said, 'I'm sorry, son.' Drake took a sip before spurting a stream of vegetable puree up the wall as his stomach heaved. 'What!'

'You see, there's no match for you in our database, so you wouldn't be booked by anybody because you don't look like any famous bad boy. Unless it was a ghoul's funeral. I'm sorry. But if you have any facial work or a nose job done, come back and see us.'

Drake told the man where he could put his poxy job, his stinking business and his whole useless, rotting body, blowing any chance with the girl who stood by her dad while Drake poured invective over him.

He made his way home on two separate buses and through rain which didn't give an inch and poured off his shaved head and into his clothes. His mum's front garden was already half full of water and a man across the road was piling sandbags round his front door.

Mum and that small-fry Pedro kept asking how the interviews went as if their lives depended on his answer. Not in the best of moods, Drake went out after his tea to see if his favourite standby girl was around.

She wasn't.

Next morning, he walked, huddled in an old anorak, his head under a plastic bag – one of a dwindling supply now they'd been banned.

The Replicar workshop was easy to spot, even through the rain, because of a wooden car mounted on the fascia of the building. Already, the wood was showing signs of water damage.

He was given a short, guided tour of a workshop by a man who'd worked there all his life. Or so he said. The smell of wood was over-powering and Drake realised that it was pleasant, one he could enjoy as he worked. He was asked about his experience on chainsaws, electric saws, cutting timber, measuring, designing and making things to order.

He had none. The employee must have gone deaf because he seemed not to hear anything Drake said. Well, there was background noise from saws, chisels, polishers, sanders, forklifts and people shouting.

Another workshop 'over there' was identical, just different people working on different projects, he was told. A roped-off section of the workshop they were in had a bed and a cupboard of medical supplies.

'This for the people who accidentally chop off their arms or legs, is it, mate?' Drake asked. 'We have the very best employee care here,' the man replied.

Drake was expected to admire the gallery of actual or pictures of finished furniture, boats, cars, torture implements and unusual doors, frames and window shutters.

He made noises which the man took as overwhelming approval. Within fifteen minutes, Drake was on his way home, having been told he had a week's trial and to come back tomorrow and see them.

Having been given no guidance on what to wear or bring, Drake put on the same t-shirt as for the past two days – it'd been thoroughly washed by the rain. Same jeans, same trainers. Same wet walk and same entry to the Replicar building.

This time he was met by a managerial, officious looking woman clutching a mini pad. Her ears were muffled but she heard everything. She looked Drake up and down, her face a picture of disgust and disappointment. Without checking his name on her device, she barked:

'Workshop next door. You should have been told that. Don't come in this way again.' He was pointed to the side where a pair of double doors was being guarded by the woman's replica. Very appropriate. 'Name?'

'Drake.'

He was pointed into an almost identical working palace, but here staff wore bright orange jump suits and the medical area was three times as big and filled with workers nursing cuts and severed limbs. Drake looked around to protest when a third woman with a pad stood in front of him holding up an orange jump suit and ordered him to 'try this on for size, if you can get your big head through it.'

Realising that his appearance had led managers to conclude that he was a criminal and should be in with the people paying back to society instead of being locked up, he tried to explain. While she heard, she ignored him. She gestured to a toilet where he could change and only when Drake was not looking checked her device.

She promptly turned back, yanked him by the shoulder from the toilet door, snatched back the orange jump suit as if he'd been trying to steal it and pointed him back to the first workshop.

Reprimanded for lateness by a man not unlike the one he'd met yesterday, he approached the point of telling them where to stick their shitty job. But a sudden heightening of noise from an electric cutter as a massive timber trunk was fed in, rendered speech pointless.

A group of four other recruits were being given the safety talk which amounted to little more than 'watch your fingers if you're fond of them. There's compensation for loss of fingers after the first two and generous payouts for loss of your heads.'

Drake stood with them and heard the supervisor explain that they had to make fifty garden boxes and bird tables for an order followed by twenty five coffins this week. They had a huge commission to build a replica Noah's Ark, but that would have to wait till the bread and butter jobs were done.

Drake said, 'we should build an ark, or we'll be washed away,' in an attempt at worker camaraderie. They agreed an Ark would be useful, given what was outside. And increasingly inside too, as the endless deluge found holes and weaknesses in the roof; one waterfall was horribly near an electric switch.

'We have to make the small stuff, first. Bread and butter, you know. Anyhow, someone I know reckons the rain will stop soon and the water will drain away. No problem.'

Apart from expressing that hope, the older guy made a fair job of demonstrating how to read a plan, cut wood to size with minimal wastage, make joints, add strengthening and work in pairs where necessary. To his surprise, Drake found himself absorbed in the challenges of turning planks of wood into useful boxes.

Next morning, his mum was amazed he was returning to Replicar. She wasn't surprised he wore the same clothes, but none of her washing had dried so she let it go. She took over his attempt to make himself a sandwich of sliced cold potato and non-animal meat and slipped a can of beer left from the barbecue into his bag as he squelched to work.

As days passed, Drake learned woodwork and enjoyed a little banter with his workmates. He especially liked the money they gave him after a week. Since the abolition of cash, he checked his online balance, smiling happily.

'Plenty more where that came from, if you keep up the good work on the bread and butter stuff before you start on the big projects,' the supervisor told him, watching the medical section where one recruit was staunching blood from his thumb.

Drake went out at the weekend, dolled up in a clean t-shirt and his second-best trainers, seeing people he'd not bumped into for ages, all surprised that he was still working. He saw a couple of cousins at the bar, but as he couldn't recall their names ignored them. His friends enjoyed his treating them to drinks before he stopped.

Keen to keep enough to spend on wine, women and song for himself, he made his excuses and dashed through the flooding streets to another club. His money went on cheap beer substitute and a prostitute who'd been flooded from her home, needed to be persuaded to step out of her wellington boots and who charged extra for music in her dimly lit room but wasn't fussed about protection.

Drake worked most of the following week; the flooding worsened. His way to Replicar was blocked, the sea had risen above its previous flood height and nobody ventured across streets swirling with increasingly fetid water from blocked drains and backed up toilets. A crowd of youngsters broke into a small shop looking for food. Once he'd have joined in.

He came across his supervisor, staring sadly at the Replicar factory in the distance, water lapping around his feet. Side by side in amicable silence, they stood till a wave from an inflatable rescue dinghy washed over, driving them back.

'Ah, Drake. Doesn't look like we'll be working today.'

'No, it doesn't. Or ever again, I reckon.'

'You're probably right. Should have listened to you. We should have built an ark all along.'

Drake nodded. 'Too late now.'

'You're probably right again. We never listen till it's too late, do we?'

'We?'

'Human beings. Always think we know best.'

9. Sallumus and Tolbanes

Preparation for my annual address to The Porter Society began immediately after delivery of the last one. No resting on laurels. The next one was always most important; coming up with new ways to talk about Porters.

I'm trawling *The Bible* this year, where I found a reference to two men in the *Apocrypha*, at *1 Edras 5:28*, identified as 'sons of Salum and Talmon'. By *1 Edras 9:25* they were listed as *the porters*, Sallumus and Tolbanes, who along with many men had taken 'strange wives.'

Other versions have it as 'foreign' wives that they took. While this was rich soil for speaking, it was fraught with danger in our sensitive times.

Glancing through previous talks, I smiled at my coverage of the Shore Porters Society, established in 1498 and now the world's oldest storage and transportation company. Hardly award-winning, but I'd received enough kind words said to volunteer again the following year.

My Cole Porter talk was well received with a group of enthusiastic amateurs from our local players singing his classics. I added a footnote on the singer Gregory Porter and the songwriter, producer, cornerstone of the Stax record label in Memphis, Hall of Fame inductee, David Porter.

The year I chose Katherine Anne Porter (1890-1980), American novelist, short story writer, political activist and Pulitzer Prize winner wasn't so lauded. Two family members had the temerity to suggest I was running out of topics. This, even after my friends in the local amateur theatre group read extracts from her book, *Ship of Fools*, 1962's best US-selling book.

But I had to stop digressing, focus on my next talk.

It's possible that Tolbanes was actually Talmon in *Nehemiah 12:25*, where he was noted as a guard of the storerooms at the gates of Jerusalem. It's equally possible that he was Telem listed with Shallum as gatekeepers in *Ezra 10:24*.

Shallum may be a variant of the name Sallumus, the son of Jabesh who killed Zachariah, King of Israel who'd sinned in the eyes of the Lord and became king himself for just one month before being assassinated. Was this too much background for my talk?

And there were mentions of a Shallum as the husband of a prophetess, a descendant of Shesham, a high priest and, wait for it, the chief of Porters at the Kings' Gate, the east one of the temple in Jerusalem!

Talmon was listed among the 212 porters in 1 *Chronicles 9:17*. So it seemed reasonable to assume that the pair was temple gatekeepers from the tribe of Levi. I'd found my topic.

Despite their important jobs, they'd married strange or foreign wives. It happened a great deal in the Old Testament, men marrying women and girls from the wrong tribes.

We also knew that Gatekeeper and Porter are mutual synonyms, and that Porter is nowadays a deep, dark craft beer, once widely drunk by the working classes. That was my theme two years ago and went down as well as the samples I brought in, at some personal expense.

Shakespeare placed his Porter scene in *Macbeth* between the murder of King Duncan and the discovery of the body. The unnamed servant was responsible for opening the locked gates; repeated outside knocking and his drunken responses created humour and light relief between sections of grim and bloody tragedy.

That was last year's talk; my friends in the local amateur players had performed it for us. Went down a storm.

Well, that was enough; too much research kills an idea. I'd discovered The Tavistock Archives, a 'great misanthropic trust' with its dislike, distrust and loathing for humanity. There was a reference to The Porter, a 'Grade A sociopath. Nothing about this guy is worthy of praise. Best to waterboard the ape and think about it later.'

Just for a moment, I wondered if he'd be more interesting than old Sallumus and Tolbanes. The Archive went on to state The Porter is 'violent and prone to dangerous balcony-based monkeying about with the fine line between stupidity and insanity. Regularly makes outrageously generous promises, which he never fulfils. He's impossible to kill - one can only hope he will destroy himself. Always in need of fresh underwear due to soiling tendencies.'

Wow! Yes, that one was for next year. Could the society be The Tavistock Society of Psychotherapists? But the Archives contained templates for use in a 'wiki' way. One of my young descendants explained to me, a wiki is put together, amended, improved or deleted by everyday people.

I liked that. History may be written by the victors but can be deleted by common consent as if it never happened.

Settling on my first thought, I decided to imagine a day in the life of a couple of porters bearing great responsibility keeping the gates safe but being handicapped by having taken strange wives.

I wrote a little play, or glorified sketch. Two male characters, Sallumus and Tolbanes were solid, long-term friends who worked as senior porters guarding some gatehouse. Their women were Donyell (God is my judge, wife to Sallumus) and Zillah (shade, married to Tolbanes).

There was also an official with the role of ensuring correct paperwork was available for inspection on demand. His name was Amos, which means weighty. He was a large, fat, over-dressed, lump of lard with a pomposity second to none.

Humour arose because Donyell and Zillah didn't speak the language of their husbands and were making a slow job of mastering it. Their 'strangeness' also stemmed from the fact that both would have felt at home in an English Victorian mental asylum.

How they ate, stared at people, horded food, carried out daily chores and supported the men with children was alien to everybody, particularly Amos who took it on himself to train them to behave as wives of senior porters should.

Several old friends in the local amateur actors group agreed to perform my little play at our next annual gathering of Porters. It was my first attempt at scriptwriting.

It had to cater for all my family, downwards from my own six children, through their spouses and offspring, my 11 aunts and uncles, my 29 cousins and our dear old Matriarch who'd also feel at home in that same Victorian home for the insane and demented.

Everyone gathered at the farm of my Uncle Todd who used the money we contributed to turn out a massive buffet spread in his second barn, laid out on trestles. His home-made cider, fruit juice and well water washed it down. Puddings were brought by families; lots of meringues and cream.

Nobody needed go hungry. Nowadays he slipped in meat-free, dairy-free and gluten-free foods to satisfy changing tastes and fads. But I never said anything.

After the meal, family volunteers cleared away the food remains, dishes and cutlery. There was tea, coffee, yet more juice and, again, herbal infusions have crept in along with alcohol. I've grown used to the smell of cannabis and have learned it's always safer to say nothing, just be grateful so many Porters spare the time to come for a day.

Once the trestles had been nosily dismantled, we crammed together for a set of compulsory photos taken on their mobile phones and available on family social media instantly. Children under 12 were then excused to go and play hide and seek on the farm and in the orchard.

The youngest remaining Porter was asked to recite the names of new arrivals to the family – in baby or marriage form; the oldest beside Mother was invited to share names of family members who'd departed through death or divorce.

And then I, making a ridiculous pantomime of being reluctant but giving in to calls to speak, stood by the last trestle standing and normally spoke for a reasonable half hour. It was a cross between best man's after-wedding speech, funeral oration and audition for a part in a TV show.

'Dear family, dear Porters... You may not be familiar with Sallumus and Tolbanes, but they were porters. Senior, important porters with responsibilities.' I then got my Biblical history and details out of the way fairly quickly. I just wanted to set a scene.

My actor friends shuffled on beside me, centre stage. I noticed some audience quite pleased that I'd finished; others were less happy at seeing the amateurs strutting yet again. They may also have feared I'd return to round everything off with more words.

The little performance started well enough. Sallumus and Tolbanes were seen at work, carrying bales, guarding the gatehouse and supervising 'others' in the form of universal dogsbody, Pete, who took on anything players needed, a task he'd carried out since 1969 when he joined as a young thespian.

This drama would see him play slaves, porters, officials who helped Amos and a crowd. And all without change of costume. In fact, he did everything without change of voice or expression, either.

We saw Sallumus and Tolbanes in a bit of banter and a few in-jokes, establishing their personality traits. Next, their strange wives Donyell and Zillah went about their domestic duties, hanging out a line of washing and revealing how weird they were. They talked in fast gibberish and followed a set of obscure customs and rituals.

Amos arrived, rolling his fat belly as he shuffled one foot before the other. He demanded, pompously, to speak to their husbands. A scene of misunderstandings and misconceptions ended with the arrival of Sallumus and Tolbanes needing their lunch.

Amos repeated with even more pomposity what he'd told their wives that all the paperwork was out of order and the women would be deported back to Strange, thinking that was where they came from.

It was at this point that any self-respecting amateur players would forget lines, fluff cues, break a prop or forget to come on. But not this one. Oh no. The thing had to suddenly descend into dark, surreal, unintentional farce.

Sallumus held Donyell tightly to stop her spouting nonsense at high pitch and volume. The actor playing Amos took exception at this because he'd been having a secret relationship with the real-life Donyell who was married to the actor playing Tolbanes to the horror of the actor playing Zillah as she fancied Tolbanes and was now ready to say so.

As secrets spilled left, right and centre, copious face slapping, hair pulling, clumsy stage combat, spitting, shoving, high hysterics, shrieking, attempts to claw eyes out followed as the actors got carried away. Even Pete was drawn in because Donyell was his daughter-in-law.

Our Porter audience loved it, forgetting my Biblical times scene setting that this was a serious topic with undercurrents of correct thinking to suit the times. They just enjoyed the unplanned fiasco unfolding before them.

Immediately I was praised by some early teenagers as being cooler than they'd thought, while I got hot under the collar. Small comfort under the circumstances, but any praise from a youngster was worth treasuring.

Someone must've told old Uncle Todd his barn needed cheering, so he'd placed mini bouquets of seasonal flowers everywhere. Recognising one as a handy weapon, Zillah grabbed it and brought it down on Tolbanes' head which produced a lovely shower of broken petals.

This was the cue for everyone to grab flowers and set about each other, including, I noticed, three members of the audience who joined in readily.

As I wondered how to bring it to an end, the actors knew instinctively that it had run its course, so in turn, each stormed off, slamming the barn door which creaked back open every time, so the effect was rather lost.

Amos even had the nerve to spray a few harsh words in my direction as if this was what I'd planned. On a flourish and a shout that I could whistle if I thought they'd ever help me out again, he too stormed off, leaving Pete to sweep up the flower mess.

The applause was deafening, the ovation was standing. The cast returned to take four bows, which was three too many. Sallumus and Tolbanes had got a bit forgotten, but they'd inspired the whole thing.

Follow that next year, Mr Porter.

10. Seven Henchmen

I know. I know, many would find it unfair and unreasonable, that I turned from an entire political party just through the actions of a handful of their functionaries.

But I'm like that. If someone's not for me, they're against me.

Many years ago, I was rejected for membership of the Approved List of Candidates. I reached the shortlist and then somebody put a spanner in the works because *he* didn't think I was candidate material. Not even to fight a hopeless council seat.

So, I quit. I walked away. I didn't join the Other Side to get back at them, because I loathed that lot to a man and a woman. Instead, I became 'apolitical', somewhere between an agnostic and a cynic. A plague on both their houses.

What hurt as much as the outright rejection was the cavalier, off-hand manner of my dismissal, coupled with the sense that they'd done me a favour even to consider me.

However, I shouldn't blame Jeremiah Smith personally.

By the time he was crowned Party Leader and romped home in a General Election, I was established in my alternative career as a political journalist. Hostile to every politico, questioning everything, every motive and every response to every issue, I was the everyman journo.

Jeremiah, the new 'first among equals' had worked his way up a variety of different ladders from mine, of course, yet we had something in common. We both hailed from the same neck of the woods.

He, naturally, went away to private school and a big-name university; I, the son of shopkeepers, served my time at our local grammar school and a small-name university. Our paths only crossed in the Youth branch of our favoured political party.

There I watched how even as a teenager Jeremiah instinctively worked a room, cracked jokes with the boys/men and flattered the girls/women with a continuous charm offensive he could switch on and off at will. I struggled to make eye contact with the girls, who seemed to find me faintly amusing.

Eventually I left, having stuck out like a sore thumb at one too many cheese and wine events. He, of course, thrived, the youngest district councillor in a generation, speaking out on whatever put him in a good light. He led a march against a factory closure and took credit for putting right an injustice through his Party contacts.

He went on to become chairman of this, local big wig of that and beacon of hope for those who loved his unstuffy, go-getter ways. On the local TV news and in the corner of the odd press photo I noticed that he always had an adviser hovering nearby, a man with ginger spiky hair and staring eyes, who missed nothing and made notes on a clipboard.

This was Norman 'Spike' Raven' who looked an older version of his weird, loner 14-year-old self I remembered from school.

His first fifteen minutes of fame came for inventing an insurance scheme pupils could pay into for sixpence a week – half a crown payout for detention; five shillings for the cane. Only potential offenders joined, but it was a roaring success for a month.

The local media splash was followed by the regional and national boys. At that point the Headmaster summoned Spike into his office and put a stop to the scheme. I knew then that Norman 'Spike' Raven was an original thinker who'd do well.

My career path after university was modest - a journalism training course before landing an apprenticeship at our weekly rag. I stayed local, secretly nursing hopes of doing 'something' in politics. And the only thing really worth doing was becoming an MP.

As a junior reporter I grew adept at reporting council meetings, funerals of the great and good and sniffing out unusual stories to lighten up a humdrum town life. My prospects were deputy editorship, the editor's chair followed by a senior post in the regional office and a seat on the board when I retired.

So, while I waited, dreaming of canvassing, the hustings, my victory speech and sitting on the green benches, on the quiet I became a stringer for several national news outlets, scouting for stories they'd blow up into scoops and scandals. Occasionally I thought about Spike, but we'd never been more than nodding acquaintances, so I looked out for a book he might write or a new appearance at the shoulder of somebody famous. Like Jeremiah.

For ages Spike publicly and clearly served as his closest adviser. I assumed Spike drafted if not wrote Jeremiah's speeches, co-ordinated his appearances and fed the media with nuggets from Jeremiah's World.

Just as Jeremiah reached the foothills of Everest by securing a seat in Parliament, I made it to the Press Gallery for one of the national dailies.

At that point adviser Spike suddenly disappeared but I suspected he still conjured unexpected ideas from the ether. Without evidence, I believed he still worked for Jeremiah but out of sight. Behind the scenes, behind the arras from where he could stab people on Jeremiah's behalf.

I had only one chance encounter with Jeremiah while he was a backbencher. When Division bells rang, Members' lobby was cleared of staff and journalists. We loitered in corridors hoping to snatch a word with an MP and get a new lead, unless it was near the end of the eight minutes and they were in a hurry before the lobby doors were slammed shut and locked in their faces,

With a good four minutes left I caught Jeremiah in an affable mood after a fulfilling dinner in the Members' Dining Room. He stopped when I wished him good evening.

After my name I revealed we came from the same home area. He was delighted, thumped me on the back, roared approval and promised to talk to me whenever I wanted to know something.

Flinging his arms wide, he dredged my face from his memory and our shared youth activities. He hadn't noted I was on the fringe, but good politicians neglect those on the margins at their peril. I guessed that he assumed I was a secret Party supporter.

I asked about Spike, expecting an enigmatic reply, but he acknowledged Spike was heading his backroom team and doing great work. If Jeremiah ever made it to Number 10, he assured me, Spike would be among his closest.

He ended with a suggestion that the three of us should have a drink one night and reminisce about old times in our hometown. And with that, he continued to the voting lobby; we never exchanged words again.

Following the rise of Jeremiah, I discovered no references to his backroom team. At that time, I just couldn't see how I could make a story out of it.

It was four years before I found my scoop. Jeremiah somehow survived a messy and publicly waged divorce battle, several unsuitable relationships, a few minor errors in junior office and a biggie over a rashly spoken throwaway about poor people in the north and became Prime Minister.

Over three days he drip-fed the names of his Cabinet as they were pictured striding up to Number

10 and away, grinning or pretending to be on important phone calls as they walked.

There was no word of his advisers, his inner circle. So, I made a story out of that absence and was pleased other media followed it with wild speculations of their own. Once Jeremiah could hold out no longer, he announced his six-strong inner policy advice team, which I labelled his 'henchmen.'

It stuck. 'Henchmen', or 'hench-operatives' as my editor demanded they be called, described loyalty as much as the crony of a dictator or criminal mastermind. But it was unflattering, bringing to mind deviousness and orders carried out in a brutal manner.

However, I was more interested that Spike was not among them. After all, he relied on Spike and he couldn't just appoint without making it public.

Since the 1960s, SPADS, or special political advisers, have been part of the system. They're appointed as temporary members of the Civil Service, advising ministers of the Crown in a way that the regular Civil Service cannot. And, indeed, should not.

Opposition parties appoint their own advisers and these government or opposition 'policy advisers' or 'policy wonks' are fished from the full experience and temperament pools of the human race.

Business world advisers are consultants, usually commanding huge by-the-hour fees, like solicitors. The joke that if you bid a solicitor 'good morning' you would be billed for time spent being courteous and expressing advice on whether it was a good morning or not, wasn't really funny.

Humans gather advice from all over, besides friends and family – accountants, doctors, dentists and other medics, non-executive directors and even energy advisers who just want to sell solar panels or new electric car charging points.

It's the *quality* of the advice that matters, everyone says. Problems are invariably multi-faceted, so there's a need for a round, holistic approach encompassing a variety of specialisms and prior experience. And then it's a matter of judgement to take their advice or not.

The PM of the day approves all Ministerial appointments and sometimes intervenes to remove them when they fall out of favour. Many are poached from ministries to work directly in Number 10. Wise leaders choose advisers from a variety of backgrounds of life experiences, education, cultures and ages.

Some turn out to be unfortunate placings, including one in recent times who recorded and filmed every meeting, every event, kept every email and memo during his time close to the PM to stab him in the back with later, after he inevitably was removed.

It wasn't Spike.

I studied the list of the PM's appointed, four women and two men. Had Spike changed his name? And suppressed photos of himself? Where was he?

In a stroke of humour, I detected Spike's hand. An extremely tall Secretary of State was landed with very short junior ministers, so the senior man always had his head above the parapet.

In the balance of the SPADS he had a female artisan sort, a female religious kind, a female natural server and an outstanding female sage. The pair of males could be described as the warrior type and the yes-man. Again, Spike must have been involved in making that team.

Where was Jeremiah's dreamer of off-the wall ideas, his thinker outside and inside the box and his avoider of minefields, bombs and traps? Where was his man to toss a dead cat on the table as a distraction? Where was the one who saw dark nights of the soul when they were but specks on the horizon?

Where the hell was Spike Raven?

Online he was listed as 'humourist, adviser and someone to keep on your side.' He was credited with writing the 6th form sketch show, *'Bring Out Your Dead'* which I'd forgotten but contained the immortal lines, 'you want my advice? Don't whistle with blancmange in your mouth. And don't pee into the wind.'

Apparently, he trained as a teacher and survived a year in the classroom where a contemporary recalled him announcing in a staff meeting that all colleagues should be sure to check their pigeon holes the next day. Early in the morning everyone found photocopies of pigeons and little piles of pigeon mess.

A former student remembered being told, 'before you vacuum the whole house wearing music headphones over your ears, ensure the cleaner is plugged in and switched on.'

His final two recorded wisecracks online were 'if you find the queue too long, start up a chainsaw and they'll be falling over themselves to serve you. Even those with missing legs' and 'if you're caught sleeping at your desk, lift your head slowly and say, 'In Jesus' name, Amen.'

From then on, Spike ceased to exist on any social media, nor appeared in print. Explaining that I was after the story of Jeremiah's seventh henchman, I tapped my contacts, every MP who talked to me, Party officials, House of Commons staff and two Ministerial drivers who normally knew everything.

It seemed that Jeremiah was indeed served by a seventh henchman, off books, paid as a private consultant for special and specific projects. Clever.

And a year later during the night of the Great Falling on Swords of Cabinet and advisers alike after an organisational cock-up in Government, it was even cleverer. The six fell or were pushed; the seventh survived, his special task to guide the Jeremiah ship out of troubled waters.

My paper employed odd job people for various activities. I asked around over quiet drinks in different pubs. Hacking into 10 Downing Street was neither realistic nor worth the risks. We weren't, after all, enemy state operatives.

There was never any record of Spike entering or leaving Downing Street. Had they built a secret tunnel? Even explaining that I wanted to be a parasitic fly on the wall watching and listening to what must be remote meetings between Jeremiah and Spike, came back as 'nothing doing.'

On the point of tearing my scant remaining hair out, one of the black-ops girls suggested it would be easier to watch it from the other end – in Spike's house, if he worked from home. It was surprisingly simple to track him to his home address; slightly more complex to set up a fake repair team with van and cabling in hand to claim he had a tech problem.

Already vetted by Special Branch, Spike's home equipment would be state of the art. So, I suggested the team should be gas repairers checking a reported leak.

They did a superb job and evacuated three apartments on either side of Spike's to add authenticity. Within three weeks, several thousands poorer from my own savings so my editor knew nothing, I had eyes in every room of his accommodation, several on his supersized screen occupying a whole wall.

His daily routine comprised early morning coffee while sampling every news outlet going, showering and dressing casually. He then sat to a sparse breakfast of fruit juice, brown toast and more coffee.

After token exercises on a fixed exercise bike and five press-ups, his commute was a stroll to his lounge, logging on his big screen and waiting.

He scribbled on piles of scrap paper and notebooks. He played music from our teenage years. He waited for a connection from Downing Street. It came late morning, three days out of four. The PM had been briefed, agreed his diary and set his new SPADs off on a variety of tasks.

Then he was ready to chat to Spike. Sometimes other SPADs were present with Jeremiah; most days just the pair talked. If anyone interrupted, they switched to unrelated topical news items.

Spike shared first thoughts on recent events; they planned strategy and made a few chess-like suggestions of moves the public, politicos, the media, special interest and lobby groups and the rest of the world might make.

In my second week, as I sat at my home or in my office observing Spike talking with the PM in Downing Street, I realised I'd stumbled on something BIG in media terms.

Amidst the cogs and wheels of his inventive mind this one had the air of heralding his finest hour to date. It would take a special kind of person to do it all for Jeremiah without claiming credit.

It was to be a two-hour, seven nights a week, real-life, real-time extravaganza on mainstream TV and social media for a fortnight in support of a new era of open government and public education.

He'd devised a nifty giant board game screen with all the interactions anybody could desire. It had the air of a chess game merged with *Battleships*, endurance and mental supremacy. It drew on games with titles such as *Nuke Apocalypse, Dictator in the Garden, Headless Chicken* and *Twisted Loyalty*.

Spike thought it would show the PM at his best running computer models, algorithms, conundrums, chance, destiny and Grade-A decision making. He'd take on all comers with problems, global disasters, cost of living, education, health difficulties, pet theories and mad schemes and show the world he was the master at work in the service of the Great British Public.

There was a beneficial spin-off. Jeremiah and his program were available to other countries around the globe. For a small consideration. Not money. No, nothing so mercenary. In exchange for fossil fuels, rice, wheat, vegetables, technology, water or carbon credits, Jeremiah Smith would save the world.

The grand culmination was a declaration of war in the name of high moral ground that had all the appearances of being for real. He had a standby ready – reintroduction of the death penalty for crimes against humanity, war crimes and others as yet unnamed.

Spike foresaw those crimes would be hijacked by the gender, sex, religious or social reforming brigades, so he added 'vexatious irritants' to the crime list and death penalties would be carried out in public. Or it would be war as well as death.

Either way, Jeremiah would become even more inevitable than he was, thorny problems would be consigned to history and life would be amazing.

True to form, Spike dreamed up onion masks as a fun element. It was desirable to entertain the mass of citizens so they could appreciate how good their lives had become.

Well-designed onion masks would hide who was doing what. Each of the clone players (real or simulated) could keep peeling off layers to find the same face over and over again.

Not onion masks for hair growth or to deal with dandruff, not onion hair masks, but Spike's masks would make everyone look like they were wearing an actual onion and stay totally anonymous. Nobody had an unfair advantage. Only Jeremiah was seen and heard by everyone. Continuously.

It seemed they hadn't yet come up with a name for this circus. Spike favoured Big *Brother* as it smacked of fraternal strength and big-heartedness. Jeremiah with more of a sense of the lessons of past history than his adviser rejected that in favour of *The Jeremiah Game* or *Democracy*.

They tried it out on the other hench-folk. Nobody understood it, but that was the point.

While citizens were trying to work it out bad news was buried; necessary but unpopular and strange measures were enacted.

To break that story before the government's news machines would be the making of me. The summit of my career. I could retire on the payments from public appearances. I could write my autobiography. Somebody would make a film about my persistence.

I'm still waiting.

For that drink with Jeremiah and Spike. For my onion mask to arrive. For my editor to grow a pair of balls and publish my scoop. And for my trial for 'vexatious criminality' to be concluded.

11. That Turpentine Tree

It's said that every choice has consequences. 'They' also say that for every love story enacted on a stage, behind the scenes there's a hate story.

Many hold to the belief that the show must go on. And still others swear that life imitates art, art is a template for life.

Well, bearing all that in mind, the play *That Turpentine Tree* is now one that superstitious people refuse to name, like 'The Scottish Play.' This one became 'That Hanging Play' and everyone knew what it meant.

Its final performance before it was deemed unlucky to act in, was staged at the old Corn Exchange, cheek by jowl with the ghosts of 18th Century merchants who once thronged there.

It had four characters in four acts. Some writer has since rehashed it by adding more, so that no two actors are ever alone together backstage.

A turpentine tree presented practical difficulties to designer and director. They settled on a huge symbolic structure cobbled from rusty metal, old rails and mesh, screwed to wheels like a gigantic supermarket trolley.

Branches protruded - disjointed robotic arms at random angles. One was strong enough to hang a man, as events proved.

The artistic vision was explained in a program note. There was a paragraph on 'what is a turpentine tree?' penned by A Teacher of Science from the local high school. It was the terebinth tree, common in Palestine and the Middle East.

She wrote stuff about resinous secretions, turps, herbal remedies, medicines and poisons. She got a tad nerdish explaining pines, important for turpentine production, enthusing about maritime, Aleppo, Masson's, Sumatran, longleaf, loblolly, slash and ponderosa varieties.

By then most people switched off. Indeed, some never got beyond resinous secretions, thinking seminal, blood, sweat or tears. Sketches of a trunk being debarked and V-scored like 'cat-faces' as resin drained down confused many, thinking they were looking at a reproductive system of a swamp-fly.

She should've added a section on what happens to a human neck while a body is stretching on a gibbet. A Teacher of History could've contributed a potted timeline of public execution hanging and hangings as suicides. A Teacher of Religious Studies and Morality could have droned about the one Biblical reference, in the *Apocrypha, Ecclesiasticus. 24:16.*

The Teacher of Mechanical Skills could have told how turpentine is an excellent timber for dance floors, constructing plywood, laminated beams and bench tops, for joinery, parquetry and boatbuilding.

The Teacher of the Crystal Ball would have ensured all that was in the program notes; but nobody knew or guessed. No teachers were in the audience. But that's the danger with happy stories on stage; nobody spares a thought for misery behind the scenes.

Out front, the love triangle story was simple. Character A was the protagonist; Character B was one suitor, Character C another. B and C both loved character A, competing for A's attention and affection.

Character A loved both B and C but could choose only one to be with.

Character D, the antagonist, was secretly fond of C but showed scant patience for any. D loathed A.

A and D were men; B and C were women, but there was variety and fun to be had in swapping roles or having all of one gender.

Out front they were stereotypical, totally flat. Once in that backstage world, however, their real personalities shone through. Old enmities flared; forgotten wounds and slights re-emerged, fresh and raw.

The tree, Character A's delight, was wheeled onto the stage whenever the setting moved to his/her house. It was a symbol of the love Character A had for B and C, a wide-spread affection that looked beautiful, smelt interesting and appeared when something meaningful was to be conveyed.

It was supposed to be brought through by a crew of stagehands. But of course, there weren't any. Whichever actor was not needed in that scene dragged it on and slipped back into the shadows.

In Act 3 there was one moment when they were all on, so Character A had to appear with it trailing behind and look natural and completely at ease doing it.

During Act 1, A shared his dilemma with the audience; his impossible choice between B and C. D created a wall of high-horse disapproval of A. Both women had a fair period of time together offstage.

And Beryl and Caroline shared a mutual dislike in real life.

Some of this was evident while they waited for their next entrance cues. All actors develop a way of communicating with others while listening carefully for onstage progress.

Beryl's real-life backstory was that she was a personal assistant cum virtual secretary to whoever bought her research, organisational and planning services. Of average height, she exuded energy, bounce and joy of life that entranced most people she met.

She'd managed to push to the dark corners of her mind an unhappy single-parent who died and grandmother-raised childhood. Determined not to let that define her, she'd made a success of her life and knew she'd find the man to father her children when the time came.

Caroline was woke, on trend and mixed race, frequently apologetic for the white half. She set out her targets and went for them. Like the Terminator, she never gave up. She too had shrugged off excess baggage from her past, her dysfunctional siblings and prison-held father. Having set her heart on the man Beryl had chosen, she relished the challenge.

So, it was in a sense no surprise that this pair, feisty in contrasting ways, beautiful, desirable and confidently aspiring to the same man, should be the trigger that sparked the tragedy that followed.

After a frosty silence during the first act while the two men on stage established their territory-claiming techniques, Caroline demanded in a calm and reasonably quiet voice, 'hey Beryl! Did you actually go for a drink with him last evening?'

Beryl fiddled around, smoothing out her next prop, a large fan of black feathers. 'Who told you that, Caroline?'

'Don't answer one question with another. Never mind who told me. Did you?'

Beryl looked straight at her.' Yes, I did. And very nice it was!'

Caroline stepped closer. 'The drink or what came after?'

Beryl, with a smile, stepped back, 'Oh we're in high school, are we? Teens squabbling over the captain of the rugby team?'

'If that's how you see it, Beryl,' Caroline hissed, moving closer again, 'for me, it's more serious than a bit of fun.'

Outwardly, it was no more than a few pent-up feelings. But deep down, it reflected an increasingly toxic jealousy of each other's successes and of Adam's continuing relationship with both. His inability to decide allowed him to enjoy, in his masculine way, the fact that they adored him.

Small and lightweight, a man of Asian heritage, Adam was clever and assured of finding someone to fulfil his wants. With no apparent racial resentment chip on his shoulder, there was a weakness for flattery and admiration particularly from his string of young females that he found irresistible.

He held some job that he'd never speak about, something important in research. He kept fit with twice weekly gym visits. He'd entered the London Marathon twice, coming in within the first two thousand entrants each time.

Damian wore more of a chip on his shoulder, like a badge, a big heavy chip. Living in a time when people claimed membership of a white working-class background to bestow credibility, he was lower middle class – his parents had owned and operated a caravan holiday park.

He enjoyed boxing, martial arts and extreme sports and a court had made him undergo two courses in Alternatives to Aggression. Others suspected he was an armchair sports enthusiast but as he never saw anyone socially from the acting or his work worlds, nobody knew. He liked it that way. Nobody needed to realise he sold miniature historical battle kits online.

He held onto grudges. He suspected Adam was a thief - Damian's girlfriend at school, money from his pocket during rehearsals and now Caroline. Fascinated as he was by her, she'd barely looked at him, being so obsessed with bad boy Adam.

No person asked, even later, whether the director, a non-disclosed ethnic minority binary in a wheelchair, deliberately mixed skin colours or were characters cast colour blind? We'll never know because after the tragic events, they/them never spoke in public again.

During the 2nd Act on stage, the characters shared old stuff from school, their early days of working, neighbours, people they knew, interpretations of current news and past issues – all at loggerheads.

By midway through the act, they were in a my-dad's-stronger-than-yours mode, each outdoing the other onstage. In the wings, Adam's prowess in bed and his turn-on skills became the topic of heated debate through clenched teeth, as what had happened the previous night increasingly annoyed Caroline and Damian.

It was in the 3rd Act that things came to a head between the men. Adam, finally fed up with being told Damian needed to approve how he lived his life, snapped and prodded the bigger man.

Although the backstage area was relatively tidy, it was a matter of a short time before Adam stumbled to the floor from a changing bag.

And despite the proximity of his next entrance which was to a pub where quarrels and disagreements were to be settled in a form of truce that Character C dreamed up, Adam leapt up and went for Damian.

They fought like cats and dogs, like school kids, like men who'd had too much to drink. D found a metal bar, a surplus tree branch which he swung round, emitting yelps as it sailed through the air, closer to Adam's head on each swing. Suddenly with a sickening crunch it hit Adam on the side of his head. He went down, whimpering.

Damian spat, 'you're making sounds so you're not dead. Either get up and fight. Or get on stage and mutter your lines.'

Caroline came off stage just in time to see Adam, groggy, dazed, pull himself up on a stool in front of the make-up mirror and crawl towards Damian. 'What the fuck...?' Caroline said, alarmed. The distraction allowed Adam to find some energy and grab the metal spike.

His sweeping circle above his head forced Damian to retreat. He got to the wall and Adam struck with deadly force. It took out Damian's lips and his front teeth. He crashed to the ground, doing his best to contain his pain silently.

Caroline grabbed Adam's shirt front, 'We're on. Now.' They left Damian to recover as best he could. He sat for a few minutes, listening to the deterioration in relationships on stage and then grinned, a huge, bloody, open-gap grin that was both funny and scary.

It was as if inspiration had occurred. Hiding the metal spar in the prop cupboard he delved around, emerging with a ready-made noose from a nostalgia poetry show they'd performed last year.

While he waited, he looked at himself in the mirror making no attempt to stem the bleeding. He gave himself the bloody grin every few seconds.

Returning, Beryl was shocked and could only stare while her mind whirled to the next part of the drama. She only had a second before her cue arrived and she returned onstage, leaving both a shake of her head and a pointing finger.

They were exhausted. Adam had survived his little scene, ignoring his forehead trickling blood down his face. He slumped in the battered old armchair and considered his options. The women on stage spouted lovey-dovey lines of sisterly love and time they'd had or wanted with A.

Damian waited till Adam appeared to relax, closing his eyes for sleep. He wandered up to the tree that was to go on soon and with his back to Adam, attached the noose to the strongest branch.

Wheeling round suddenly, Damian seized Adam by the throat with both hands and yanked him towards the tree. Caught off-guard and still shaken, Adam put up little resistance. That was easily overcome with a pair of groin kicks from the knee and a resounding slap across the face.

Stood precariously before the tree, Adam offered no fight as Damian reached for a rickety wooden chair and pulled, pushed and hit Adam till he climbed on it, Damian's grin adding to the ghastly terror of the moment. As if in a nightmare, Adam allowed the noose to go round his neck.

Damian kicked the chair from under his feet. Immediately, Adam danced, kicking the air, desperately trying to get his hand between rope and neck.

He stopped. Adam hung, gently dangling. Nodding, pleased with himself, Damian caught his breath while listening to the stage action through the backdrop.

It was the 4th Act. Damian trundled the tree onto the stage, the body still swinging. As he caught the first gasp from the audience, the big, jagged grin returned to his battered face.

The women seemed frozen; no words scripted or otherwise emerged. Much of the audience laughed, unsure if it was meant to be funny or if it fitted what had now become a totally surreal play.

With Damian grinning and Adam's body horribly realistic, the laughter faded. Some cried; one screamed. Later, witnesses disagreed whether it was the knowledge that a man was dead or that another man grinned which caused their biggest revulsions.

That Hanging Play was abandoned, breaking the theatrical superstition that a show which has been started must be finished.

12. Person of Interest

It was once a classic study in the detective exams, requiring both consideration of the evidence and a bit of professional judgement.

The question: On balance in this scenario, which Person of Interest is most likely to be guilty?

1. Name: Thomas Peyton deceased, 39 years old.

Some information:
Thomas Peyton's body splashed a hysterical woman and her toddler in the car park of Severalls House, a 21-floor block of top-end housing. Enquiries suggested that Peyton had fallen, jumped or been pushed from the 18th floor where he lived in an up-market apartment with a balcony facing west.

Some evidence:
We discovered an alleged suicide note typed on an antique manual Remington typewriter hidden in the dressing room. The letter 'f' had dropped and 'o' was cloudy with the centre filled in. His home office contained a state-of-the-art copier and printer, but personal documents that were outside the computer network at his business address were typed and copied sparingly. The suicide letter was found in a card folder labelled 'The End' and dated a week before he died. It was typed on that machine, but whether it was his fingers that pressed the keys is not proven.

'My name is Thomas Peyton. I was almost five and a half feet tall. By the time you read this I'll be little more than a heap of human matter, bones, muscles, skin, brain and blood. I'll barely fill an A2 carton.

Many of you will wonder how I was able to throw myself off the Severalls Building when I was always so afraid of heights. Well, desperate times call for desperate measures.

I've betrayed all of you long enough. The shadows of my past crimes and sins are closing in. I've reached the point where I can take no more.

Nursing a massive carbuncle on my private parts through my careless indiscretions, robbing one person to pay back another and becoming overwhelmingly weary with it all, I've taken the ultimate walk of shame. Down 18 storeys.

Following careful observation and joined-up thinking, Selina alerted me to financial problems we're facing and a huge debt we must repay. I know we cannot begin to do that.

I believe that my Crock Initiatives business partner, Omid Salomi, has been skimming from the proceeds of our joint venture and submitting false accounts to cover it up. I have challenged him several times in recent months. He always lies, diverts attention or brings up my own small indiscretions so I have felt unable to go to the police or engage Matthew Newman, our heavy from the local underworld, to sort him out.

The final straw was notice that Her Majesty's Tax Stasi are about to open an investigation into our business. I die at my own hand, at a time and place of my own choosing. I ask Theresa to forgive me and pray that in time she will.'

2. Name: Omid Salomi, joint owner of Crock Initiatives.

Some information:
38-year-old, fit, tanned, sports-enthusiast and astute businessperson with a number of directorships and a chairpersonship to his name. Married, lives in Hertfordshire with his wife, Selina and three children of school age. Has never come to the attention of police, HMRC, social services, DVLA or any official agency. He's a school governor, member of his local church Parish Council and volunteers at the St John Ambulance brigade.

He was visibly shaken to discover what had happened to his business partner when he arrived at Peyton's apartment for a 10am meeting that was in both their calendars.

His statement, taken an hour after police arrived at the scene:
I am Omid Salomi, business partner and close friend of Thomas Peyton. We've known each other since Nottingham University where we studied economics.

We set up Crock Initiatives soon after graduation. The name came from the American expression, 'a crock of shit,' because at first, we traded in waste, sewage removal and cleaning. Once we'd got a bank account and letter headings printed, Crock Initiatives stuck as the name, like shit to a blanket.

And we've done well over the years. There's money in rubbish, cash in shit, if you like. But we now also sell second-hand cars, trucks, clothes and anything pre-used. We buy holidays from tour operators that have become unusable through sickness or death and sell them on with a discount. And profit.

We have our offices in north London, as you know, but when we wanted to discuss business privately, we met here in his apartment.

Yes, I was aware that Thomas was paranoid about data crimes, so used an old typewriter for private stuff. No, I never saw anything he typed, but he'd often start typing as our meetings ended, even before I'd left.

I don't think it helped him sort out his jumbled private life at all. Liars need good memories. Thomas's was imperfect. Everyone says that Theresa is a saint to put up with him, but she has a fearsome temper and I suspect she is jealous of his younger women. I think she could commit murder, yes, but to be fair, I've never discussed it with her.

He's always been driven by his sexual needs and got himself into lots of unpleasant situations at university and since. When I realised that he was skimming off the top and presenting false accounts, I guessed he was paying off a woman, her husband or an abortion clinic. He'd done it before.

When we got the notice last week that the tax people were launching an investigation, Thomas fell apart, losing all rational behaviour. I urged him to take a few days off.

Yes, it was quirky that he handwrote or old fashioned typed on his old Remington things he didn't want shared or hacked into. As far as I know it worked, nobody ever saw anything he wanted kept private.

No, I don't know but guess his files are in that cupboard. No, never.

3. Name: Theresa Hopley, in a relationship with the deceased.

Some information: She is 42, slightly older than Peyton but as she was resident in the apartment and clearly they were sharing the bedroom, she was happy to be styled as his 'live-in personal partner.'

Her statement taken 20 minutes after police arrival at the scene:
I've been living here with Thomas for about eighteen months now. We met through business. I worked for a local authority consortium responsible for buying in waste disposal services. Now I work in the special services department of Crock Initiatives.

Before you woke me, I had another half hour before I was ready to get up and prepare a working breakfast for Thomas and Omid. These happened about once a month, but more recently.

Yes, I heard rumours about Thomas' relationships with women. I accept him for what he is. Was. He's a remarkable man, so loving, so full of great ideas and solutions to business problems. I adored him. And I have a huge capacity for forgiveness.

Yes, he accepted me for what I am. Twice divorced and a traveller on the road to sexual exploration. My mother, a love child of the 1960s, inspired me.

The typewriter? I suppose he used it once or twice a week. Usually when I was out or asleep. He filed everything on old fashioned card files and he maintained an old index card roller thing.

Did it work? Well, I could easily see what he typed and filed. No, I didn't look that often. No, I certainly didn't see the last note he wrote.

4. Name: Selina Salomi, nee Peyton, sister of the deceased, aged 32.

Some information: Married to Omid Salomi; mother of their three children, she sits on the board of Crock Initiatives and describes herself as a 'housewife.' She is kept informed of business matters by her husband and late brother but appears to take no part in the day to day running of the company.

Her statement given five hours after the discovery of her brothers' remains:
I still can't believe what has happened. When Omid came to tell me, I just couldn't make sense of it. I know he had his problems, financial and

occasionally personal. But Theresa seemed to be good for him and I thought things were looking up.

There's no way my brother jumped from that veranda. He was scared of heights, really scared, shaking, sweating, unable-to-move scared and never went near the edge of the balcony. When he bought the place, I was puzzled but he said he had to try to get over what was an irrational fear. It was Omid's idea to buy it, and Thomas bought it from a developer's plan before it was built. Omid persuaded him it was a great investment; property only ever goes up in value. Of course, Omid had shares in the company, but even so, Thomas loved it.

Somebody pushed him over. No, wait, If someone pushed him, he'd have to have been near the edge. No way would he be, even to retrieve something valuable that was blown there. So, he had to have been picked up by somebody strong and thrown over.

Yes, yes, I'm absolutely sure. I know him. I know him better than anybody, even Theresa, even all his women. And even Omid, even my lovely Omid. Thomas and I were raised together, closely, by our grandparents when Mum and Dad were lost in that US plane crash over Nebraska when I was five and Thomas was twelve.

I'm telling you, he was chucked over. Like rubbish.

I last saw him a couple of days ago. He was waiting at ours when I got back from the school run. We talked about all sorts. Yes, he was worried about the tax inspection. But not suicidal. Not Thomas. He loved life too much for that.

5. Name: Matthew Newman, 49, freelance special assignment operator, occasionally employed by Crock Initiatives.

Some information: known to police as a fixer, cleaner up of unusual waste and arranger of special activities that sail close to the legal wind. Served prison spells in 1985-6 for grievous bodily harm and in 1991 for failing to report a suspicious death.

His statement taken nine hours after the discovery of the remains, when Mr Newman was invited to the police station to assist in enquires:
I ain't got nothing to say. Yeah, I worked when needed for Crock. I work for lots of companies who have special requirements. I'm good at it. I'm well paid.

No, I ain't never been in his place up the tower block. I went into their office or got a phone call to say when I was needed. I then quoted them a price.

Mr Salomi usually gave me instructions, Mr Peyton dealt with what I heard someone call 'the bigger picture.'

Some of the lads did an April Fool prank by sending him a ticket for a roller coaster ride. Not me, mate, not me.

No, I didn't throw him off the balcony.
No, I didn't push, knock, hurl, dump or frighten him off the balcony.

*No, I ain't ever been there.
No, Mr Salomi did not pay me to throw him off.
No, nobody else in Crock paid me to throw him off.
No, I did not know he was afraid of heights.
No, I thought he was a straight up guy, full of ideas for business.
No, I'm a capitalist, I believe in the free market.
No, I ain't got nothink else to say.
No, prison was a long time ago. I learned my lessons and never again.*

6. **Statements from others**:

a) The office secretary, Ms Sylvie Watson, 25 years old, in command of the back office at Crock Initiatives, claimed that she'd been Peyton's extra-curricular entertainment for a year but had called it off when he mixed her up with another woman, Ms Sandra Wilson, 19. She was aware of his fear of heights, spiders, snakes, chickens, moths, hedgehogs, fast cars and germs. She had full praise for Omid Salomi's patience in dealing with Peyton, but felt unable to trust Mrs Salomi when she came into the office.

b) Peyton's neighbour in the apartment below, Raymond Abel, claimed to know him reasonably well through encounters in the lift and the car park and tolerated his frequent parties which Abel suspected were drug fuelled and occasionally lasted 24 hours.

Abel and Peyton had an altercation last Christmas when Abel knocked on the door to complain about loud music as his son was sick and needed to sleep. He described Peyton as aggressively swinging his fists, urging him to 'come on then, prick, come and take me on.'

He'd met Mrs Salomi once and thought her 'stuck up, up herself.'

c) Mr Archie Fenner, antiques dealer, stated that he'd sold Peyton the old typewriter, had tried but failed to correct the f and the o and reported that Mr Peyton had asked him how was he supposed to write 'fuck off' properly? He struck Mr Fenner as impatient, restless and 'darkly troubled by something' or why else would he use an old typewriter when his office was stuffed with computers? He never met Mr Salomi but had sold his wife antique carpets and candelabra at a bargain rate.

The question: did he commit suicide; did he slip or who murdered him?

The answer: It was concluded that Peyton committed suicide while the balance of his mind was disturbed and despite his often-repeated fear of heights. And because he was no longer around to challenge what others said, he was unable to add more lies to the mix that soon became fact.
13. Tumbleweed Corner

It's on record somewhere that I first knew the world was completely mad when somebody was fined for allowing the shadow from his parked car to go into a parking space reserved for disabled drivers.

Just how it is these days. Leaving that aside, I guess all wasn't well when I realised that the postman was someone I'd known for years. I mean, he was a regular deliverer of our circulars, bad news and bills, so of course I knew him. But close up, I realised I KNOW this man.

He had a run-of the mill face, I'd say. Well worn, creased round the eyes, leathery surface in need of soothing cream. His mouth quite weak, but hidden beneath an Edwardian style moustache, so nobody was sure.

He walked in an ordinary way. Well, he would with tramping door to door over three decades.

He gestured with his fingers curved into a hook, as if he wanted you to come closer. Hear his tales of woes. His rejecting female advances through his keen conscience. Jokes he'd picked up doing his job.

'I didn't realise you were a postie,' I muttered, in some confusion.

'Ha ha,' he laughed, 'very amusing.'

Puzzled, I continued my day. The next person with that face was the attendant in the self-service garage. I had to queue for the last petrol pump as electric charge points had replaced them. Nobody wanted a charge; nine cars waited for petrol.

He had an everyday face, I'd say. Well lived in, folded round the eyes, dark surface in need of massage. His mouth hidden, beneath an Art Deco style moustache, so nobody was sure.

He walked in an everyday way. Well, he would with all that perching on a stool over three decades while operating the pump and taking payments for fuel, drinks, sweets, smokes and occasionally flowers and condoms.

He gestured with his three fingers curved into a hook, as if to show you what survived his industrial accident nineteen years ago. Hear his tales of mishaps. His hopes channelled to a smutty calendar on the wall behind the cash register. Jokes learned moonlighting for the refuse collection service.

'I didn't realise you were a garage operative,' I cried, in wild confusion.

'Ha ha,' he laughed, 'very comical.'

Puzzled, I continued my day. The next person with that face was a fellow customer, coming in to pay for the carwash.

He had a round-robin face, I'd say. Well read, bleached round the eyes, spotty surface in need of medication. His mouth unfortunate, but hidden beneath a Victorian grandee style moustache, so nobody was sure.

He walked in a circular way. Well, he would with holding his balance on fishing boats as a lad and the illegal smuggling boats he now gigs on today.

He gestured with his fingers curved into a gun shape, as if he wanted you to keep your mouth, ears and eyes closed or he'd shut them for you. Hear his tales of victims. His rejecting advances through a predilection for the seedy and sordid. Jokes he'd created doing his job.

'I didn't realise you were a customer,' I whispered, in some fear.

'Ha ha,' he laughed, 'very dead man walking.'

Puzzled, I continued my day, ignoring the fact that everyone driving and all the walkers looked identical. Then, there was my boss, parking next to me in my space at the clinic.

She had an angelic face, I'd say, if you'd seen a lot of devils lately. Smoothed out, like a Chinese mask, hiding pock-marked skin that needed grit blasting. Her mouth hidden, beneath child's party clown lips, so nobody was sure.

She walked in an exaggerated way. Well, she would with all that bossing about while encouraging underlings.

She gestured with manicured fingers curved into a hook, as if she wanted to whisper in my ear that I needed to shape up or she'd ship me out. Hear her tales of cash flows and side-pocket investment expectations. Her new code of practice about safe distances and approved conversations. Jokes she'd scraped from Alternative Jokes.com.

'I didn't realise you were the boss,' I chortled, hungry for a donut.

'Ha ha,' she mouthed, 'very strange.'

Puzzled, but resisting commenting that it wasn't as strange as her face that had become the postman's. I continued my day trying to do my work which made no sense any longer, realising that everybody owned the same face.

Colleagues, those people who came and sold sandwiches and drinks for lunch, the cleaner who was running late, the lab techies as I walked through carrying a single sheet of paper to look busy and the contact in Anaheim, California who was having breakfast when I called late afternoon.

And I told each identical face, some teenage spotted, some so filled with snake venom injections they could only mutter, that I didn't realise they were ... whoever they claimed to be. Especially with the clip-on moustaches, false lip sets and three or more beady eyes, nobody was sure. Well, I wasn't.

After walking in a three-legged style, well they would if they were mounted on wheels, they gestured with seven or eight fingers as if they wanted to claw back what they'd lost. Their moans set to organ music. Their human temptations stolen from a psychotherapy manual. Their unfunny jokes.

I was told I was very naff, very out of date, very confusing and very droll.

Going home was a carnival of identical faces, but bizarrely not bodies. All houses around and near mine were from the same architect, the same builders. All faces watching from their front rooms or bedrooms were the boss and the garage man.

I live on the street corner. It's known as Tumbleweed Corner because nothing much happens. Nothing out of the ordinary. No mass murders. No hostages taken. No door-stepping news teams. Just a roll or two of tumbleweed blown from a garden up the road.

I get the east wind straight from Siberia, the westerlies when a storm is visiting, the northern gales to freeze the testicles off every brass monkey we have and the southerly howlers when the moon is right above and big.

Parking outside in my usual space, a late delivery van driver asks me to take in a parcel for my direct neighbour since he was carted off last week.

'I didn't realise you delivered parcels,' I managed, looking closely.

'Ha, ha, I also deliver meat, milk, eggs, vegan meals, diet meals, cakes, party food and jokes, which you need with a face like that. A coffin plate face, as somebody once said.'

I open my regulation blue front door to release the dog, who's in urgent need of a walk. Trouble is I'm certain that every dog walker will wear the same face. It's either that or dog mess in the lounge.

I look at it; does it really need a walk? When the dog you've had for five years wears the same human face as everyone all day, then you must accept something is awry.

When even the goldfish you keep for sharing your secrets looks at you through the same face, it's time to check yourself in the hall mirror.

There is an outline of your head, your hair, your ears and your chin. It's not really you, after all.

What a relief!

Only trouble is - you have no face at all. In fact, where your face should be is blank.

It's just how it is these days. Somebody rings your approved doorbell, somebody who'll ask your old mum if you can go out to play with your mates? They promise to take good care of me.

14. Several Slices of Slime Pie

During one of the coldest, bleakest Augusts in living memory, stall holders and business owners on and near the seafront half joked that they should have opened during the unseasonably warm January instead of waiting for this Siberian summer.

At least the lack of business from happy holidaymakers gave Silas Shreiber time to mull over the meaning of life and other imponderables. Loads of time. Time to fill with random thoughts jotted in his summer notebook. Time to kill with his ideas for brightening up his stall in the light of the machinations of his imagination.

For hours he stood, staring out to sea or unnervingly right through people in front of him, blinking the grit from his eyes. Short-sighted, he refused to wear glasses. Just over five feet, and sparse of frame, a slight stoop, thinning hair too long at the back and usually dressed in grimy T-shirt with an old army greatcoat when it was chilly – that was Silas. He gave little else away to onlookers.

Even when he didn't seem to be listening, his radio blared incessantly. Occasionally, fed up with commercial radio's endless adverts, moronic announcers and diet of people expressing opinions, badly, he switched to cassettes and played a selection of old pirate radio tapes complete with forgotten jingles, dead disc jockeys and songs from the best ever years of pop – 1966-70.

For days he'd been pondering what to call this disastrous year. *The Curtain Rises on Catastrophe. Bankruptcy Calling. Permanent Winter, The Deckchair of Humanity. The End of the Matter. A Length of Rope, a Beam and a Chair.*

Titles matter, Silas understood. In fact, what a book, a film or a song was called was the most important thing. The title makes someone want to read, see or hear the thing. However, a better title for his retail outlet would not have helped this particular year.

Unmoving, he watched the wind hurl his specials board from the side of his ice-slush machine across the prom and against the coin-operated telescope mounted on a swivel facing out across the turbulent North Sea. Dragging it back, he decided it wasn't worth the effort of refreshing the chalked offerings.

Top of the day's bill was *Several Slices of Slime Pie*. Customers asked how many 'several' was, instead of wondering what was in a slime pie and why anybody would eat it. That was the thing, he'd observed about people, they were often surprised but not always in a nice way.

In fact, Slime Pie was his whimsical name for a fish-based chowder he sold hot or cold. It was liquid, so was never a pie capable of slicing. Last year he'd called it *A Meal of Calories, Fat and Gristle*. The year before that was *Fungus on Toast with an optional Diarrhoea Side*.

It allowed him to stand out from the endless ice creams, donuts, candy floss and imported pasties at neighbouring stalls. He served no fish and chips, kebab and chips, chips with/without scraps or plague and chips, either. In fact, that had been stolen as a title by a writer who dreamed stories about the prom.

He declined to operate a little kiddies' roundabout outside. Or turn his private car space into a crazy golf course. Or remove the East Coast Vomitorium he'd created from recycled cans as a conversation piece. No beach furniture, no windbreaks, no buckets and spades were had from Silas Shreiber. Hand trowels to discretely remove or bury anything undesirable on the sand, yes.

He 'maintained', if that's not too strong a word, a handful of assorted chairs to the side, three wobbling round an old garden table, wedged upright by stakes driven into the earth, lashed to the legs. Above the table flapped a wind-destroyed sunshade, last serviceable in the 1970s.

Most customers preferred to eat on the sea wall or one of the council provided benches on the actual prom. There resided council waste bins handy for surplus food and any heavings that arose. Seagulls rarely dive-bombed to steal slime pie.

Windblown litter was a regular backdrop to the endless fun to be had on the promenade. Rare indeed were days when other people's detritus sat where it was dropped. But less rare than the occasions when waste removal teams ventured down the prom, preferring to concentrate their efforts on smoothing the beach.

Silas also treasured the old industrial sausage machine he'd bought from a scrap dealer. Labelled a Seagull Shredder and mounted on his roof, it was staying put. *Cream of Seagull Soup*, with or without beak and eyes, was popular among drunks and teenagers. Not for him the jellied eels, whelks and crabs brought in from North Norfolk.

The normal rules of customer-shopkeeper service had no place at his ramshackle stall. He told the odd customer – customers were never right – to dress properly, to remove his flip-flops or just to fuck off. Other customers loved it; promenade theatre at its best.

Gradually, he hired 'resting' actors, dole queue beneficiaries and the hopeless to be the recipients of his abuse. They were paid in the *Dish of the Last Day*, served in a chipped Victorian bedpan. Few people, however desperate, worked for long. They never knew if he was joking or not, whatever he said.

Around his opening in the spring (Easter) and his closing after the chilly October Half Term, he served *Meat and Veg with Vomit Gravy* to warm up running obsessives and dog walkers. He planned to add variations of his summer menu this autumn. *Buckets of Bile and Scum. A Portion of Slime Pie. A Serving of Scum. A Bucket of Bile (and Scum).*

And to wash it all down? Well, tea with standing spoons was a best seller. However, he was known far and wide for his cracked glasses and chipped cups of *Unspecified Liquid #1* or *#2*. Again, they could be sampled hot or cold.

The year he'd started out, local TV news filmed him nursing a heavy dripping cold, slopping food into bowls, wiping cutlery on his sleeves and scraping bird droppings with a spatula from his cooking shelf. They also caught the line of hungry enthusiasts he'd paid to queue to buy and rave over the slop.

That exposure brought from the woodwork an old flame of his, now very old and arthritic who took to limping along the prom once a week for a meal, which he made a point of charging her for.

'Hello, how are you?'

'I'm alive. How are you?

'Well, I seem to be alive, as well.'

''You can't believe everything you see.'

It was an identical conversation every time she appeared. With no particular favourite, she landed on a dish that was unavailable that day or he'd just sold out of. He tried not to focus on how they'd been when young and active. What was the point? Not now they were so old and useless.

During his quasi-religious phase, he fished a few morsels from *The Bible* for his titles. A large, blinking neon sign above the shack read, 'Food Adventure – as though a man fled from a lion only to meet a bear.' (*Amos 5:19*)

He liked it because it was true, but also his middle name was Amos. But for all that, all his wisecracks and culinary catastrophes, Shreiber was aware that the business tide had turned. The man was increasingly jetsam left on the beach when the tide went out.

No matter that flotsam was debris in the water not deliberately tossed into the sea, while jetsam was rubbish thrown overboard to lighten a load when a ship was in distress. SOS, Save our Shreiber: next year's banner.

Free council toilets opened daily during the summer from 10am to 4pm, so Shreiber made use of them then and hoped for the best till he closed at sunset. When nature called him by name, he took his cash from the till and invited a passer-by or a person he half knew to stand in for him and serve while he relieved himself.

At the end of the day or the close of the season, Silas Shreiber made his way from the prom, across a main road and to a terrace of old, once-grand houses overlooking the sea. Most were now homes in multiple occupation – flats and student digs – with a couple that their owner kept for the down and out.

That owner was Silas himself. The house and its neighbour had belonged to his family in better times. He sold off Number 18 after a hard couple of years in the 1970s. It was a move he always regretted, having been raised to believe in the sanctity of property ownership.

He was left with Number 16 with a basement apartment, a ground floor one which was his with two floors above of tiny units he rented out. The pair in the attic was for really struggling people. It had occurred to him that he himself might be better off up there, when one next became empty.

One was taken by a man aged 60 plus who busked in the towns around and Shreiber often thought he did better than he let on. He hated noise from others but was happy for them to endure him practising songs and guitar. He was part time bozo, probably on something, Shreiber concluded.

The other was occupied by a woman in her late 30s, outwardly normal, but inside a full-time nutter. She had an unnerving habit of staring right at people, blinking as she was short-sighted but had never got glasses. Just over five feet, and sparse of frame, a slight stoop, wild hair that had never recovered from blonde, ginger, purple and red dye and usually dressed in grimy dungarees with an old hippie parka when it was chilly. She gave little else away to onlookers.

He'd taken her in at the request of a man he knew in social services who helped him out with warnings about health inspections. This man was particularly useful when he warned that the Food Police were looking for inaccurate food descriptions. He made a replica menu board with what his great titles actually were in small print in brackets.

The man also advised him to submit tax returns as tax officials had draconian powers. Silas found it cheaper to pay the fines and tax estimates than have proper returns done on his behalf.

The female needed accommodation; Shreiber let her have Attic One, with an excellent sea view from the window.

It was the same window that she threw herself from to the street below one winter Sunday afternoon, just before dark, when she suffered an episode. Miraculously, she lived.

During five months in hospital and convalescence the council paid her rent, enabling him to rent out her space by the week. She took longer than expected to heal because they discovered she needed mental health work on top of the physical damage.

Once off her crutches, she dragged herself painfully up and down the narrow stairs to and from her home from home, after he'd returned her possessions. Needing daily exercise, she took up hobbling along the prom twice a day, with an inevitable stop at the Shreiber showcase.

She not only learned to swallow reduced rate slop, sludge and swill without spewing, but was asked to stand guard as he went along to the toilet occasionally. Her favourite dish was *Botulism Light with Chunder Sauce* on rye with fat free margarine.

Her name was Mariette. Officially Mariette, though Shreiber could imagine it was a fiction. An alias adopted years ago when she lived her teenage and twenties in various parts of London, she said, in hostels or prisons.

She applied a disconcerting, penetrating gaze when she stood at his counter of delicacies. What she'd decided was that he'd do just fine, as if she was choosing a husband; what he thought she'd decided was how can I skin this man without him noticing? Nonetheless, he gradually began to trust her, not only with guarding while he nipped to the toilet, but with advice and practical help on the internet.

Mariette played the dumb airhead to perfection when it suited her. Shreiber suspected she sold favours to the musician next door, to a man four doors down, a guy from above the shops in the main street and a bloke he thought was a Muslim, but evidently not.

Occasionally, very occasionally, it crossed Silas' mind he could join the queue going up and down to her and they'd come to a deal on the rent. Surely, he wasn't past it yet?

But she gave no hint that was on offer, so he kept quiet. It seemed desirable till he thought about the sheer physical hard work it would involve. So, he was past it, after all.

What he didn't know was that if any customer asked, she claimed to be his daughter with the same surname. Only once did it slip out. She had ordered human teeth to decorate a shelf of treats to enjoy toothlessly after a trip to the dentist.

'They're ordered, Dad, and I got a two-for-one offer.'

Immediately realising her slip, she glanced at him, but he said nothing, a half smile playing on his lips.

She shrugged, blew him a kiss, peeled on rubber gloves and went back to the washing up sink where cooking pans languished in tepid slimy water.

A dab hand at the internet, she used his, initially to help with his accounts including submitting a respectable-looking tax return and sourcing unusual ingredients. While probing deeply she was able to buy a birth certificate, council tax bill and exam results to prove she was Mariette Shreiber.

They enjoyed a quietly friendly relationship with him taking just enough interest in her life and plans to be polite but not over curious. She seemed to enjoy listening to his assorted ventures to earn money over decades and talking about his off-the-wall ideas, new ingredients and effective if controversial banners and posters.

One day she asked him, 'What's the stall a front for?' He checked he'd heard right. She repeated it.

'How do you mean, a front?'

'Well, a nice but unusual retail outlet like this, on the seaside, quiet, unassuming. It must be a front for drugs, strong-arming, fencing, slave trading ... Are you secretly running a people smuggling racket off this coast?'

He sat down to get a good look at her to see if it was a joke. She went on, changing tack, 'I've been here a while now, and I would've noticed what was going on behind the scenes, so what's the game? Or are you what you appear to be?'

'Well, not a bad idea, what you're suggesting. But I'm just a Great British Eccentric, neither more nor less.'

'Mmm,' she smiled, unconvinced.

'And what's your front hiding?'

'Well, it's not really hiding anything. I just want to be settled with a family, roots and a job with physical activity that keeps me fit while I use my brain in my business venture.'

'And what's that?' he asked, genuinely interested.

'Well, as the digital world goes on, relentlessly, the need for data is so consuming that even the real world of billions of people can't produce enough to train artificial intelligence systems in the future.'

He helped himself to a glass of something sludge brown. 'Go on,' and he swigged deep.

'Well, I have a start-up that makes synthetic data that's automatically annotated so that the machines of tomorrow can learn from it. It's imagining every single person on unbiased, speeded up hyperactivity using every human facet, quirk and intelligence that it has and more.'

'Now, I think I'm about to step into some world where I'm lost.'

'Well, it doesn't matter. I'll keep at it, while helping you here. This is my keeping fit and physically healthy.' He nodded, thinking that her unspoken activities with men here and there was also part of that.

'My brain is alive with AI, and here I can work when I want to without disruption or unreasonable expectations. Thank you for giving me that.' She volunteered to experiment with new dishes. She got his nodded, though lukewarm, approval as he digested what she'd just said.

'It's not so much what you put in them but how you title them,' he informed her several times as she noisily set up former industrial catering equipment on the prom and in his kitchen. Had she two friends, he pictured Macbeth's three witches mixing a potion.

She spent ages beavering away in a swirl of foul stenches punctuated by occasional delicious aromas. She learned how to get into the dark web, courtesy of a man she picked up at the railway station one night when she needed company and a few quid. Thus, she bought aconite.

This was made from monkshood, a plant also known historically as wolfsbane, which poisoned even through touching the leaves. She wondered about slipping the aconite into a plate of stewed mushrooms which she could claim included a bad one.

But having watched Silas over time, she decided to supplement his daily sugar fix. She broke meringues, sprinkled in milk chocolates doused in cream and came up with *Sweepings and Droppings*. Unsure how much aconite it would take, she stirred in half of the packet.

Very little persuasion was needed. He sat down to it; the stall had another hour to go. Toilets were shut but how bad could her new pudding be? He tucked in greedily.

She perched opposite him, scoffing the leftovers of a vanilla cream cake while he assumed she was eating the same as him.

'This is not bad, Mariette,' he enthused, cream on his lips as his remaining teeth crunched meringue.

'We can start selling it tomorrow,' she smiled, dropping her spoon and bowl into the leaking metal sink. 'I'm going back now, Silas. Got someone to sort out.' One of her paying customers, he assumed and was on the point of mentioning it.

'I'll lock up,' he muttered, already feeling excessively hot, sweat gathering under his arms, round his neck and back. It took about ten minutes after she'd left, for Silas to become agitated and restless. Far from shutting up shop and locking it down, he felt a burning desire to cool in the sea, mad as the idea was.

The sun rising on the east coast revealed that the stall was as open as it had been the night before, the radio cassette was jammed. A little cash was still in the till. The only thing missing was the smell of food being cooked or warmed up and the sight of old Silas staring out to sea.

Mariette ventured onto the prom late morning. No queues of hungry holiday makers; nothing cooking.

No Silas. Before calling the police on her mobile to report him missing, she took safe possession of the takings.

Not till the late afternoon did anyone from the police force arrive to take down particulars. By then she'd got some food on the go, had her lunch and served just three people. She took the opportunity to blackbag the dishes she'd used to make *Sweepings and Droppings.*

She took a risk by not doing it last night, but figured if any kids used the stall for fun, she could argue the aconite had come from them. The officer was more amused than concerned – old Silas Shreiber was known as a bit of a character, generally harmless but of no interest at present.

He pronounced it too early to be worried and she shouldn't concern herself about her Dad. Missing people sometimes turned up. He gave her a crime number and his own mobile, in case.

She took the opportunity of Silas missing to establish herself in his stall and his flat. She loved his notebook. She rang her cop daily, begging for updates, wringing a few crocodile tears to make it convincing. She claimed to be struggling to hold his fort.

When his body was washed up nine miles south, she was interviewed informally at the stall and played the card of helper a bit out of her depth. She thought of telling the officer she'd met before that he was right; missing people indeed often turned up. Dead.

When he told her he'd have to look around Silas' flat, she felt he was angling to ask her out for a drink and wondered if it would be useful to have a friendship with a policeman. He made no move when he came with a plain-clothes detective to look round Silas' flat and then traipse upstairs to hers, just for 'background.'

A week after the disappearance, three police officers arrived at the stall to tell her that Silas' postmortem revealed he'd drowned, but he had an arrhythmic heart condition which would have eventually suffocated him if he hadn't inexplicably gone into the sea.

One of the officers was the man she'd had a drink with and already become more acquainted with. They wanted to talk to her at the station or failing that at her flat. She protested the need to mind the stall, although there were no customers in sight.

The senior office accepted the situation and suggested to her that her father had swallowed something that caused his heart problem. Did Mariette have any ideas?

She'd given it careful thought and reported the old woman who had it in for the poor man. Despite knowing perfectly well where she lived, Mariette was a bit vague but described her physically as a bag lady, old, dirty clothes, a stained beret atop an almost bald skull and wheeling a shopping basket.

The beat bobby knew her, so they set of with a spring in their steps, helped on their way by the stench of boiled socks and cabbage, Marmite and poo emanating from the latest dish on the menu, *The Bowels of Hell, second helping half price.*

It was in the papers and on the radio next morning. An old woman was found dead in her house beside half a packet of aconite. She was connected to the late Silas Shreiber, stall holder, recently discovered drowned on the beach.

Over the next few weeks, police enquiries continued. They searched the stall and surroundings; they went through his flat and her little apartment. Nothing was found; not even the notebook was still there.

No relatives came forward, so Mariette soldiered on, taking up with the council official who helped Silas, getting him drugged so she was able to take an incriminating photo of him. Then he was putty in her hands.

The story dropped out of the news. The season ended and by the time the next one came along, her false documents had proved she was his only living relative, so she'd rented out her old apartment and moved into his.

She persuaded local TV news to cover the reopening at Easter, where they were thrilled to find a human-interest story about a daughter who carried on her father's wacky dreams and ideas after his unusual death.

Tomb With a View was clearly going to be a success. She organised a seafront summer mini festival of graphic Punch and Judy, circus acts, illusionists, escape artists and contortionists to go with it.

That first summer was a belter. The weather was kinder, customers liked her meal titles and she put in a tax return to keep officials happy. By the autumn she was asked to lead the local Association of Seafront Attractions and Entertainments.

She stayed in Silas' old flat, thanking him silently each day and not wishing to flaunt the incoming wealth from her synthetic data company. And she gave up the sideline of selling half hours to desperate men. Almost completely. She was sure that's what her dear, late, much-missed old Dad would have wanted.

15. Waiting for Idiots

The door swung open silently.

It's time. Time for Don Pedro Bella de la Questa to leave the room, clutching his notes before him and make his way to the ornate dining room which nowadays doubled as a courtroom with three spotlights.

His talk was to be a cross between a sermon and self-improvement lecture. There would be a dash of stand-up comedy and Best Man at a Wedding speech thrown in.

The Lowestoft Society for Mountain Climbing hadn't told him that's what they wanted, but he'd sat through enough such presentations from nervous members to know that was needed. In fact, in this day and age of distrust and persecution, they never told anyone anything.

People were expected to know, having swallowed the contemporary doctrines of tolerance of anything and everything provided it was on the approved list. Anything from even 20 years ago was old hat and rarely allowed.

There should be some superficial linkage to mountain climbing, of course. But the fact that Lowestoft is hundreds of miles from any mountains at all and most of its members had never been near one, was a clue to what was really afoot. At least in the old days.

Founded in 1969, the Society was a drinking club for men with a sense of humour who wanted to imbibe beer under the cloak of admiring hills and mountains. They even half organised a visit to Switzerland 'next year' which needed eternal monthly meetings to iron out the details.

Of course, the excursion never happened.

Over the years the group had expanded to include women and others. Now members didn't even have to live in the town. They'd been through a real and craft beers phase; an anti-spirits period and nowadays they accepted drinkers of anything at all, even soft ones.

The monthly talk was one tradition that had survived the decades and speakers were chosen by pulling a name from an old cash bag. Of course, until the Second Purge, it meant that some people were called more regularly than others.

In fact, a couple of years ago, the Grand Pourer, the annually elected official wearing a flowing hat of soft material that made him or her look ridiculous who presided at meetings, secretly kept one person's name out of subsequent draws, because she was so dull and tedious.

However, since they'd been designated an Approved Neighbourhood Hub, the only people making after dinner speeches were those being tried for heresy or false thinking. But pulling their names from the bag persisted.

At the end of each meeting when the landlord called 'Last Orders' they used to prime their glasses, drew out the name of the next speaker and toast his or her health before everyone dispersed.

Now the Society had transformed into a Civic Watch organisation, a cross between the Nazi Third Reich and Orwell's Big Brother world. A snooper's charter. People were denounced as traitors on the whim of children; their trials a travesty of justice, their disappearances never mentioned.

The door swung open silently. He was in a library where the history of the town, of the nation, was stored.

He knew that old standards had been swept aside in the First Purge, another name for a bloody and raging rebellion against law and order. The Second Purge was low key, silent, creeping up on selected individuals. He had no time for any of them, but thought he'd kept that to himself.

Don Pedro Bella de la Questa was not, naturally, his real name. He was Colin Jones. He'd adopted what he imagined was a Spanish name upon being told as a child by his paternal grandmother that he carried one thirty seconds of Spanish blood in his veins.

The accompanying tale of his ancestor marrying a glamorous Spanish lady against his family wishes fed his imagination. How she was in Lowestoft over a hundred years ago to be met and married remained an unanswered mystery.

He first used the nickname in a classroom talk at school and continued with it. Gradually people accepted it, apart from all his relatives and teachers. Sometimes friends just called him 'Spanish,' 'Bullfight', 'Costa' or even 'Package Holiday' on rare occasions.

Away from the town to study psychology at university, he was popularly hailed as 'Inquisition' or 'Nobody Expects.' What people in his club today expected of him was a reasonable talk to follow the regular dinner they always enjoyed. That was another surviving tradition.

Nothing beat a choice of roast meats with the usual trimmings and a hot dessert with custard or a choice of ice-creams while sitting in judgement on one of their number who'd suddenly fallen foul of someone somewhere.

In his case, the idiots running society now argued that to have so many aliases was itself suspicious leading to anti-social thoughts and avoidance of reality. He knew he had no choice but to play along with their silly games. If they were going to execute him, he wished they'd get on with it. Waiting was worse than anything else.

The door swung open silently. More blank paper was brought in.

He chose to start his address with a question and lead up to a rousing condemnation of their regime. He planned to call them all idiots at the climax of his speech. That would show them, shock them, that someone already condemned would have the effrontery to insult them.

Start with a question - that will throw them. Nobody expects questions, rhetorical or otherwise.

'How would you wait for something or somebody if the room was full of angels watching you, angels ordinarily invisible to you but now you see that they see you? How would you wait for something knowing you were watched?

Well, in today's surveillance society you are watched. We all are.'

'How do you wait for things?
Are you patient? Resigned? Restless? Angry? Violent? Unreasonable? But how do you play life? Waiting is one of the trials of life. The entire human existence revolves around waiting.
Waiting for the missing relative to unlock the door and enter.
Waiting at windows, by a door or staring into space, itself waiting to be filled.
Waiting to grow up, be tall, have a whole set of teeth.
Waiting to get through those spotty teenage years.
Waiting for Christmas, birthdays or winter to end.
Waiting your turn.
Waiting for instant gratification or recognition.
Waiting to fall in love.
Waiting for bureaucracy to grind to a conclusion.
Waiting for traffic to clear.
Waiting for a baby.
Waiting for enlightenment.
Waiting an entire life for meaning to show up.

Waiting for Godot.
Waiting for a job, an interview, somebody, a tradesperson, an appointment.
Waiting for a phone call, for a text, for any sort of news.
Waiting for a bus, a lift or someone to treat you seriously.
Waiting for an ambulance or the dizziness to pass.
Waiting to win the lottery, to get a promotion or to pass a test.
Waiting for a rich uncle to die.
Waiting to move or somebody else to die.
Waiting for technology to catch up with your dreams.
Waiting for people to stop telling you patience is a virtue.
Waiting for dental plates, strong glasses, hearing and walking aids.
Waiting to die.
Your family then must wait to bury you.'

'Or, if this is an old-fashioned sermon, waiting for God.
Waiting on the Lord to move in His time and ways.
'You believe that you are your mind – restless, impatient, anxious.
But your mind is ruling you.
Waiting is not a shutdown of activity; it's being ready for a new command.'

The door swung open silently, admitting a chill draft.

'Most people wait only seconds before giving up on a video loading or for a queue to dissolve. We will only stand in line a short time before we are overwhelmed by the feeling that our lives are slipping away. We'll never have that time back again.'

It was a rather long intro, but as time was running away, it would have to do. Now he just needed the meat, the main substance of what he wanted to say.

The door swung open silently. They brought no meat, just a prod stick to make him say something. Anything.

But the truth was that he didn't want to say anything at all. He wasn't going to beg not to be thrown from the roof, his blood licked by savage dogs. He wouldn't plead for his life.

He was still thinking about his finale when the door swung open silently. He sensed them filling the tiny cell. 'Ah, greetings, the idiots I've been waiting for have arrived,' he yelled as he was dragged out.

'How was the roast dinner this week? Did you have ice-cream or a pudding with custard?' he asked as he was hurried along to the dining room. Staff were clearing the detritus of the meal and serving coffee and sickly sweetcakes to those who fancied them.

The Grand Pourer stood to welcome him. He was positioned at the top table where a place had been kept empty. 'This is Colin Jones. Welcome Colin. Colin has numerous aliases, as many of you will know. Spanish, Inquisition, Holiday Package and Nobody Expects to name but a few.'

The Pourer was intending to say more about Colin's long service to the Society and his good work promoting approved beliefs after the Second Purge. He was going to regret that Colin had become a criminal facing charges.

But Colin cut him short. 'Ah the Grand Pourer in a silly hat. Oh, what idiots you all are. There is nothing evil in having your own thoughts, unless someone says it's wrong. That's why you're all idiots.'

The door swung open silently. Two flunkies staggered in bearing a heavy wooden lectern. They were waved away in irritation by the Grand Pourer.

His outburst upset several in the room who began to murmur. As he sat in the empty chair, he grasped a glass into which he splashed water from a jug on the table. The murmur rose and became a chorus of keening voices without words.

To rise above it, he stood in his place and read from his notes. 'How would you wait for something or somebody if the room was full of angels watching you, angels ordinarily invisible to you but now you see that they see you?'

The noise began to subside. 'How do you wait for things?' Nobody answered, naturally.

The Grand Pourer regained some sense of importance and authority and stood beside Jones. 'Sit down, Colin, that's quite enough. You're not permitted to make idiots of us all. Of anyone, in fact.'

'You do that yourselves. I can't make you more idiotic than you are. You and this wretched way of living we now must endure.'

The door swung open silently. He sensed them filling the dining room. 'Ah, greetings, the idiots I've been waiting for have arrived,' he yelled as he was guided into the room he thought he was already in and sat at the top table next to the Grand Pourer.

'Looking forward to the roast dinner this week? Will you have ice-cream or a pudding with custard?' Staff were serving the top table first, where his place had been kept.

After clearing his throat and swallowing a mouthful of bitter, the Pourer looked around and beamed. 'Welcome to our 5th anniversary of the founding of the Lowestoft Society for Mountain Climbing. For five years we've spread the cause of mountains, hills, abysses, rocks, summits and clamps. I believe we are appreciated. We have a waiting list!'

He got a cheer and a round of applause. 'This is Colin Jones. We all know Colin, one of our keenest members. Colin has numerous aliases, as many of you will know. Spanish, Inquisition, Holiday Package and Nobody Expects to name but a few.'

Colin didn't stand at that point, he waited. Waited till the silence became uncomfortable and several thought he'd lost his mind. Then he became animated, stood and asked them all:

'How do you wait for things?

Are you patient? Resigned? Restless? Angry? Violent? Unreasonable?

How would you wait for something knowing you were watched?

Well, in today's surveillance society you are watched. We all are.

But how do you play life?

Waiting is one of the trials of life.

The entire human existence revolves around waiting.

Waiting for the missing relative to unlock the door and enter.

Waiting at windows, by a door or staring into space, itself waiting to be filled.

Waiting to grow up, be tall, have a whole set of teeth.

Waiting to get through those spotty teenage years.

Waiting for Christmas, birthdays or winter to end.

Waiting your turn.

Waiting for instant gratification or recognition.

Waiting to fall in love.

Waiting for bureaucracy to grind to a conclusion.

Waiting for traffic to clear.

Waiting for a baby.

Waiting for enlightenment.

Waiting an entire life for meaning to show up.'

It really served only to confuse his listeners. 'Ladies and gentlemen, I've dreamed that in the future this association will be part of a repressive machine that controls people's thoughts …'

The door swung open silently. He turned to face it.

It was a journey of about a minute to the floor above, a rooftop terrace. Meekly, he went, surrounded by a cohort of his idiot peers.

The door swung open silently again. The party of idiots returned without Colin, without Spanish Inquisition, Holiday Package, Bullfight or Costa.

16. Hollow Gurning

Perhaps you know that feeling people occasionally get when a certainty about someone grows and grows. You feel it in your waters. It's borne on the wind, not letting you go. Till it becomes fact.

I'd started to hover outside my house faffing about with my car on the drive or weeding near the gate whenever my neighbour went out or came home. She had a regular schedule, which I discovered she needed, leading the sort of life she had built for herself.

We exchanged greetings, a few words about the weather, something current and then about her children, work or some family issue to do with her husband or her elderly parents.

At 45-ish she was quite a stunner. Medium height, lovely shoulder-length blonde hair, fashionably tinted with a central parting, just what I'd delighted in when I was young. Nice legs and a confidence that was appealing. She had a range of three business suits and bright, flowery but tasteful frocks and expensive accessories, depending on the weather.

I'm two decades older than Sheila Matthews. Once I realised that I fancied her and wanted to be part of her busy life, I set to researching. Marvellous things, the internet and social media. Companies, schools and friends innocently give away so much detail, it's quite encouraging to someone like me.

I began to steer our brief shared conversations around to the busy lives people have, the excitements they must crave and/or miss out on. And the regrets they must live with.

With her, I revealed just enough about myself, stressing my intellectual experiences, my achievements in the arts and the community. I guessed that Bob, her husband, was of the professional class, but was clearly not doing much for his wife.

He'd started to take the kids to school in the mornings, as she went off to work quite early several days a week. That made me smile. Something was going on.

I found out about her lover by following her to his place and then to their work. Certainly, I wasn't surprised that he was a tall, rugged Alpha male, practically dripping testosterone. I guessed he worked out and played rugby at weekends. However, I could be the addition to her life she perhaps didn't yet know she needed.

'Nothing is obvious unless it's happening to you. Nothing is obvious that is not happening to you.'

At the end of our chat about hiding things from people, Sheila came up with this pair of truisms as a justification, if she needed one. She shared them as if imparting profound, higher-level thought; I nodded in agreement. Cracker wisdom or not, they were accurate enough in her case.

I watched her settle her pert buttocks into her new generation electric Mini and set off to her lover for an hour before work or before she picked her kids up from school and cooked tea for the family, including her husband. Evenings they either watched TV or she regularly dealt with bills to be paid for her elderly parents.

She was a juggler. The more balls she had in the air at any one moment, the happier she seemed to become. Even against a headwind of opposition, difficulty and going solo, Sheila managed.

Given a fair wind, she could cope with whatever came her way and then some.

She was a thinker when she had time in her over-busy life, I'd gathered that much. Her children were young – the boy was only five and his sister was nine. Reassuringly bright as they were, they certainly depended on their mum.

Bob, her husband of 12 years, was also pretty dependent. Dull but reliable in some lights, he was unimaginative but as a financial planner he provided well for the family. Two holidays a year.

Rather stuck in his ways, I knew by watching the cameras I set up in their house when I broke in. Well, they left the key under a flowerpot for a plumber who was due later, so I borrowed it long enough to have my own copy made in town.

She carried her work laptop off each day, but I was able to have a good look round her home device. This private one opened to me when I got her password right after a couple of minutes – Sheila1. She clearly didn't expect Bob to crack that.

My observations turned up that Bob was a sex-on-Saturdays-and-Wednesdays sort of man. But Sheila needed to go out to work to absorb some of her energy and brain power. Her salary was pocket money.

At work she'd met and hooked up with Mick, a big, brawny truck driving foreman in the waste disposal company where she sorted the office out and was soon sorting him out, too.

Living alone since his third wife left him after one infidelity too many, his flat became the rendezvous for Sheila and Mick to meet early mornings and late afternoons.

He depended on her in his own way, knowing he was her bit of rough. He kept a single mum supermarket worker on the side, just in case things went pear-shaped with Sheila.

I often wondered if she smelt of sex at work; if they had an afternoon encounter, did she stink as she cooked for the family? Bob never noticed.

It made no difference to her daily life. Having considered it, I assumed she enjoyed flirting with danger. Disease, pregnancy, discovery, shame – it was the elephant in her room, but she ploughed on regardless.

She could easily accommodate me from time to time. Bob was often out on Rotary business. The kids were abed quite early. I decided to press on the busy angle and told her it surprised me how much people can fit into their lives when they want to.

'If something needs doing, ask a busy person,' she came up with to transition into the car for her date.

'If someone acts as if it's all fine, it will be', I added, with a smile and nod. She knew what I was hinting at, I chose to think.

One of my biggest and strangest discoveries about her was her party trick. Doesn't everybody have one, I imagined her asking?

I caught her at it over the fence on a sunny evening when she was playing with the kids before their bath and bed. She half explained it from the fence and filled me in on the rest the next morning.

Her speciality was out of character, but she'd copied her father in his younger days. He used to gurn. Gurn for Britain, he could. He made distorted faces, twisting his lips, chin and eyes into unnatural postures, often as protection against people's curiosity or nosiness.

Her mother used to tut at him, she told me, wearily spouting a truism from her own parents' youth – if the wind changes direction, you'll be stuck like that.

The day he found his wife of 49 years unable to move after a stroke, his gurn to bring her out of it stuck. The wind must have changed direction. He thereafter grinned at everything, unable to respond in any other way.

When her babies arrived Sheila naturally started gurning at them in the pram, cot and on her knees. They gurgled joy. Even when they were older, they'd enjoy the sight of Mummy's face twisted into ridiculous, impossible, comical mis-shapes.

Bob, by her account, loved it when they first met. He liked everything about Sheila. She was a delightful powerhouse wherever they went. And she was his. People were drawn to her, enthusiastically laughing at her jokes. Even her gurning.

After a time, he emitted a hollow dry-laugh. It just wasn't funny any longer. I sympathised and thought nor would it be if her lover was discovered. Nor would it be if anything happened to upset her finely balanced lifestyle.

Hollow gurning, she called it.

Last Tuesday. it looked from the window a fine summer morning; outside there was a chill north-easterly breeze that made people anxious to keep moving.

'The wind has changed direction,' I told her as she hurried out of her house, on time but keen to press on.

'Good job I'm not gurning, then' she replied with a laugh, a warm, friendly one that made me sorry she was already in the car and starting up. I'd have liked to make her laugh a bit more.

About mid-morning a police car pulled up outside. Two female officers knocked and waited, looking around to gauge the locality. They saw me emptying my waste basket into the requisite black and blue wheelies. So, I felt obliged to walk round to the front to see if I could be of any assistance.

'Do you know if Mr Robert Matthews is about, Mr …?'

They always want everyone's name. I told them that he was at work and gave them the address of his offices in town. I added that the children were at school and named it along with their class numbers.

If they were surprised I knew so much, they didn't show it. I hoped they'd think I was just a helpful neighbour imparting information to the law. But why hadn't they asked about Mrs Matthews? Had they arrested her or was it him they wanted to collar?

Of course, they weren't going to tell me. As soon as they'd gone, I was indoors as sharp as my legs would carry me. On with the news, cameras in the Matthews' house, street views of both their places of work and the school.

It was frustrating. It looked as if I'd have to wait for the local lunchtime news. I found on a social media feed from a woman receptionist at Sheila's company that tragedy had struck.

A sudden gust of wind had blown a cyclist into the path of her car a street away from her lover's place. She had stopped to help him and a lorry had overtaken her car, the driver swearing at her, and taken the door clean off as he passed.

She was pushed along the road, her head bouncing, life blood draining from her. Sheila was declared dead at the scene; the cyclist was in intensive care with life changing injuries.

Over the next few days, the lives of her dependents changed for ever. Distraught, Bob had to be taken to a special hospital, unable to handle a thing. He was at her funeral but was helped to his seat and stayed staring at her pictures placed on her coffin, mouthing soundless words.

One photo was of their wedding day, another was a more formal one taken for ID while the third and most appealing was her playing with the kids. They were laughing at a giant gurn that filled her face.

The kids were swiftly taken by a grandparent and moved away. They were spared the funeral, but I suspected they might regret that in later life.

Mick went along but stayed at the back with others from the company, uncomfortable in an ill-fitting suit and black tie screwed round his bulging neck. He was devastated, I could see.

On the other hand, when I saw his supermarket woman, I knew he'd be fine.

At 25-ish she was quite a stunner. Medium height, lovely shoulder-length blonde hair, fashionably tinted pink at the ends, just what I'd delight in if she liked. Nice legs and a vulnerability that was appealing.

I'm three decades older than Janice Smith. Once I realised that I fancied her and wanted to be part of her bland life, I set to researching. Marvellous things, the internet and social media.

Companies, schools and friends innocently give away so much detail, it's quite encouraging to someone like me.

I began to shop at the supermarket where she worked, sharing brief conversations. I accidentally happened past as she came off a shift and had a longer chat. I was keen to find out her party trick, her specialism shared with others.

It turned out she was into taxidermy, stuffing dead animals.

That made me smile in a twisted sort of way.

17. Life's a Beach

A sickness ran through the veins of Ozymandias' family. Sooner or later, at some point in their lives, one generation of his family destroyed the one above it.

Speeded up evolution, the old giving way to the young. He knew that at some time, it would happen to him. Facing it became one of his decisions, when he was still a teenager.

The family were comfortably well off, as if the curse of the dynasty was countered a little by incredibly golden touches in business and commerce, property and creating fiscal monopolies. That gave him choices in life.

While he didn't welcome what he'd be driven to do, he was resigned, so as a man, he avoided his father as much as practicable. His grandfather had died recently of falling in a vat of bleach that was parked outside the family mansion before a deep clean.

Father inherited the fortune and got away with whatever he did to his own dad. It looked like an accident. His great grandfather had perished by falling from a helicopter he was trying out and his son was piloting. Again, it was declared an accident.

Money passed down, no waiting for a parent to grow old and doddery, demented or a nuisance to others. It had much to commend it.

When Ozymandias first booked a cruise, his family thought he was having a holiday. In fact, he apparently disappeared in one of the ports the ship visited, nobody was sure which. Enquiries were cursory. This was before cruise ships checked everyone off and back on electronically.

He actually lived on several ships for twenty years, going ashore when he had to, saving a fortune on running a house and avoided killing his father. He was rather fond of the old boy, in fact.

Each week he adopted a new persona, a fresh backstory to explain his base on board a ship and refusal to live in his homeland for years. He didn't disguise his name, though, he simply created other identities, sometimes even being but a subplot in somebody else's tale.

Ozymandias was not his real name, but it was certainly memorable. As he passed through people's lives, some recalled his investing in the money markets, betting on horses, going on grand tours while using every minute to write feverishly. But to a person, they remembered that ludicrous name.

His middle moniker was Oswald, after his father, grandfather, great grandfather and great-great grandfather. So, he was called Ozzy, which in adulthood he insisted became Ozymandias.

The great English poet Percy Bysshe Shelley published a sonnet in 1818. *'My name is Ozymandias, King of Kings, look on my works, ye Mighty, and despair.'* It was intended as a warning to people that whatever one man achieved, it all crumbled to nothing.

It's a poem about transience, nothing lasting forever. All things must and will pass. In the years since, it's been cited by dictators and power mongers anxious to demoralise their enemies and potential foes. Look at my works, and despair. You can do nothing so grand, so don't even try. I'm omnipotent.

It was a case of something meaning one thing becoming its opposite. A poem about humility became one about hubris.

Using his time on the ships productively, he read copiously and widely. He knew a little about lots. The internet enabled him to self-publish a clutch of novels under the name 'Ozymandias', each about a different aspect of his life, real and imagined. The few who knew this considered him a clever sod all round.

In youth, he'd rashly called himself a humble young man. With plenty to be humble about, some friends jeered. Older and wiser heads didn't like it. 'You're not humble, Ozzy. Only Jesus has ever been the world's truly humble man.'

It was a lesson he took to heart and while on two back-to-back Mediterranean cruises, he formulated a theory and wrote a novel based around it, that when someone is in a very low place, he or she is invisible, never seen or heard. People think invisibles give them nothing, so they ignore them. Condemn them. Forget them.

In a dog-eat-dog world, important people walk over unimportant, overlook and exclude them, brush past them in irritation, discontinue them, grumble that they're using up oxygen and space. Let the low-lives wallow in their pits, never complaining or explaining in case others are hurt, forgiving rather than making an issue of anything.

He read that humility is the soul, coming from the inside. Humiliation is the place we learn humility.

Ozzy bored a fair few passengers with that dance of words. Some bought him a drink on the back of it, either to get away or to wind him up. He was the Ancient Mariner, the man who foolishly shot the albatross with his crossbow.

One day, looking around a collection of listeners in the upper deck bar, he was inspired to find a handful of the arrogant and bring them down a few pegs. He started small - a trip here, a cut-off in mid-sentence there. He often pretended not to understand English, so his target had to explain something all over again before Ozzy yawned in his or her face.

One night, on a spur of the moment, he graduated to a full push overboard of one man much the worse for alcoholic refreshment who demanded of Ozzy an instant beer top up, as if he were a waiter.

He'd thought to raise the alarm to avert suspicion, but a nosy old bat beat him to it, so he melted away back to his cabin. Only then did Ozzy realise the man had reminded him of his father. He feared that he was actually rehearsing to fulfil his destiny.

His final ship-drafted novel remained unfinished. He intended to complete it in the care home he'd selected to look after him, feed him and give him some peace. A murder in a care home by someone who pretended to be totally paralysed.

The germ of the idea was inspired by a conversation with and observations of an elderly man on a cruise who was spending the last of his savings before cancer stopped him doing anything, even breathing. This man, Alfonse, had shared the hope with Ozzy that one day someone would steal him and his chair to put an end to his troubles.

Ozzy thus had an opening for yet another novel.

'*His carers left the old man strapped in his wheelchair outside the shop while they nipped in to buy soft drinks, crisps and chewing gum.*

It was dead against all the rules, but the old man said he was fine, it was a nice day and he was good to sit and watch the world go by. So, chancing it, Paul and Paula left him and went inside. Who'd steal an old man?

Three minutes later they burst out, laughing and joking, tearing the crisps open, and to their great relief, the old man was still there.

However, his wheelchair had vanished, and he'd been plonked down on the pavement unable to describe the miscreants.'

After reflection, he decided to change the oldie victim into a woman. Most of his writing was about men, so this would be different. He sold a handful of his books in a year and he had perhaps two regular followers. But the important thing was to get the stories out there in the world. It was as if he wanted to leave something behind.

A pair of former carers lost their old woman they were supposed to be taking care of. It was in the park, and they must have been followed as the culprits knew a lot about them, including the care company they worked for.

The spotty girl (Fallow) and the gangling youth (Cyrus) who were paired that day by the case manager, fancied a bit of practical biology in the bushes by the overgrown tennis courts. Elsie didn't hear all they said to her, but picked up, 'we won't be long, don't wander off.'

When they emerged, brushing grass and twigs from her back, Elsie was gone. And so was her wheelchair. She'd wandered off, was their excuse notwithstanding that she couldn't walk, never mind wander.

There was hell to pay at the office. Managers were livid and gave them notice on the spot. Police were called and found it difficult to take seriously the theft of an old lady and wheelchair.

There was some relief when the office received a call four hours later saying that the criminals had kidnapped the oldie for ransom and wanted a hundred thousand to return her safe and well.

This news the police took with more concern. 'We never give in to ransom demands,' they said. Several times.

Local media soon got wind of it and launched a caravan of media types around the offices, blocking pavements, ignoring yellow lines and pestering everyone in sight for news and/or comments.

That night the kidnappers called again to say if the money wasn't paid by noon the next day, the price would double. The police remained adamant no money should be paid.

A big-shot hostage negotiator was sent from London to show the provincials how to do it.

He got nowhere. In one call, they threatened to return the old thing in several bin bags if at least twenty thousand wasn't paid. Nobody could understand why the price had dropped.

News outlets ran wall to wall coverage of poor old Elsie's kidnap, her life story and the distress of her loving family. All of whom, turned out to be in prison or dead.

The senior cop, hoping for a career in broadcasting, grandstanded through regular four-hourly press conferences.

By the 5th day, social media coverage dried, and the journalists had drifted off. It was clear the story was dead. And so was Elsie, most people quietly thought.

Then came the bombshell. The criminals rang to open negotiations. This was electrifying.

And even more so when it turned out they were offering twenty thousand to hand the old woman back. They couldn't stand her or her voice any longer.

Then one turnaround day Ozymandias suddenly grew tired of the routines, the endless streams of faces climbing aboard every week, the sameness of some of the ports. He finally came ashore permanently.

He checked into a residential care home, still in his fifties. They quibbled, but fees and a half bought off their qualms about caring for such a 'young' man.

It was another opportunity to reinvent himself for the hundredth time. A fresh sheet, with a new backstory carefully edited to suit the role of a retired businessperson who'd ridden the financial storms and wanted only to read and write in his dotage.

If anybody cared, they'd be interested in his big contradiction - wanting to be unnoticed yet promoting his name and being memorable to hundreds of people. This 5 feet 3 inch, overweight man with thinning hair and grey eyes behind double thick lenses was an enigma. Like most humans, he thought.

Keeping his name, he simply took on and lived till he got bored, other histories, some true, many false and a few amalgams of real people and invented shadows. Like most writers, he thought.

Of course he travelled about, often at night. He occasionally went to look at his father from a distance, playing with the top of the range tractor he'd invested in.

As soon as he arrived at the old folks' home, a letter from his solicitor caught up with him, dated six months previous. His father had fallen prey to an unexplained mishap. When driving his tractor late at night during the summer harvest, he'd fallen off and it had cheerfully driven over him. Twice.

Police investigations found nothing odd except the fact it went over him more than once. However, with a sudden rash of hate crimes to exhaust their time and energies, his father's case was filed under COLD. Nobody would ever know that the blunt object blow to the back of his head wasn't caused by hitting the tractor steps.

After the condolences, he was informed that he'd inherited his father's fortune. By this time, he'd burned his way through two thirds of the wealth his grandfather had left him. He'd hoped that with interest and judicious investing, it would see him out. Now, suddenly he had another pile of money to play with. He could have his own private suite built onto the care home and live a relaxed and safe lifestyle.

Until or unless his child found him.

He had just the one, allegedly. She was the product of a one-night stand with a dancer on a cruise, who kept him informed of the girl's progress through life in return for a monthly standing order he increased annually. The dancer named her Louisa, after herself, her mother, her grandmother and great grandmother.

Years before DNA, he accepted the fact at face value. He was unaware of any females in the line who'd caused an accident to a parent; only the men. But he intended to take no chances.

Maybe it was the comfort of his care home, where his life was more like a private hotel that caused him to lower his guard.

Last week, when my mother, Louisa, was away for a few days of 'relation hunting for a novel' two things happened.

First, I learned everything I needed about the family accident rate, the fortune and my probable destiny, too.

And second, it was news that Ozymandias, the modern sphinx, was declared missing from his room in the care home. Of course, he was free to come and go as he wasn't suffering dementia so didn't forgot where and who he was. He just vanished.

They found him two days later in the garden greenhouse. Hanging from one of the roof beams. A stool kicked over beneath his feet; he swayed gently in the breeze through the open door.

My mother's return from her trip, nursing burns on her hands and a dislocated shoulder, brought refusal to tell us where she'd been or how she'd used an interest in genealogy to track him down.

She claimed she wanted to write stories for a living and sometimes needed to go off and find ideas. My guess is that she nagged him into putting the rope round his neck and hoisted him off the ground.

They checked the height of his feet from the earth and from the top of the stool. He couldn't have stood on it. He was murdered by his own flesh and blood.

And I found it all in one of his early novels which I've started reading avidly, a story about grievances stretching down through generations.

My biggest worry at present is how to spend a great deal of money. I'm attracted to neither cruises nor care homes.

Oh, and I've just discovered I'm pregnant. That's a worry.

Life's a bleach. Ain't it just?

18. Repairer of Broken Walls

Characters:
Perry, church elder
　Robert, former MP, now church big-shot
　Sheila, retired Headteacher, now church finance officer
　Charlie, jobbing builder
　Josie, assistant at local funeral parlour
　Lucy, recent convert to the faith
　Jonno, itinerant musician, leads church worship
　Paul, a youth at the church

Charlie:
As a builder I've been offered weird jobs over the years. Some wouldn't stand scrutiny from building control officials. Like digging up forgotten drains and relics, replastering DIY abominations and adding extensions.

　Lucky for me, the gradual renovation of the old church, piecemeal as funds allowed, coincided with a spate of local, publicly funded restorations which handed us several small jobs from the taxpayers' largesse. My entire team is me with a pair of old boys who've seen it all from fishing deep sea to hauling vegetables to burying the dead. We're doing OK.

　For their old, discontinued Methodist place, the young, energetic Hope Church of the Saints next wanted a new stretch of crinkle-crankle wall to keep the patch of garden and backyard semi-secure from the passing public.

Records showed there'd been one there for at least 100 years, from before its incarnation as a church and right back to when it was a slaughterhouse, herring smoke house and a barrel-makers' storehouse.

Crinkle-crankle walls are ribbon, snake or wavey walls built for strength. Possibly of Dutch origins, crinkles are widespread around East Anglia. To build them takes skill, though they use fewer bricks than traditional walls that require buttresses, And they sit firmer on sandy soil, withstand the easterly winds that regularly rock us and look nicer.

We'd hardly started on the foundations when I was taken aside by a senior in the church. I thought it was a joke. But seriously, this person wanted the hush-hush disposal of a body, part under the new wall and part under the old building it adjoined.

Perry;
It happened most mornings when we were washed in early sun, breaking at dawn across the beach and over the town. I thought of *Psalms*, as you do. Well, I do in my role as lead pastor, senior shepherd, top interpreter of the Word.

'From the rising of the sun to the place where it sets, the name of the Lord is to be praised.'

Good opener for a sermon. Trouble is, I used it already. Twice.

But that's my business, praising the name of the Lord. My people expect me to have integrity, not to lie or deceive, to speak truth to power, to resist the Devil and his works and to obey the law of the land.

Robert:
While being rightly proud of all I did to put this community on the map, to iron out difficulties, correct misapprehensions ... to be defeated at the polls? Well, that was years ago; I'm supposed to have accepted and moved on.

I've absorbed in large measure. Just occasionally it washes over me what a loss I am to public life.

However, I was asked to head up a big festival, a push to increase public awareness of the asset of Easton, a town suburb and once more powerful than its bigger neighbour, Seawold.

Charlie:
I think it was Perry who named me, 'repairer of broken walls.' Quite suitable really. He drew attention to me in one his many 'few words' uttered at various opportunities to promote the Awakening of Easton project, 'Easton's New Dawn' or some such.

Robert said he admired my handiwork and craftmanship, while quoting a Bible verse. They can never resist.

Sheila:
It was Charlie's prowess in building that crinkle-crankle wall that gave me the perfect hiding place. It could only be hidden in plain sight. Perry spouted *Isaiah 58:12*

'And your ancient ruins shall be rebuilt; you shall raise up a foundation for many generations; you shall be called the repairer of the breach (of broken walls), the restorer of streets with dwellings.'

Then I knew I'd get away with it.

Lucy:
I love the Old Testament, in some ways more than the New.

I adore the poetry, the rich language, the blood-drenched stories, the power of God and his people, yes.

And when old Perry came out with his reference from *Isaiah 58*, I think it was verse 12, and applied it to our builder man, Charlie, I rejoiced in how the old so often describes the new.

Robert:
It fell to me to pull together the data for the historical section of the book I'd arranged to be printed to support the project.

Well, there was nobody else I trusted.

OK, Sheila was a retired Headteacher so should have been capable. But I'd begun to wonder if her loss of recent memory wasn't the harbinger of dementia. Either that or she was pretending to be a bit loopy, for some reason.

One of her relatives, Tom 'Horatio' Nelson, vanished into the twilight zone a few months back, She showed early symptoms.

So, there we have it. I did the history.

Josie:
Because I work in the funeral parlour just near the church, I attend more than enough religious services. I mean I'm not a Senior Mourner or Event Commander, or anything like that, I just help where I can and am pushed to the front if the deceased is young and they want a younger person in support.

Ours is a run-down, pokey little office onto the street. There is also a tiny staff room next to the toilets and chemical stores. To the side and rear is a series of hanger-like bays where we do the work. Receiving, dressing, in display or sealed lid family vigils and loading for the final journey.

A few are still embalmed, more from superstition than serving any practical purpose as far as I can see.

We're a respected, long-established business and have laid to rest many generations of local families. It's a strange job for a woman in her twenties, I know. But it's a job. I'm useful, I make a difference; I enjoy helping people.

Funeral parlour is a bit grand and I'm not sure it's appropriate. You get beauty parlours. Nail parlours. My granddad reckoned there was an ice cream parlour on the seafront when he was a boy.

But funeral parlour? You can't do much with a decaying body. There's a limit on how normal you can make the face of a crash victim.

Anyway, I aim to visit the church in my own time, Maybe once a month. I like the atmosphere; I enjoy worship music, and I can bear most sermons. A welcome change from endless speeches that move a person in death to sainthood they never achieved in life.

There's a young man I like, raised in the place by his parents (his father was a customer of ours last year). Paul. We smile, we talk, we sometimes laugh. We could go for coffee, a drink, a film but he hasn't asked yet.

I'm sure he will when he gathers his courage.

And speaking of that, when I was asked for advice by that Sheila about disposing of a body so no smells arose after a time, nothing that would interest a sniffer dog, I was amazed.

Then I was intrigued.

Paul:
Josie is so popular, it's hard to ask her something privately.

Robert:
In dry, local government terms, Easton lies south of the bridge along the seashore to the Sunnyfield boundary, down The Avenue and in the west to the Navy and Filcher ward boundaries.

When some look at Easton today, they see the award-winning beach, the Triton statues, the

Vaudeville and South Piers, the Yacht Club and an intermittent tourist industry.

Others become overwhelmed by its faded glory, employment challenges, frequently poor aspirations, transport needs, houses in multiple occupation, free school meals, crime, immigration, mental health, drugs and alcohol issues.

But it wasn't always so. Easton was once an independent village mentioned in the Domesday Book, home to a fishing industry that employed most people and shaped their lives, linked closely to the village of Sunnyfield to the south and Seawold to the north.

Some historians dismiss Easton as of limited importance, but the fact is that once it boasted fine housing, factories and places of employment; it was more than a Seawold suburb, greater than a rather sad gateway to the bigger town.

Easton once housed a huge windmill which gave the name to Mill Drive and the modern Easton Mill Health Centre. In the 1840s, it enjoyed piped water and gas ten years before Seawold.

The Grand Cinema in London Lane South, where now stands Easton Community Centre was built onto Victoria Hot and Cold Seawater Baths and Gymnasium with a 90-foot pool, topped up with fresh seawater on every tide.

The Grand opened in 1920, the emptied pool under its floorboards. Seating 1000 people, it was the first to show sound movies in Seawold. Later it became a roller-skating rink.

The Playhouse Theatre in London Lane South was originally a saleroom, then a dance hall and then a repertory theatre in 1927. It later showed films. It burned down in 1946, was rebuilt in 1948 and Seawold Corporation offered £10,000 to buy it to replace the dilapidated Seagull's Nest Theatre.

The great flood in January 1953 submerged the Playhouse under six feet of dirty water. The Corporation withdrew its offer. Today it's the East Coast Cinema.

Those floods that claimed dozens of lives in Norfolk, Suffolk and Essex and huge swathes of Holland, drowned nobody in Seawold but deluged 400 homes and overwhelmed much of the old Beach Village.

A former net store in Keel Road to this day bears a mark indicating how high the flood reached. St James Church built in 1854, sheltered 40 people including children who had to be rescued.

Sheila:
As a local, I was asked by Robert to check his draft of the history chapter of the Easton book. Pompous ass that he is, or rather was, asked me because someone had the temerity to suggest it should be proofread.

He asked in such a way that suggested it was all perfect, so I needn't trouble myself. In fact, what you read now is a much-improved text, polished and tidied by little old me.

Paul:
I'm Paul. I like sitting next to Josie. I'm going to hold her hand next time.

Robert:
On the outbreak of the war, St James's spire was thought to be a landmark to enemy bombers, so it was disguised in black canvas and wire netting before the wind scattered it all away. Built from sandstone, it was subject to salt and water erosion. By the late 1970s it was demolished before it blew away.

Across the road stood the stables and, on the seafront, The Royal Hotel, glorying in its heyday amidst three acres of private seafront grounds. It was described and I remember it as a handsome building.

Miraculously it survived German bombardment from the sea in the First World War and German bombing from the air in the Second. It was requisitioned by the Admiralty in 1941.

It's thought that Charles Dickens visited; it's known that King George V did. Even so, by the 1970s it failed fire regulations and it too was demolished.

Sheila:
For goodness' sake. This history stuff is available in any one of several local history collections. All written better than this drivel.

Robert:
Suggestions for the site included a conference centre, bowling alley, amusement arcade, casino, police station and a Christian college.

Instead, in 1993 the Royal Green was laid out as public open space and the Dawn Pavilion was built at a cost of £1.3 million. It may soon be demolished.

Next to the stables, from 1913 was the Palace Theatre which became a cinema and then bingo hall till it was destroyed by fire in 1966. Part of it became Catchpole's Auction Rooms, where my wife and I bought a step ladder just after we were married. Today there's Catchpoles, a club, I believe, with the address 1 The Royal Thoroughfare, a reminder of its past.

From the bridge up to the Fish Lab mixed dwellings line one side of the road locally known as Middle Drive, because it ran between London Lane South and the prom, on which cars drove freely before the war.

There are records of Seawold's MP Albert Biverton (1934-45) watching his car parked outside the Vaudeville Pier overturned by fishermen angry they'd lost the market for fish to Russia.

There was a Promenade boating lake and where the South Pier began was Children's Corner with a more open layout before the current sea defences went in. A Punch and Judy stood there all the summer days of my childhood. That's the way to do it!

Much of our heritage is thanks to the great millionaire entrepreneur and one time Norwich MP, Sir Samuel Morton Peto. Peto purchased shrubland to the south of the bridge for two hundred pounds. The Easton we've had for the past 160 years is due to his brilliance and foresight seeing the potential of the harbour and the railway taking fish to the cities and bringing visitors in.

Sheila:
I think you'll find Peto overstretched himself and went bankrupt.

Robert:
Primrose Collis, our oldest church member, recalled as a little girl having tea at the house of Miss Peto in Marshes Road. This may have been Morton Peto's sister or one of his 8 daughters.

Josie:
I remember the send-off we gave Primrose Collis. All the church attended, lots of flowers and recorded music. It was quite pleasant. They hired the two black horses and carriage — now that doesn't come cheap.

Nice oak coffin with silver handles carried by her two great-grandchildren with our professional attendants. One of them, Royston Hills, had a stroke at the cemetery. It made the local paper, got a brief mention on regional TV news.

Paul:
I'm going to ask Josie if she'll have tea with me in Crimean Gardens. I hope she'll say yes. She's a lovely young woman.

Robert:
After a lifetime in politics, I see the political angle on businesses closing, often despite rigorous campaigns to keep them open. Locally famous Easton names which provided skilled and non-skilled jobs for generations of families, created its culture and put Seawold on the map, are now faded memories and old photos.

Perry:
In a book about Christian activities in the locality – more specifically, our church – I'm not sure about all this history. But Robert insisted and what Robert wants, Robert gets.

Comes from a lifetime in politics, I suppose.

Robert:
On 23 November 1913 Edward Benjamin Britten was born at Easton Cliff, almost opposite the Edward Hotel. His father was an oral surgeon; his early schooling was in Seawold. He became a global household name and was a son of Easton.

Two hundred yards to the north at Victoria Dip almost opposite the Oswald Hotel on 16 April 1948 was born the man who would become MP for Seawold from 1987 to 97. He did **not** become a global household name but is a proud son of Easton!

His parents started in business in Easton; later in life he taught at Easton High School for a season. Easton is the blood that ruins through his veins.

While this book isn't a study of local history, nothing happens in a vacuum. We're all tied to our past. To make sense of the future we must understand the present; to grasp that, we must see how the past affects us.

Perry:
Robert always sounds as if he is, or is about to, deliver a speech. Or a sermon. He once criticized my way of imparting information! By the way, I got this funny story for next Sunday. A man visits Heaven and Hell to book his place ahead of time. In Hell everyone sat round food-laden tables, all hungry because the spoons were too long, so in frustration they starved.

In Heaven, same set up, food galore and long spoons. But they're contented and full. What's the difference? In Heaven, they're feeding each other! Priceless!

Robert:
Most things leave a legacy. The stories in this collection are summaries, synopses, nutshells and highlights of lives lived in so many ways that serve as inspiration, warnings and amusement of other people.

Easton itself isn't a single community. It's a web of local communities of people of every age, size, shape, nation, belief, talents, skills and flaws, joined and touched by others and contributing to this great shared diversity of today.

The wind from the North Sea has brought fish and flooding over the centuries.

It hardened locals to deal with life's difficulties and it's been a hallmark of the community that was known as 'The Grit.'

Religious revival came in 1921, brought by the Scotch girls who followed the catches down the coast to gut and pack the herring.

After years of words and prophesies about Easton, Hope Church of the Saints staged monthly prayer meetings in the old Methodist Church and prayer walks, knocking on doors asking people if they'd welcome prayer.

Perry:
Robert let me write the last paragraph of the introduction. I thought that was kind, till Sheila pointed out he was keeping me on his side while he did his own thing.

I wrote: 'One over-riding prayer for us as a church was that our legacy would be to help foster, support and develop those modern day, diverse communities. Not to establish a church as such, (though that is what happened) but making connections with people, praying for them, helping address their needs and gradually revealing the saving grace of Jesus in all our lives.'

When this Easton project was first mooted, I felt stirred. I also had a powerful feeling about our future in Easton from *Isaiah 58:12* and buttressed by the word from *Ezekiel* 36: 33-35.'

Robert:
I had to stop the fool there before he quoted chapter and verse that I'd already used properly in the right place in my narrative.

Sheila:
He can't give anyone else any credit at all.

Perry:
In fact, I used the Bible quotes myself in sermons at the time we were launching the Easton project. It's quite wrong of Robert to criticise me.

And I was not a little miffed that he should start to direct what I was saying, but there we have it. That's Robert.

After months of regularly praying, we, the church, realised that inviting strangers to ask for particular prayers for their needs was a way of building bridgeheads into their lives.

Some homes became base-camps or power hubs. And this was to be the way a move of God would be birthed, not necessarily by starting a formal church in Easton.

It was *Matthew 10,* really, Jesus sending out disciples 'as sheep in the midst of wolves' – go rather to the lost sheep... heal the sick, raise the dead, cleanse lepers, cast out demons...'

He urged them to acquire no gold nor silver nor copper; to take no bag, no spare tunic, sandals nor a staff for the journey.

They were to stay in peace in a house that was worthy till they departed. If the occupants would neither receive them nor listen to their words, they were to 'shake off the dust from their feet.'

He warned that it wouldn't be easy – in fact, it could be quite harmful to them. He had come to bring a sword, to divide. People are either for him or against him. And as we all know, bringing the good news of the risen Christ can provoke some people to anger and hostility.

But the disciples would be obeying his great commission, to make fishers of men and women. He urged them to have no fear, for he was with them.

Robert:
I've asked some trusted church friends to check over the first chapter, before it's printed verbatim in this book I'm co-ordinating. Well, it's an after-dinner speech at an evangelical dinner we're hosting with other churches in the town.

They want my testimony.

And my life reads well, a damned good yarn told fluently.

I'm naturally confident at public speaking and have entertained crowds of all sorts, filling in and timing my remarks to the second as required. But I don't want this to come across as arrogant or pompous.

Sheila:
It does. On both counts.

Robert:
During my years of teaching at Easton High School (1998-2011) students would often respond to my telling them that I'd been born in Easton that they had, too.

However, unless they were born literally in an Easton house, they generally arrived in this world at the Jenner Hospital in Bleak Point before coming home to Easton to live.

I, however, *was* born at 16 Albert Terrace where my grandparents ran a bed and breakfast guest house. It was there because the tiny apartment my parents lived in above the shop they ran round the corner in London Lane South, was just too small.

Jonno:
When I was asked to contribute my Christian journey to the book, I thought others would be given the same space. I never knew till later when it was actually too late, that it was really a book about Robert.

Robert:
Yes, but I didn't dream Jonno's would be such a long, rambling monologue boring everyone to death. Lord, would that half-wit Paul be better?

Jonno:
I do think Robert would like me to stay silent till *he* has said it all.

Robert:
My birth came a few months before the National Health Service that most citizens have now lived their

whole lives under. My mother spoke of how long and hard labour was. At one point it was touch and go whether she or I would survive.

Charlie:
Blimey, I've heard this before. Do we need it again? He can certainly infuriate, can old Robert. You'd think a politician would be more careful about who he upsets.

Robert:
My parents, George and Margaret met on Boxing Day, 1946, at the Palais ballroom on the seafront in Easton, now the fisheries laboratory.

Margaret, a secretary at Godwin's the builders, 5 foot 1 inch, typist from Coventry who'd come with her parents to Seawold's sea air for her father's health.

George, Seawold-born, Black Dog Grammar School educated, a bit taller, black hair combed back and later a small moustache, served his apprenticeship at Bridge Marine, Seawold. During the latter part of the war he served in the Royal Navy in the Far East.

On his discharge back home in Easton he'd set up a bicycle and motorcycle sale and repair business.

They were married in September 1947 in what by all accounts was not a joyful occasion for the families – my mother was subject to his family criticism for being very young, among other things.

Lucy:
This is all very interesting, but ...

Charlie:
He's going into his problems with his feet, his primary school, secondary school. No, it's too much.

Robert:
At birth, my feet were normal but when I was about five or so, they noticed the curled hammer-toes and high arches were beginning. The label of Charcot Marie Tooth condition came many decades later.

My Dad's feet were identical, so it was thought no more than a nuisance. The doctor had no ideas beyond breaking and resetting every foot bone and starting again!

Dad lived with it; he managed. Curled toes, standing in the shop for hours, horrific corns and blisters – all part of him. I adopted the same attitude later and got on with it but was blessed to be born in an era of medical welfare.

Sheila:
All this should be in his autobiography, not here.

Oh, it is.

Robert:
My sister, Rebecca, arriving three years after me suffered chronic asthma. By then, our parents had moved the motorcycle business to the High Street in the north of the town.

My childhood was unremarkable, loving and in keeping with the times. I attended Macmillan Infants School, near the football ground, the first intake at a brand-new school. From there at seven, it was to Macmillan Junior School. Rebecca was walked to and from school by me from what would be considered a shockingly early age nowadays.

In the climate of those days, schools were steeped in Christian values and Bible teaching – they were part of the fabric of life, if not always explicitly.

My sister and I spent hours about the town, north and south, roaming with a freedom unthinkable nowadays. A favourite trip was the train to Grand Headland, or to Bleak Point and over the ferry to the funfair and back.

In the mid-1950s my parents borrowed to buy and build on a bomb-site in London Lane North, just into the prime shopping area. We lived in the big two-storey flat above.

The scooter craze brought prosperity and later they bought the large Dreadstone House in Short Lane. This was what Dad had dreamed of.

1959 was a landmark year: I turned 11 (adulthood arrived at 21) and just passed my 11-plus exam to admit me to Seawold Grammar School and moved from the Cubs to the 14th Seawold Scouts.

Perry:
Sheila, can't you do anything to stop him?

Sheila:
Now there's a phrase that could be misinterpreted. Like 'Let him have it' and 'Rid me of this turbulent priest.'

OK. I'm vetoing any more of this personal testimony. Ask somebody else to give us a different experience of coming to faith.

Josie:
Someone who can keep it shorter?

Robert:
I'm ignoring the whispering and hostile looks from others.

I date my first interest in politics to the General Election of Thursday 8th October, also in 1959. I was aware it was on; there was talk in the town, in the family and at school. After all, we were a Grammar School and supposed to be interested in current affairs. We saw the results on a borrowed television.

Charlie:
Sheila, did you want to ask me something?

Sheila:
I need to talk to you about that crinkle-crankle wall of yours, Charlie.

Robert:
My ordinary, lower middle-class life changed dramatically and horribly on Tuesday 18th February 1964, a cold, dreary winter day. It was half term – just two days. Dad was going with one of his staff,

Billy Armes, to London to buy cars as they progressed from selling two wheels to four.

He suggested I went along to learn, but I decided I had to revise for my O-level mocks. Rebecca was out riding her horse. The police called mid-morning and took Mum away, saying only there'd been an accident.

She was gone ages, leaving me alone, worried sick and without any information. She returned with the police officers. My father was dead. Killed on the A12 near Darsham. No other vehicles involved, he'd left the road and when the car bounced along the verge and hit a tree, he was thrown out.

No seat belts in those days. He'd died instantly, so they said.

There was barely time to tell my sister before hysterical grandparents, aunts, cousins and friends started arriving. It was well into the evening before we were alone trying to take in the day we'd just endured. Suddenly, Dad's dream house, expanded and fashioned as he wanted, felt too big, too empty and too pointless.

He was 40. Mum was 34. I was 15 and Rebecca was 12.

Josie:
I saw that Paul watching a funeral last week, watching me helping people into the cars.

Paul:

I love the black clothes Josie wears, and that shiny top hat.

Sheila:
Robert, none of us feels we want the soap opera of more of your life. I know it was hell for you. It always is when a child or teenager loses a parent. But the book and the whole Easton project are more about the future than the past.

Charlie:
Yeah, yeah.

Robert:
But I haven't done my testimony, my Parliamentary life or coping after the loss of my seat.

Perry:
Robert insisted I told the following section. God gave them special and unique family time and closeness after losing the seat. He gave Robert a job teaching Drama at Easton High School, where he stayed 13 years – the longest job he ever did. And I believe he loved it.

In turn that provided him with exam and writing work that meant he is neither retired nor ready to be so.

He's very much a work in progress. Isn't that a wee bit too much? Through his natural self-discipline he has no trouble in reading the Bible daily – indeed, he is one of those misunderstood souls who read a different version of it from start to finish in a year.

Robert: Thank you, Perry. Too kind. And, you know, there're times when I rebel at the way things are. If someone tells me to stand, I instinctively stay seated, partly through a physical inability to stand for long and partly through my sometimes stiff-necked response.

I pray. I give. I do what I can. I am thankful for Penny, our family, my life's rich experiences, travelling, the arts and relationship blessings which God has showered upon me.

I'm aware that even in this season of my life there's more to give and more to be done for the Lord, even for somebody with reduced mobility but a mind that's busy with ideas and plans and dreams.

So, my message is that we are ALL works in progress. Nobody is a perfect Christian. But without that hope of the resurrection and forgiveness for our sins, there is no hope at all.

I say to you: you can ask Jesus into your life and you'll be forgiven, saved. Feel free to applaud.

Lucy;
To say I was shocked when I heard about this, is to understate it. While I knew some of his past, I never had much to do with Robert, but I felt his burning passion for self-promotion got out of hand shortly before he vanished.

Perry:
It should be about the future, with a nod or two to the past and how we got here. Let me share this incident. In Britain there are periodic auctions of ancient manorial titles. People buy them a) in the hope they include rights to valuable land, b) as investments or c) out of vanity.

In 2018 a clutch of titles was offered which included the Lordship of Easton.

It became obvious that Robert was daydreaming about it. How fitting, to be Lord Easton! Never mind that auction estimates were in the region of £6500, plus auction premium, legal and conveyance fees.

Several of us, including his long-suffering wife, Penny, pointed out that he'd be a laughing-stock and cautioned against it. We were right.

An old title in the ancient locality of Easton means nothing when there was so much to be done with that money, time and energy and that sense of purpose.

Robert: Hear this, then. Some of the core beliefs I've learned as a Christian:
I believe there is a God. I believe that God made everything, including us and this world. I believe in his risen Son Jesus Christ who died for our sins. I believe we've all been made individually, although we're all human beings with common shared characteristics. I believe everyone comes to Him by different journeys and so we all have a unique story to tell about our Christian walk that may help and encourage others.

Josie: Amen.

Paul: Josie, would you …?

Robert: That's why my story starts this collection of unique, different and absorbing stories about the outreach work Hope Church of the Saints did, is doing and will do in Easton. In His name.

Sheila: And I believe that he who bores for Britain shall be subject to a mighty storm, a catastrophic visitation of forces that'll crush him.

I can't believe we had to endure this tedious testimony. I mean, come on. What does it tell us?

Well, I had it out with him on the Monday before his death on Wednesday. He said he could accept it as an appendix, but it must be part of the book.

Perry:
Jonno, my friend, change the topic for us. Tell us about your journey.

Jonno:
I'm the 39-year old musician, old boy of Easton High School and worship leader at Hope Church of the Saints. When asked, I speak warmly and passionately of a God-given vision I was given years ago.

I saw a large building somewhere in Easton beneath the banner – 'Seawold Community.' It was the hub containing the bases of a host of groups and projects from retraining the unemployed to caring for the vulnerable. There were advisors in money management, carpentry, mechanics, teachers of English and spiritual input on hand for anyone and everyone.

All ages, those with families and none, immigrants to the area and well-established locals – all are welcome to share what the brand that is Easton Community can give.

I envision a place where people can go for encouragement and help to do what is possible, to make things happen. It's a powerful dream which I feel compelled to speak out.

Lucy:
I love those services where people take it in turns to give their testimonies and what has been happening to them recently.

I think I suggested that Jonno is asked about his story and I'm glad they listened. We've heard quite a bit about Robert, when all is said and done.

Or is that heresy?

Josie:
Has Paul gone to sleep? Should I ask him to go for a drink?

Paul:
I'm waiting the right moment.

Jonno:
Born to Christian, Salvation Army stalwarts Greta and Hubert Temple in Eastgate Hospital in Grand Headland in 1980, my older brother Malachi and I lived in Lower Stoney. Hubert was coming out of the second-generation family bakery business and studying to work in the labs at the chemical giant Elefant in Norwich.

My childhood was fun despite hydrocephalus, an overlarge head, and the fear that it would be a serious problem as I grew older. With my communication also hampered by a bad stammer, my parents were deeply concerned about me starting school.

I credit the power of the prayers of many that led to my head being cured 'instantly.' From that momentous event at the age of four I learned two things – 'God is real and God is good.'

My grandfather closing the bakery led my parents to move from worshipping at the Salvation Army in north Norfolk to the Bethel in Seawold.

When I was about three a breakaway group (who'd experienced the Holy Spirit in their lives but little on Sunday mornings) set up the new Hope Church of the Saints, hiring space for meetings as and where they could.

Therefore, I was among the establishers of the new Church. It was an exciting time. There were children and teenagers. There was life. There was a sense of being different, breaking a mould and being obedient to God's prompting.

I've always loved music. I was drawn to it on TV, on record or at worship meetings. Songs I could connect with filled life at home and outside whenever possible. Music speaks to everyone, whoever you are, wherever you've been in a personal and unique way.

The family moved to Sunnyfield, so I started at the primary School. My struggle with the basics became a theme that clung to me through my years of education, particularly when it affected my behaviour.

I fondly recall watching while the Headteacher frequently played the piano with great gusto to the school, while I slowly slipped behind my peers. I was a late developer.

At nine, I moved up to Sunnyfield Middle School where I found encouragement in music through the Head of Music and played bass guitar in the school orchestra and in a concert at Snape Maltings, while I mastered trumpet and violin.

Besides music, I was good in technology, but didn't fare so well in other subjects. While accepting I was 'a bit thick', my real problem was motivation.

Both my dad and Malachi loved cars and it was my desire to be a car mechanic. It was inspirational teacher Mrs Boniface who told me that I could be a car mechanic, of course. But I could *be a car designer* if I set my heart on it. She saw something in me.

Halfway through Middle School, Headteacher Mr Thompson caught me dancing on a table in the classroom when I should have been sat at it studying. I was on report and labelled a perpetual troublemaker.

Dad often took us boys out for together time on a Friday evening. One night, sitting in a car park in Bleak Point, following a strong suggestion from a church member that we could and should be filled with the Holy Spirit, Dad prayed. And I *was* filled with an overpowering sense of the love of God.

Something had changed. I was still me, but the fruit was not just feeling different but living life better. In effect, it turned me round.

I had a new understanding of the value and need for work and application. Not that I suddenly became the class genius, but life was different. And music spoke even more loudly. Music theory downloaded itself straight into my brain with new depth of knowledge and the ability to help classmates who struggled with music lessons!

While watching a video of a worship band in Los Angeles, God spoke to me. 'That's what I want you to do. Play bass guitar. That's what I want you to be. A bass guitarist.'

Robert:
Thanks so much, Jonno, that was inspirational. Now …

Jonno:
At 13, I started at Easton High School, a huge and challenging establishment of over 1200 students serving the whole of south Seawold. Previous poor behaviour and attainment levels put me in the lower sets for main subjects, but I no longer misbehaved.

In the bigger school, I was drawn to other students like me, all interested in music. I hit it off with 6th former Donny Shelton, who's a professional drummer to this day.

When I was 14 the 'Toronto Blessing' swept across much of the earth. Coined by British newspapers, it described Christian revival evidenced by being physically and emotionally affected as the Holy Spirit fell on people in waves.

It hit Seawold in the early summer. I already knew the power of the Holy Spirit, but I too was caught up in the phenomena of what was also called 'falling down or being slain in the Spirit.' Hope Church of the Saints has always been a Spirit-filled church.

I achieved a single GCSE – in music, naturally. When I said I wanted to be a musician – I was already earning a few quid playing gigs here and there - one teacher said that in that case, I'd be touring a lot so should study travel and tourism. I lasted two sessions.

Grand Headland College ran a decent A-Level in Music Technology so off I went to resit my GCSE Maths and English at the same time. I moved on to add a BTEC in Commercial Music and an HND in Performing Arts (music specialism) to my qualifications. And I played in the award winning, Europe-touring East Norfolk Jazz Youth Orchestra.

My friends were Christian and non-believers alike.

Lucy:
It's worth pointing out that there's a natural ease and charm about Jonno, a boyish openness that people warm to. He played in the church band most Sundays and established himself as a central, young church member.

Charlie:
I remember his dad telling me that when Jonno reached 17 and started driving he gigged in Norwich, plugging into the lively city music scene before being invited to join the prestigious Norman Pettifer Band

as a bassist, following a call to help them out one night for a gig.

Jonno:
I lived and supported my family on self-employment in the business. It's living on a knife-edge, it's cut-throat. If you get a gig, someone else hasn't. But then you're disposable, good till someone better comes along. Literally 'living on a prayer.'

Looking back on my earlier years and then my adult life in music, it's right to ask if I always knew I was Christian and how I kept to it. Resisting secular temptations in the life of a teenager and then the often blatant drugs, sex and rock 'n' roll of professional musicians since then, I've been able to reject temptations. My faith has been strong and sustaining.

I was once offered cocaine by a band I gigged with and turned it down. Later the members apologised, realising I didn't need that. Relying on God rather than myself has worked.

I married local girl Jane when I was just 21. Some thought I was too young - people often feel free to pass comments on others. But it's worked and we are raising two Christian sons – Moses and Isaac – in a loving family.

Easton is on my heart. There's something special about it. I recall being in Salt Lake City supporting The Blessings on tour. The radio played '*I Believe in a Thing Called Love*' by a 4-piece band called The Grit, three of whom hailed from Easton High School.

Ordinary people from Seawold became global music stars, yet their first guitar teacher lived on our street. Yes, it was a tough neighbourhood and school, but many former students achieved great things in life.

Lucy:
I know the next bit. Poor Jonno. Poor Jane. Poor boys. Now this is real suffering. Robert? Are you listening?

Jonno:
In 2017 I was diagnosed with stomach cancer, from which many patients recover. With bad indigestion and not feeling myself I'd been ill the previous year on tour in the USA. There I swallowed water during a swim and was sick, sick with blood in it. Back home, I saw a doctor who thought it might be an ulcer.

I was sent for an endoscopy and on my return to the hospital for what I expected to be a routine prescription for ulcer tablets, I was met by a doctor and two nurses clutching Macmillan leaflets.

The effect on my family of the horrendous, frequently dark journey of the preliminary operation, rounds of heavy chemo, drastic diet changes, I've written and spoken about. With such local support of prayers and words of knowledge from God, I still well-up when I look back.

A prophesy over me said that God intended me to fly. My cancer was a turning point; I was the butterfly emerging from the chrysalis.

Lucy:
That's so wonderful.

Robert:
I think he's nearly done.

Jonno:
We delivered letters to our immediate neighbours telling them about my cancer, how faith got me through and letting them know that I'm always available to pray for them, to help them. It's one tangible sign of how my family live and work with God in the Easton area we absolutely know we were born to serve.

Robert:
Great stuff, Jonno! Thanks so much! Wonderful testimony!

Paul:
My plan for Josie is to go easy. Get to know her first.

Josie:
Think I might have to look further than this church.

Sheila:
My plan for Robert had three distinct phases.

First, I had to square away all trace of conscience, guilt, fear of being caught and people hating me afterwards. Robert's allies could emerge from under the rocks and become my problem.

Why was I doing it? Because he was pompous, arrogant, cocky, boring, self-centred, cynical, ungrateful or unsympathetic? Yes. All of those, of course.

But also, because when I was teaching before I became a Head, he visited my school and received a guided, VIP tour. Once the local paper photographer had finished, he couldn't wait to get away.

He pleaded other appointments and was shown out, obliviously passing the foot of stairs up to my lab where I and 24 teenagers had set out an interesting experiment, making a volcano.

He waved to me at the top as he dashed out and I went back into the lab to tell the students that their MP had something more important than climbing up to enjoy their experiment and talk with them.

Second, the actual accident he'd suffer. The mechanics of accidental death were one side, but the when, where and what about unexpected people and events played on my mind.

I was overjoyed to hear that he and his aging dolly bird wife were having most rooms renovated in their fancy house. They'd camp there each night but go out every day to let the builders get on. She visited various 'friends'.

Robert had no friends, of course, only business acquaintances, so he took over a table in the corner of the Church lounge area all day and evening, working self-importantly.

During a late working evening, old Robert would find himself stumbling and falling as his legs became entangled with a loose coil of wire some fool had left amongst other rubbish.

Just to make sure, if he pulled himself up on the table, I would be close by kitted in my surgical gloves to make out I was supporting him while smashing his head down with mighty force against the corner.

If he actually died, I'd leave his body overnight. In the event of discovery, it would be blamed on local youths with nothing better to do who came in through the door I'd carelessly left open. Oops.

Third, disposal of his putrid body. If still undiscovered by morning, I'd be in early, wrapping the deceased in an old canvas sail I'd bought for the purpose. I'd booked Charlie to start work even before his first cuppa.

He only had to dig the space under wall and corner, slide the wrapped corpse in and start the infill before his team arrived an hour later for their cups of tea.

I told Charlie it was waste I wanted out of sight as we couldn't afford to pay the council to remove it. When he remarked how it looked and felt the right weight for a man, I upped his fee, praying he had more sense that he appeared to have to keep totally quiet.

Charlie:
I've reached the point in life when it's time to clear my conscience of all the things I did wrong. Those women who came my way from time to time. Some

would now be called special needs. Others were merely restless with their daily lives.

I've learned that even Christians can and do fall into temptation to sin. Of course, I never saw it as sin. What others don't know don't hurt, I always said. And it was true.

Perry:
Old Charlie had a fit of conscience. We're not that sort of church. I don't hear confessions and dish out penances and forgive them on behalf of the Lord. No, no. But I listen and advise. Or just listen when a heart is troubled.

I said we're not that sort of church, but I do recall learning that sins fall into two categories - sins of commission (bad things we do) and sins of omission (good things we don't do).

I'm not sure about what's under the crinkle-crankle wall, to be honest. Perhaps best we don't investigate. I mean the man disappeared. Let's leave it at that.

If he turns up under the wall, well, he didn't put himself there, so they won't rest till they've found out who did it.

The police in fact did a thorough job of investigating. Sightings of him were followed up endlessly. His home was searched; Penny questioned several times. We all were.

For a time, I wondered if he'd faked his death for insurance or devious reasons. He was in politics, so nothing surprised me. Until the end, I couldn't see why he'd give up being a star around here.

Perhaps he was murdered? Someone from his past, the past he spoke about endlessly. Was that a clue?

Josie:
I first heard that Robert was missing when I realised I hadn't seen him around for a bit. Neither had I heard anything of him. People usually had something to say about him when his back was turned.

Then when I heard that his wife had reported him missing, it was hell in church. They searched everywhere, not thinking he was in the building, but just looking for clues as to his state of mind.

Speaking of which, I'm trying another church in the north of Seawold, where Gerald has a lot more about him than poor Paul.

Jonno:
When I first heard about Robert's disappearance, I thought it was one of his 'look at me' moments. Even when his family floated about like ghosts begging for news of him, their tear-stained faces masks of misery.

I assumed he'd gone off the rails mentally and he'd show up soon enough. Living in Bolivia disguised as a missionary. Or lost in London among the down and outs, hoping his wife would soon claim on his life insurance.

Charlie:
I first heard that Robert must actually be dead when he was on the news a lot, then not. Nobody mentioned him. They wanted me to repair the roof so that kept me busy.

The world just carried on without him, former MP or not. They say it does that. Carries on like a river.

Paul:
It felt odd that Robert was no longer around. But then most weeks, Josie wasn't either. Lucy told me she'd gone north.

Was it something I did? Or didn't do?

Lucy:
I was thinking about poor Paul's infatuation with Josie, when I overheard people whispering about where Robert had disappeared to.

The gossip suggested that one of us had done away with him. Deserved, undoubtedly, but really? This is a church. These are believers! Surely, they wouldn't do anything like that!

Josie:
I first suspected something had happened to Robert four days after his disappearance when I noticed Charlie and Sheila separately examining the join of the new wall with the old church building, pushing it, spending more time staring at the ground than anybody normally would.

Then I remembered that question about burying bodies so they don't smell or rise to the surface.

I'd expect it of a politician, but not people around me on Sundays and social gatherings. Time for me to move on.

Gerald got carried away after our dinner out last week, when he promised hands on heart that he wouldn't. But he did.

Sheila:
Did I have any feelings of Christian remorse?

I went through a phase of hating what I'd done, the longer I got away with it.

How could anybody who believes in God the Father, Jesus his son and the Holy Ghost commit murder, even indirectly?

And even worse, how can such a person cover it up, lying as required. Well, it's easier than most people think. You must remember what you said and stick by it. And keep remembering as you go on lying.

Eventually you come to believe that you didn't do it. And shouldn't someone deal with old Perry, long past his retirement date, who'd become such a bore I can hardly look at him.

What is Charlie working on next?

Charlie:

Robert always said that the book would be called *Repairer of Broken Walls* and it would be, in a sense, a tribute to me.

I once overheard him talking to people after church on a Sunday and running on about his legacy from all the things he'd achieved in life. So, I understood what he meant about a legacy.

Only now he's gone, Sheila has taken over the finishing of the book because there is a cost element and she deals with church money.

She it was who changed the name from *Repairer of Broken Walls* to *The MP Who Vanished*, on the grounds that it would sell more copies.

In the end, it's all about Robert but I don't think his final disappearance was what he wanted to be remembered for. But if one day it is, well that will be quite something for his grandchildren to know.

19. Unclean Till Evening

In the small hours, three nurses, two residents and five visitors remained awake.

In Room 11/02 of the Bright Star Twilight Home at the end of a dark corridor, four silent people, mainly older, framed by their grey-black coats and long dresses, shuffled in and waited by her bed.

They just waited.

He'd been invited to investigate in the home. The old woman was the only thing out of the ordinary. He noted her silent visitors.

The thought came to him from his long-gone Christian teaching (before it was culled a decade ago) that the question when tempted by some sin was this. Would you continue doing what you're up to if the room was full of angels watching you, longing for you to turn to the good?

She couldn't see their faces. She saw the backs of their heads, long straggly hair greasy in the gloom. Labouring to catch her remaining hundred or so breaths, she knew, absolutely knew, that when they turned to face her, it would be time to go.

He touched her face to make sure she was gone.

Clods of earth and stones rebounded off the coffin lid. The spotty-faced apprentice Funeral Assistant struggled with a fit of the giggles, picturing poo dropping into a box, till he was rescued by a sharp elbow prod from the Chief Mourner.

'There is a season to scatter stones and a time to let go.' The priest paraphrased the text in his bumbling way, emphasising random words like a TV announcer. He'd always wanted to be a poet. He continued, 'a time to *scatter* stones and *a* season to le*t* go.'

Wind stirred; clouds presaged heavy rain. There was an absence of birdsong, despite this being the countryside. Deep silence copied that over any of the concentration camps that survive as museums.

Only a few weeks later, the grave having barely settled, furtive activity materialised in the middle of one night. She was exhumed, the grave covered by a mini tent to keep away prying eyes or prurient camera lenses. The grisly scene was lit by a handful of high power solar-charged lamps.

The gravedigger's caterpillar was trundled in and proceeded to scrape out clods of earth and stones.

When the coffin was reached, they attached a harness and watched as the machine lifted it clear and reversed out of the tent to lay it on the ground.

First spatters of rain hit the coffin lid. They quickly dragged the flimsy tent across to cover the mud-caked box, one shiny handle glimmering in the lights.

Screws turned under the electronic driver. The lid came up. They stared down at three house bricks and a dead cat somebody'd tossed into the mix embedded in foam. But no old lady.

Did it matter, the moment that Artificial Intelligence took over the world? Most of humanity has died off from some virus AI engineered to keep vermin and weeds at bay.

Well, it was 3.24pm on Friday 29th, six months ago, when AI became absolute. Up to a point.

Recently it had become obvious that AI started to exhibit human traits, expressions and errors. Old things crept back. AI showed signs of dotage that humans used to display.

Something went badly awry. Got out of hand, in effect. Errors compounded like bacteria. In a three-way fight, one ran from another. Another hit a third. A third caught one and was crushed.

The sort of mess up of a woman being exhumed who wasn't there was now commonplace. AI couldn't keep up.

In a nearby road rejoicing in the aptly name Anguish Street, some residents had gone to seed. One, Ron, a little wizened old grump of a man had filled his garden with old signs.

They weren't needed any more, as AI was supposed to do what it was told. Keep off the grass. No ballgames. No loitering. No hawkers, no sales people, no cold callers. No parking. No entry unless you're tired of life.

Some collected antique cars. All petrol and diesel models, now illegal, of course. But they could be kept as playthings on drives and in gardens.

One car was a store for drugs belonging to the local warlord. Another was used by a woman who flogged personal services on Friday nights, all day Saturday and Sunday up to about 7 in the evening.

Climbing off her and tucking himself away, he relished for a moment the seediness. The creaking suspension. The next bloke waiting furtively by the overgrown hedge. 'How did you get into this business?' he asked as she wiped herself as clean as she was going to get.

She tossed out the wipe. 'I was happily married, believe it or not. My man got a gambling addiction with one of those early speaking human look-alike robot things. I offered to do it to pay off his debts.'

'I never quite paid them off. There's always something we need. And then our ancients passed away in the same week. My mother in that care home the taxpayer paid for, his father in Plague Cart Alley, back of Anguish, beaten up by a stranger who lived across town. I had to cover both funerals.'

'Do you know how many men I have to fuck a day to keep up the repayments?' He didn't, and as he was now keener to get away than hear anything else, he didn't ask.

And he didn't enquire what he'd made the visit to find out. Any news on the local grapevines about why an old woman was dredged up after death?

He recalled some Old Testament rule about being unclean till evening for any man who had an emission of semen or had touched a dead body. He'd had and done both.

They'd assigned him the case because of his connections with the Bright Star Twilight Home. Housing both parents and an aunt there formed his opinion that the Home managed the confused forgetful with no-nonsense fairness and compassionate concern.

Missing from the permit was the reason someone had ordered her exhumation. That was AI these days. Less than complete. He wondered if their apparent human-like fatigue was the natural consequence of being made in human images. Or if the failings were programmed in to make everyone feel cuddly towards the damned devices.

No simple household appliance was anything but an AI operated thing. No human action was undertaken without the approval of the AI system. He suspected that no independent thought was possible without AI leadership.

OK, so he had the case. What exactly was required of him?

Was the old lady almost the last of the few all-human, aged beings and they'd forgotten to do tests on her before burial? Could it be as simple as that?

AI would have everyone believe life was simple under their benevolent dictatorship. In fact, it was anything but simple.

In the evening, he went along to his approved recreation. Aware he was unclean till evening, but nobody else knew that.

Sniping was fun. He'd learned precision and accuracy, stealth and cunning. He'd exercised mind and body. He'd made acquaintances who might one day be friends.

Dressed in regulation black hood mask, black clothes from head to toe and wearing no identification whatsoever, he arrived at the club to be told they were sniping from the water tower. The club boasted 52 authorised sniping locations, so each was visited no more than once a year.

The water tower was an ugly grey concrete structure sticking up like a finger with a big wart on its end, above the low, flat and level surrounding dwellings. Built to provide pressure to domestic water supply in homes to a radius of 60 units, it was a useful landmark.

Those who couldn't climb the vertical metal ladders screwed to the side of the tower and traverse the barbed wire loops, were hauled up by block and tackle and willing hands.

Security cameras disabled; guns delivered by drones. The gathered members were an assortment of the half-baked, delusional and disillusioned sorts that AI society had little place for,

As long, that was, as they kept themselves out of mischief, broke only a handful of minor laws and didn't openly entice new recruits.

It took about an hour to snipe the entire area around the tower. Anyone walking an artificial dog (real canines had been culled a decade ago) was liquidated, a shot to the head. An old man putting rubbish in his bin and not using the automated disposal unit was hit by so many shots that he virtually disintegrated before their eyes.

With no more people about, they took to shooting blind through the curtained windows of houses within range. Screams, wails and the sound of one or two below shooting back reached the top of the tower.

The flashing of blue lights and howl of sirens ended the session. Leaving the guns for the drones to collect, they returned to the ground as they'd left it. Within seconds all had vanished and the security forces found nobody, of course.

Scores were circulated remotely. How many kills, maims, levels of terror generated or accurate shooting through windows were rewarded with points. None of it was real, but simulation was so realistic, it felt like they'd done it.

Keeping to the shadows, he made his way to the back of the Twilight home. A few moments passed before the woman came out the staff door, the shift changeover under way.

New to care she loved the work but was always on the lookout for extra income. That's why she did weekends in the old car on Anguish Street.

Performing mutual perfunctory fondling in the alley, she offered up the details of the backs of the heads of four familiar people that had puzzled him. It was an illusion fed to residents in their final minutes to make them feel comfortable about shuffling off into the arms of friends.

While he was giving the woman one, she further explained that the old lady was one of only three real humans left in the place. Now there were two.

When he wondered why they bothered to generate and run a facility for AIs at all, she said they still needed to attract in any stray humans left in society, especially those of great age, wisdom and experience. Unless they were loopy.

He walked her to the pickup point for the all-night transporter, holding her hand in a quaintly old-fashioned manner. She used the other to book a seat on her device.

'I wasn't there when they screwed her into her box,' she told him, still referring to the old woman. 'So don't ask me why she wasn't in there.'

'How did you know that?'

'One of the cemetery workers told me.' He guessed the circumstances of that pillow talk, 'And yes, he mentioned three bricks and a dead cat.'

'Why she wasn't in there is one mystery. The second is where is she now?'

'In the lab, I guess. Someone I know told me they received a real old human. It must have been her.'

After waving her off, he was not tired enough for bed, so he made it on foot, keeping to the shadows, to the lab. Security saw him coming, his face was scanned, the data base searched; he was admitted at once.

The system knew what he wanted, so he was lit into a small room with a large screen, a simple chair and nothing else. He asked the screen, 'Where is that old woman now?'

A voice replied to accompany images from the old lady's life. 'She is being renovated. Restored, you might say.'

'But why?' He wasn't supposed to question decisions, but he couldn't resist. He wanted to know. Perhaps to understand. He'd been in the dark long enough.

'You're unclean till evening.'

'But this is evening.'

'You touched a body and had sex.'

'I'm clean now.'

'How little you understand the assimilation of old laws with new, old customs with modern ones.'

A flash of pictures of his friend from Anguish and the care home. She was being restored.

'29% of humanity remains. 71% are clean now.'

Walking back through the cemetery, daylight beginning to show an interest across the horizon, he noted that the old woman's grave had been restored. Renovated. She may have been put in it by now.

At the side stood an old figure, facing away. All he could see was the back of the head, greasy hair and shoulders. He knew that when the stranger turned, he would see the old woman.

But there'd be no turning until he was clean. He had no intention of being clean.

At the first opportunity, he returned to that old car off Anguish Street. She looked different. Cleaner. Clinically clean.

Climbing off her and tucking himself away, he considered for a moment the sterility. The silent suspension. No next bloke waiting furtively by the overgrown hedge.

'How did you get into this business?' he asked as she wiped herself spotlessly clean.

'I don't know,' she replied honestly. 'I have no memory.'

'Am I unclean till evening?'

'No, this doesn't count. You're clean. This will be your last day. By evening, the 29:71 ratio will be 23:77.'

20. Everyone Needs a Cause

Everyone has a story. It may be quite mundane. They lived, worked, paid taxes, raised a family, got old, became decrepit and died. That's a story.

Everyone is on a journey. For some it's a great adventurous frontier-stretching journey lasting decades and facing every danger known to man. For others it's a circular trot, from where they started to the finish. The same point.

Everyone needs a cause. Even if it's trying to live quietly with good teeth and not doing anything that anybody notices. Or remembers.

Everyone needs a god. Or God Himself. They may hear His voice, a prophecy, a teaching, from friends, their personal conscience, quiet reflection or a sense of coincidence.

Everyone needs a name. Or nickname. The Water Carrier, the Gate Keeper, the Jezebel, the Tent Maker, the Well Digger, the Shepherd, the Mean Power Monger or the Man or Woman with a Plan, with a Problem, a Castle, a Secret, a Limp, a Habit, No Friends or No Love.

And it is said that everyone needs a challenge. Well, try this.

Here's the scenario.

The first body part appeared in a flat pack furniture box, placed alongside the top, three legs and extension bits of a dining table.

Delivered to a family in Lewes it caused a stir locally. Next to the table legs was a human left leg, the bloody end bandaged up.

Police were baffled; forensics found no identity to go with it.

The man who'd opened the box was shocked to say the least and began psychiatric support at once.

Three months and many miles later, the family in Bedford who ordered an expensive, top of the range flat pack wardrobe freaked out when they discovered amidst the panels and doors, the right arm and leg belonging to the same victim.

Bloody ends bandaged, but this time both limbs were tightly wrapped in plastic, as they would have smelt otherwise.

One local journalist, later criticised on social media, wrote that it gave a whole new meaning to the expression, 'costs an arm and a leg.'

And still neither police nor forensics came up with an identity, and no clue as to how he'd died. All they had was that he (Caucasian male) had been segmented by a chain saw.

The plastic wrapped head that must have been frozen, appeared on a spike among a collection of torture chamber props and set that an am-dram society in Yorkshire hired for their production of *Welcome to My World*.

By now the entire country was agog, anxious for fresh news, the missing bits and some answers.

Police enquiries of delivery company employees, factories, neighbours and the missing persons lists produced no joined-up thinking. No solutions.

A bored girl lying on her back in a south-west haybarn while her boyfriend had his way, was the only person who saw the torso go into a pig pen.

She watched two men unload it from a van and dump it, as oblivious to what she was seeing as she was to the boyfriend.

She told nobody, even the self-satisfied boyfriend, and so the torso was lost forever. The pigs said nothing.

Police established a small, specialised unit in London to co-ordinate the findings from the parts. One of their first tasks, having fed everything into the system, was to search the profiles of known serial killers, including those deceased, in case anyone was playing copy-cat.

There were no obvious matches. So, they concluded that they could only wait for either their man to be reported missing or the killer to strike again.

They didn't have long to wait.

Just a day after the dedicated unit was disbanded, a head, naked torso, two arms and legs were discovered laid out in order in a park in outer London, partially hidden by a generous wooded area.

The most shocking aspect for the hastily reformed police unit and forensics was that each body part was from a different female. Six separate women murdered and butchered and laid out.

The parts must have been carried in a van or large car which nobody saw and didn't appear on any CCTV cameras.

Once the media got hold of it, the only cry was – where are the other parts? A national search was launched to discover more limbs.

And who were the women? Missing persons lists from around the world were investigated. No obvious links there. They were in different stages of nutrition. The owner of the head had good dental care but there are no national data bases of teeth.

A handful of run of the mill tattoos revealed little. The torso showed that one woman at least had given birth at some point.

They'd all been severed by chain saw, were all white women in their twenties and thirties. Only one appeared in the system. She'd been arrested for shoplifting in Croydon three years ago.

Police were unable to link the women to each other, much less the man found earlier. The owner of the right arm had been dead longer than the others by several weeks.

Here's Solution 1.
This is a training program for detectives. There is no solution, but candidates are asked to explore the given evidence, ask pertinent questions, decide what further information they need and come up with some possible explanations.
There are no right answers.

Here's Solution 2.
This is the gist of a pitch a would-be unknown woman writer made to executives at a TV production unit to secure a first step on the narrow ladder of writing absorbing television crime stories.
There are no solutions yet.

Here's Solution 3.
This is the confession of a madman talking to a psychiatrist as part of an assessment before the judge passed sentence.
Nothing is right or wrong.

Here's Solution 4.
It was the very vivid dream that a prophet woke up from and shared with close followers, who immediately thought it was a warning. They set off running round in crazy circles.
They had no clues as to what to do.

Here's Solution 5.
It's part of a test at a university Sensitivity and Woke Course in which candidates must rewrite it for a contemporary, aware/woke audience. Suddenly it's filled with non-specific genders, mixed races,

misogynistic men and a police force that ranged from fascist to gentle artificially intelligent creatures.

The androgynous adviser found at least one fault with every single suggestion and failed everyone.
Well, Man with No Time, there are no second chances. You have exhausted all answers. None is right.

Here's Solution 6.
A former policewoman, raised in a house near the abattoir her father ran, killed six women and one man over a year, keeping their bodies in deep freezers before disposing of them.
Her research was immaculate and her observation skills excellent. Having chosen her victims, each was followed without ever knowing about it.

The man was an adulterer, of course. The women were too weak, too pathetic, too strong, too greedy, too selfish or too ungrateful.

She blackmailed five men who'd picked her up in bars –if they'd all been asked to describe her, they'd have answered differently. Adept at disguises and accents she was wealthy enough to stage whatever scenario she fancied.

They did as ordered, of course. Two worked together though they were strangers. The human bits still unaccounted for went into five different pig pens around the country, none witnessed by a girl in a hayloft.

Everyone needs a story. Everyone needs a name and a cause. Everyone is on a journey.

Her name was Death; her cause was thinking she was God. Her journey was to Hell.
Are we sure she's not come back?

21. Liar Cesspit

Lucky I was, to get this gig. Lecturing trainee police officers in the art of interrogation – specifically, how to spot a liar.

And I didn't have to tell any porkies to get it. I knew the guy who had the work before, and when he was attacked by burglars and reduced to a cabbage with a blunt instrument, possibly a baseball bat, they asked me to step in to the breach.

Their choice was good. They invited retired burglars, hackers, rapists to lecture from their wide experiences. Made sense.

So, a speech to a police investigations team. Or, if nobody believes me, this is my address to a gathering of the Cesspit Club, an exclusive set up for habitual liars.

Still not credible? OK, this is a few thoughts to a self-help group of the Nothing to See Here Group.

Well, here goes. Whoever you are! Joke. Or shall I say, whoever I am. Another joke.

Let me tell you something of my life. Context, you understand.

I was born locally, went to school locally, worked as a local paper reporter before specialising in local crime. Very quickly I realised the best way to learn about criminality, get first wind of heists, frauds and dodgy deals, was to be a participant.

They created the 'Crime Desk' for me. Moving away from local, I supplied stories to our sister regional paper and became a well-paid stringer to one national daily and a TV station.

Alright, alright. I was born miles away and went to four secondary schools before being expelled and moved here to explore my inner psychotic. I briefly topped the MOST WANTED list.

Now I help doctors and trainees with their enquiries while they delve around in my mind looking for what makes it struggle to separate fact from fiction. Someone wanted to give me shock treatment; another was keen on dosing me with truth serum.

I was trying to remember when I first joined the Cesspit Club, full of oddballs and seekers of the murky waters between lies and boring reality. Oh, I know. I founded it!

Back around thirty years ago, when I first met my other half and ditched the others. I did it to reassure that innocently honest human I was turning over the leaf of good citizenship.

I've achieved a fair bit in my 15 years of life. To have so many white coats flapping around, anxious with concern for my well-being, is quite an achievement.

Some seemed to be saying that I was delusional rather than a deliberate liar. But what do they know?

Anyway, this year I decided to make a New Year Resolution. Weird how we make a new year the perfect time to come up with impossible ambitions. While deciding to join in was the easy part, it took a while to come up with 'giving up chocolate.'

No, I tell a lie.

I became convicted of the belief that I should give up lying.

That's quite a statement for those who know me. And that's quite a target, my resolution, for those who don't.

Talking to myself in a mirror is therapeutic and quite useful. I keep a hand-held one close by.

Lying to myself; telling whoppers to everybody. I couldn't help myself. Faced with a choice between a truth and a lie, I'd instinctively choose the lie.

And still do. This is despite having that conversion therapy and, when prompted, recite any mantra given about how effective government is, how I trust everyone in higher authority and how it would be a matter of suicide if I ever gave in to a lying temptation.

For example, a few minutes after deciding to abandon the untruth, somebody asked me if I'd made any New Year's Resolutions? Yes, I said, I'm going to give up being nice to people.

No obvious reason for my first thought always being untrue, nothing rational. It was just what I did. It was me.

I've been lucky to get away with a lifetime of deceit including a decade of bigamy. But then liars need good memories and extraordinary luck. I'm blessed with both.

Giving it up wasn't from any sense of conscience or religious conversion. No, It was just a weariness with play acting, with taking advantage of people's incredible gullibility.

How I love the stage! It doesn't have to be a proscenium with lights and costumes. An audience, any audience in the street, the pub, my home or in a work environment are grist to my mill. Do people still say that these days?

Of course, I made a few quid out of people over the years and earned a decent salary wherever I worked, safe in the knowledge that if my bogus qualifications or references ever started to fall apart, I'd move on.

Always shy, I hid from limelight, never pushing myself forward. The thought of three people in a room is too much for me to contemplate.

New passport (I have 7 currently), new name and driving licence, new look with facial prosthetics. And I'm free to pilot planes in Asia, explore the deep sea in the USA, investigate fraud in the Caymans or perform brain surgery in Australia.

If I chose, I could talk my way into anything. I could leave when things started to get hot or I was in danger of harming myself, if not others. Brain surgery might be more difficult to get away with. I'd have been mortified to be escorted from hospital in handcuffs.

I'm a black male, 6 feet and 4 inches tall, multilingual, knowledgeable, lean and lithe with a good head of fashionably greying hair. I see without glasses and eat with all my own teeth. I am fit. I walk my 10,000 steps and eat my five fruits every day.

In fact, I'm a Caucasian female, 5 feet 1 inch tall, speak only English though I can imitate a variety of regional accents. Increasingly I read less easily, and distances need squinted eyes. I have 6 false teeth on two plates. I gasp on staircases, eat my 10,000 calories and walk my five steps a day.

The truth is I am none of those at all. I'm a comedian who likes to tell tall tales, often self-deprecating ones or at somebody's expense who can take it. No, I am notoriously shy, hate appearing in public never mind speaking aloud to a crowd.

Ah, now I've already said that. Good memory, you see. No, I'm not shy. Party star, that's me. Life and soul. And always speaking up for the little voiceless people on the fringe.

My other half suggested I research information about habitual lying, psychological inability to speak truth and all about the pathological liar cesspit I supposedly inhabit. What was envisaged was some sort of giant poll overflowing with filth in which I happily splashed with other natural liars.

It's assumed that I must be in the seventh circle of hell because I am wracked with guilt at my plight. I have no sense of guilt, shame or regret whatsoever.

A whole business as big as self-help books thrives on teaching people how to detect liars. However, the fact is that human beings are lucky if they smell a rat and that momentarily. Most of the time we go on fallible instinct.

However, some behavioural ticks reveal unease in social and interrogation situations. Fiddling with face, hair, sleeves, neck, picking invisible fluff or looking away from side to side. The liar is comforting him or herself. Truthful people apparently don't do that.

However, nerves alone are not an indication of a deep lie. People are usually discomforted by being asked questions.

They say that covering a mouth with a hand is a relic from our prehistoric past, an instinct to preserve ourselves when faced with shock or horror. It is easily learned, of course.

They also say that playing for time is a dead giveaway. Cough, laugh in a non-funny way, sip a drink, be distracted by a fly on the wall or slip into a long-winded pause to recall something.

However, it's occasionally helpful to play the interrogation game back to them. They like silences which they think you will fill and give yourself away.

So never fill a silence, never spout a meaningless string of verbal diarrhoea.

However, you might ask them to rephrase a question. Or ask them one yourself? 'Are we done?' is rarely unanswered, so the silence is broken. Enquiring after their children may be OK with a friend, but not police or officialdom.

However, however, however. So many 'howevers'. Are they all stalling for time and/or covering something up?

Some lying 'experts' look for mismatching body language at odds with what's being said. Saying no while nodding is the classic, I learned.

The real lesson from mastering my habit years ago was to sprinkle my tales with as much truth as I could while maintaining the lie. The greater the truth, the more credible the lie.

One quite interesting thing is that most people are poor listeners. They appear to be all ears while thinking what to ask next or what to have for dinner. I listen outstandingly.

I don't hear too well and refuse a hearing aid. That would be too limiting. So, I lip read and pretend to understand.

People often give away dark layers about themselves which supply me with future, knowledge-based untruths or permit me to deflect from any inadequacies in my own tale.

Some bighead has postulated that the average story is around 30% build up preparation, 40% actual real meat content, followed by 30% additions, reflections and repetitions to drive home the point or the comedy.

A liar makes the build up around 80% with the meat a few seconds, dashed through quickly so the listener doesn't dwell on any inconsistencies or obvious fabrications.

Usually there's no problem. Of course, if the story is recorded it can be gone over later and holes picked in it.

Don't blame the memory! Standard liar habit, apparently. Nobody forgets a big event, so use distraction rather than blaming old age for loss of detail. Unless you want to play the doddery old fool indefinitely.

Don't use the third person! Don't say 'somebody' was walking along the street when it was you. Claim as much genuine association as possible.

Be careful of tenses. Everybody is alive until you're told he or she is dead.

One self-opinionated psychologist has claimed that 1% of the population are psychopaths who can lie all day and all of the night plus 4% who are antisocial, criminally minded and proud of it. That's a lot of people.

I'm in good company.

Of course, some people lie for a living – medics, financial advisers, estate agents and politicians, for instance. Presumably outside their work they're the very models of rectitude, incapable of even thinking of a lie.

So, again, I'm in good company.

My birthday, well one of them, is in the spring. My other half got me a set of riddles to solve online. Things like: you are a prisoner, two doors and two guards. One door leads to freedom: the other to death. You may only ask one guard one question; one always lies, the other always speaks truth.

The answer is some nonsense about choosing the opposite door to whichever is given. It did my head in. They all did. If I was setting it up, I'd simplify it with both doors leading to death and so the prisoner dilemma is solved.

But I'm not a killer.

Nor a taker of prisoners.

I spent enough time inside for murder and kidnapping not to feel a fragment of empathy for anybody locked up.

Wait! The truth is I got off and was not incarcerated.

I preferred the riddle: what belongs to you but is used more by other people? Your name.

Most people have just the one, at best two, names. A good liar has multiple names, families, backstories and ambitious plans. He nor she may need to relieve you of your life savings to achieve them, of course.

Now, where am I? Ah yes. In the cesspit with Door A and Door B. Which shall I use today?

22. A Mere Laughing-Stock Or A Donkey's Burial?

When the Government, blessed be their names, first announced that most old fogies were to be given donkey burials, few knew what they were. So, nobody was alarmed.

Of course, I knew and tried to warn people as I attended one. All old crusties are to be dumped outside the city gates, beyond the gatehouse. Let them rot there, like fish, from the head down. Just as donkeys were dealt with once they'd gone in days long ago.

Later the rule that codgers must be dead was amended to 'nearly dead.' The cash freed up for health and social care was staggering.

Anybody who objected was informed it was the fault of the previous government, cursed be their names, and people should be grateful that there was fit and proper space outside cities for dead donkeys.

The city gates turned out to be a cover-all reference for any given community. How enlightened the Government proved itself, blessed be their names. No more time wasted on send-offs and celebrations. This was the way forward.

They'd stolen the idea from *Jeremiah 22,* which pleased those who still believed till they understood what it meant.

The day they dragged old Charlie outside the village limit, I asked how old was old - Charlie was only 60, though he was ill and sucking from the public teat of healthcare more than his share.

The fact that he'd slogged all his life and paid taxes through the nose counted for nothing. Some official his junior by at least 35 years signed a form remotely that he was ready to go.

I protested that they're making a laughing-stock of humanity. For my pains, I was given a final warning in blood and told the next donkey burial I attended would be my own. But I tell you, I was not born on a beach to be scared of a crab.

I was simply trying to exercise what used to my democratic rights to express criticism of the government, cursed be their name.

Oh, I must be careful. I mean blessed be their name, of course.

They can't stomach criticism at all. Either you are for them, or you are a dead donkey.

And I was keen on the laughing-stock analogy. When a government or a bigshot becomes one, he/she/they are finished. Nobody can take a laughing-stock seriously, please may it be so.

But nobody listened. Like the Ancient Mariner I was compelled to speak, whatever danger I faced. Nip a nettle hard and it will not sting you, that's what I was told.

So, what is a laughing-stock?

If you believe the Bible, as I secretly do, then from *Ezekiel* it is what God did with those who made idols and thereby became 'a reproach to the nations, a laughing-stock to all countries.'

Sounds quite dramatic, hey? Well, it's meant to be. There is little worse than becoming a laughing-stock, a mockery to your fellow peoples.

Take public life. There're 7 stages of life for someone in the public eye. They don't read as well as Shakespeare's 7 ages of man.

Oh hell. I've just heard that Shakespeare is not to be quoted any more. He was not signed up to trans-multi-culturalism-racist-free policies. If he was alive today, he'd be a dead donkey.

Or a laughing-stock to all those enlightened people in authority, bless them all.

Anyway, first we have Obscurity followed by Rising Star for those climbing. The third phase is Taking Ground as these blessed people become ubiquitous and irresistible.

Triumph is the fourth stage, when the victorious charmed ones have reached such acclaim and fame that they can do no wrong. This quickly melds into the fifth sequence – Tedious. And that is hard to endure. Once great persons are now crashing bores.

Six is Laughing-Stock which is cruel, vicious and humiliating. So what? Live by public life; die by public life.

Obscurity is the 7th and final label. Back to the start but several decades older. I'm old now, in my second bout of obscurity.

However, I recall the 1960s and the life that went with them, when it was bliss to be alive. I daren't talk about them, not now. But lots of interesting details about the music, attitudes, fashions and dope is still vivid in my ancient mind.

I'm long enough in the tooth to have become a joke. Worse than that, I'm (shock horror) an unapologetic white man, middle class and heterosexual. I've no time for worshipping identity genders and compulsory woke views unless they contradict the current mood of intolerance. Inclusion has rejected me.

One of my grandchildren stared at my rack of over 200 CDs of classic and some rare examples of music from 1965-1990. '*What* are all these, Grandpa?' the lad asked in genuine puzzlement.

He knew vinyl records because they were back in fashion, but not a compact disk. In a way, early digital technology was still cutting edge to me. When they, blessed be the name, made it mandatory to use technology to pay bills and taxes, buy tickets and food and communicate so it could be monitored, they condemned older people to criminality.

But people with my strengths are not made anymore. I was raised in Norfolk by truly old school parents who commanded hosts of folklore to trot out when the need arose, and often when it didn't.

One I liked and still do (if that's alright with the powers that be): there's a scabby dog in every litter. It meant that every family in the world has scabs that could infect the lot.

A single person with the wrong viewpoint can spread it to everyone. In some areas it was known as the Black Sheep of the Family, but that was ruled offensive, or One Bad Apple, but that was judged over-negative.

Our problem today is that every person except a few donkeys and laughing-stocks is infected with the scabs of this age. And there is no cure.

A custom that was fraught with potential for disaster was at a marriage, the parson claimed the ancient right to have the first kiss of the bride. Any attempt of the groom to thwart it was frowned upon. We are still slaves to custom and tradition that began in the mist of past times.

One they used to press on us was 'you must eat another yard of gruel first', meaning you must wait till you're older before doing whatever you wanted to. Now, of course, that one is obsolete. Nobody's allowed to think outside the strait jacket issued to them.

We do as we're told. It's poured down our throats, down the 'red funnel', like it or not. And who does?

Don't be a gape-seed admiring the blessed government. That was when someone found a thing so weirdly fascinating that they gaped with eyes agog, mouth open.

A couple my parents got from their own grandparents. Both were about death. 'He's bare of a suit.' It meant that the person was so poor there was nothing he could be buried in. Unless he was a donkey.

And 'a plague or fever cures all disorders.' Nobody suffers once they are dead and buried. Or dragged outside the city.

Oh, and there was the horror of finding a corpse still limp before burial as it signified another imminent death in the family. Doesn't apply to a donkey's funeral, of course.

They used to say if a loaf of bread turned in the oven, if a bird flew into a room and out or of a lit candle was left in an empty room, a death would follow. Nowadays, death comes if you speak ill of those who must be obeyed.

If you watched from a church porch an hour either side of midnight on St Marks Eve (24/5 April), you'd see the wraiths of those who'd die during the year.

Before I'm taken into protective custody (arrested), let me confess my list of annoying, meaningless conversation fillers in widespread use in this society they're building. Well, they annoy me.

Make some noise for ….

Give it up for ….

A big shout out for …

To be perfectly honest

To be fair

Going forward

So … (people who start every sentence with So…)

At this moment in time

At the end of the day

A perfect storm … (what?)

A near miss … (what on earth is that?)

Reach out to someone …

You know what? …

You know what I mean?

If I said I was interested, I'd be telling a lie

I'm not being funny

Take it to a whole new level …

No problem …

No worries ....

Awesome ...

Absolutely ...

To have skin in the game ...

Blessed be their name ... (no way)

When they decreed my official diagnosis as confused, demented and a health and safety liability to myself and others. I played up. Yes, I asked questions on tiny issues; expressed trumped up fears and delusions repeatedly.

I just had time to make a list of annoying people categories: the government of course, cursed/blessed be their name, all alleged celebrities, performers, personalities and influencers. There should be a law forbidding them from uttering an opinion in public about anything except their actual performing skills.

After my requisite daily walk outside, I was taken back to my disabled-adapted bungalow to swallow my gastric tablets for hiatus hernia, heart pills for atrial fibrillation, lowering blood pressure medicine, laxatives because of the iron supplements I am on, paracetamol for headaches, blurred vision, arthritis, dodgy ears and intermittent eyesight.

A laughing-stock, if it was funny. The man who could no longer hold down a challenging job and responsibilities.

The man who, in the current mania for abbreviating everything was FOBF, living in fear of being forgotten.

This arose from some other 'popular' glib sayings:

FOMO fear of missing out
FOGO fear of going out
JOMO joy of missing out
ROMO relief of missing out
FOGOV fear of going overseas
FOSS fear of sounding stupid
FOLO fear of looking old

We've now been told we can choose – blessed be the name, choose! We are given two acronyms to live by. We must select one sequence to plan our days by. Or else.

There is EACH - exercise, admin, creative, household.
And there is ACHE - admin, creative, household, exercise.

This used to be called Hobson's choice. But Hobson fell foul of the gender expansion rules and has now been declared AIHNE (as if he never existed).

What is the outcome of all this? Am I defeated by it? Do I fall for a robot called Abishag?

Well, as I shuffle out of the shopping mall coffee shop, one hand clinging to my son's arm, the other white-knuckling an ancient wooden walking stick, I stumble as I reach the mobility scooter.

A crowd of healthy, energetic, sports-fit young people nearby roar the group laugh that comes from expecting a full life ahead with everything in order.

Maybe they're laughing at their little screens. Or laughing at me. No matter. If they clocked me at all then I am a mere laughing-stock. They don't even wait for my trousers to fall through weight-loss.

23. Three Punishments

The Boss, over-weight and overflowing from the suit he insisted on wearing indoors and out, was minding two of his little grandkids. His wife, the long-suffering Ellen, was out shopping with their daughter Queenie. What on earth they needed to buy, he couldn't imagine. They surely had everything.

And paying with good hard-earned money was anathema to Neville Statton. Not his real name, of course, but one he'd used to build an empire in which paying legitimately was a rarity.

He invariably happily accepted an hour or so of grandchildren-minding. Ellen always left him (the same) inflexible dos and don'ts. The house was huge, so they must stay in the sitting room and kitchen and use the downstairs toilet and that was it. No playing in the gardens, garage, upstairs or his study – all places they'd make a beeline for when they were older.

He loved watching his little ones play. Their pushing at boundaries, their bursts of bravery and then sudden losses of confidence amused him. Their occasional squabbles were his gauge as to how their characters were shaping up. They were his joy.

Whenever they tried to involve him in something, he just said, 'no, you go ahead, Grandpa is going to watch you.' It allowed him to be in charge should an emergency arise while giving him head space for his daily check on his accounts and time to think through his problems.

Little Tommy asked, looking up from playing with a mountain of plastic prehistorical animal replicas, 'what's your favourite animal, Grandpa?'

Not asking Tommy for his, the old man responded without thought, his mind deep in the diminished profit and expanding loss on the port operation that was not as buoyant as it should be, 'a dead one!'

The boy was upset but had to learn. Tommy was the Boss' flesh and blood. No good being soft and pussyfooting around. The kid recovered quickly, brought his grandfather a misshapen dinosaur with two of its three heads gone and put it on his lap.

'That's a good boy, Tommy. Grandpa will look after this one, hey?' He stroked it with a pudgy, ringed hand and twisted the remaining head off when the boy wasn't looking.

Satisfied, the lad went back to the floor. His time away had allowed his older sister, Rose, to steal his favourite. When he wailed at the injustice, she gave him a good slap round the head. 'That's my girl,' Statton nodded in approval. She was on the right lines, that one.

Just like her, when the Boss was displeased or wanted to make a point, he struck. He lashed out at whoever he thought, or in rare cases knew, was the guilty party. Who'd fucked up? Who'd sold him down the river?

He liked the title 'Boss'. It added respect that he felt he deserved. If anyone wanted to call him Mr Statton or Neville, that was fine but was not wise if it caught Statton in a bad mood.

He had a reputation to keep; if anybody crossed him or came up short, they had to pay. And pay they always did. He hadn't got to his supreme power without building a fearsome reputation and enforcing it.

He expected some light skimming off the club takings or a few grams of white up the nose. But anything bigger was just taking the piss.

Even those closest, often those who'd served him well over decades, would expect no mercy if they fell short.

Especially his right-hand man – Billy – who knew where all the bodies were buried, literally, was not immune. Billy in his sharp suit, lean and hungry in face and belly, hadn't been seen around for a few weeks. Nobody mentioned it, of course. It was as if Billy had never been a feature in the Boss' playground.

Statton had initially been quite taken with the cop Billy had recruited two years ago. What an asset in the operation, a detective inspector, short of the necessaries to give his girlfriend an abortion.

The bloke had been grateful to receive the Boss's help and go one step further when he tired of the girl and wanted her to disappear.

Billy took care of everything. What Billy neglected to admit was that the filth was playing a double betrayal, working for both sides.

The cop accepted an invitation to inspect the decorating Statton was having done in his second sitting room. Decorating was well outside his detective remit, of course, but the Boss needed the man standing on heavy-duty decorating sheets.

The Boss, Billy and the cop along with three sidekicks, one of whom was wrapped in a big dustcoat and held his shoulders awkwardly as if he was hiding something close to his chest, stood staring at four walls yet to be painted.

Statton offered up the evidence his men had gathered and directly challenged the cop to confess. The nerve of the man – he laughed in the Boss' face and called him a no-good thug.

Remaining calm and reasonable, Statton offered him a choice between two punishments – a permanent cure for headaches or a concrete overcoat – the man had told Statton to go fuck himself.

The grin was frozen on his ugly mug when the Boss decided for him and nodded to the sidekick hiding something under his coat. The boy in blue's head parted company from his shoulders as a great broadsword swung round in an elegant curve.

Billy sweated as he watched; he even wiped his brow, making out it was to clean off some of the cop's blood spurt. He knew the finger was pointed at him as he had brought the cop in and was doomed by association.

Characteristically, Statton let Billy choose. A gun in the mouth or jump without a parachute off the Raybuck Tower, 25 floors up.

Statton had barely got out the room when Billy's self-destruction was announced by the muffled shot. Smart move, Billy. His family would have joined him on his skydive, he knew. Statton was so pleased with the outcome he left without watching it in full technicolour.

The Boss loved choices that taxed the brain. He liked his victims to have time to really wrestle with a thorny dilemma, this death or that one.

Only Princess Lily was offered three choices. Three punishments. Three deaths. His Princess Lily deserved no less.

His youngest child, Lily had been the apple of his eye throughout her childhood. Possessed of both a terrifying temper and a truly vicious streak, she was his pick to succeed him. Come the day.

He suspected that she was setting up a rival organisation when certain people went quiet; some deliveries vanished; one load was seized by police. He thought it through, blinking his piggy eyes, and reluctantly concluded that it could only be Lily, impatient for her moment in the sun.

Unable to share his thoughts with anyone, he brooded for days on end. Ellen was exasperated.

'What's up, Neville?' That just annoyed him. He could trust nobody, not even Ellen.

Way back, soon after he and Ellen were first together, he'd suspected she was doing the dirty behind his back. The hapless man that Statton was convinced was the horny bastard was given his choice from two punishments – castration and bleeding out or having his actual wife strung up. Shitting himself, the man still protesting his innocence, chose his wife.

He got both. Statton had a reputation to live up to, after all. Ellen had already learned enough never to ask or mention the man again.

The Boss demanded a meet with Princess Lily. To straighten things out, to clear the air and to agree a way forward. He was prepared to give her a huge slice of his territory. He was a reasonable man, after all.

Turning up late, she seemed angry and aggressive from the off, asking about her mother and siblings as if she hadn't seen them for weeks. Anything but discuss the real family business her father had on his mind. She blew smoke over him as he sat, knowing her mother didn't allow indoor smoking.

Since she'd taken up with that no-good Charlie – another of the late Billy's finds – he'd sensed her pulling away from his power. From his love. And the pointless meeting confirmed it to him. She wanted the lot and if the old man had to go; it was time.

Lily had dominated his mind several times a day since then. The people who worked for and under him watched to see how he'd deal with her rebellion. They'd noted her attitude. Experts in the business, they were alert to the treacheries of others. The problem wasn't going to simply disappear or sort itself. He had to enforce punishment.

He'd thought up three for her. He was mulling over when to put them to his 24-year-old ice princess. If only she'd shown remorse, a fragment of apology on her lips. But nothing. She was determined to be defiant till the end.

His first choice was that he'd use his contacts to cut her free of all her financial support systems, accounts, income and in effect consign her to a famine. He would appoint people to watch over her and her activities. And it would go on for three years!

On reflection, that felt too harsh. Three months? On the other hand, if any other had betrayed him as she did, it would be famine for thirty years.

Next, he'd come up with a long period of prosperity and success for those she loathed and devastation on those she loved. Injuries and mutilations, breakdowns, unexplained accidents, poor medical decisions, each problem compounded by others. Three years of that? Well, maybe six months.

His third choice was direct action from his henchmen and women. For a short intense period – say three days – he'd have his thugs purge her friends. And Charlie – he was to be gunned down in a bloodbath in front of her, cut to shreds in a hail of bullets leaving her weakened and alone.

It would look as if Charlie's family had gone rogue. Nothing would come back on Neville Statton. He himself would weep openly with his daughter at every funeral.

There was satisfaction and not a little pleasure in imagining punishments on those people. But not on his Princess. That hurt. He hoped she'd show her distress and beg him to let her have the third choice which he believed would hurt her the least.

His thoughts were interrupted by the sound of Ellen and Queenie, his older girl and mother of Tommy and Rose. Queenie'd turned her nose up at the family business, but was happy with the horses, the holidays, shopping extravaganzas and the cars the wealth brought them. And now she and Ellen were laden with shopping bags; the retail therapy had got out of hand.

The kids leapt about as if Grandpa had failed in his duty to entertain them. In fact, Rose was so pleased to see her mum back she clocked Tommy one on the back of the head just for being there. She got a bollocking from both Queenie and Ellen, but a grin and wink from her Grandpa.

After a quick round of cakes and soft drinks, Queenie insisted they must make a move. Cocktails to organise that evening. She complained they'd invited Princess and Charlie but neither had the manners to respond. Statton shrugged, as if to say what do you expect with an ignoramus like Charlie.

He wanted to tell her the man wasn't down for many more breaths, but let it go. Then it was kisses and hugs all round and off they went, kids in the back, Queenie driving with two of Statton's finest bodyguards discretely following in an anonymous pick up.

Ellen went upstairs to try on some of the items she'd just purchased to give her husband his own fashion show. Statton sat thinking of his Princess and swallowed two fingers of scotch to help him think clearly. He loved her, after all.

Something stirred through the open door; he looked up. He usually heard things right through the house, but not this time.

After a moment Lily emerged from round the corner, weapon-less but followed by a group of rough-necks, some Statton knew and three new-comers. She'd recruited far and wide.

'Come to tell me your choice, have you, Lily?'

She laughed a moment till it died on her thin lips. 'No, Pa, I've come to give *you* three choices. It's time to check out, old timer. The future belongs to the next generation. Me and mine.'

He nodded slowly. Where the hell were his bodyguards? They'd let her in not realising what she was about. Or they'd seen the way the wind was blowing and joined her.

His hands seized the arms of his recliner to rise, but she waved him down. 'Stay there. Choice one: you hand over the entire empire right now and toddle off to an exile in South America or somewhere at least as far away. You'll have a decent lump sum to go with and there are cartels you might join up with. Mum stays here as my agent in this house. Most of our people will agree.'

She waited while he took in the offer. For a second, he considered it. He was getting on. The arthritis wasn't going to ease up and one day she'd have it all in any case. It also left open the possibility of revenge from a distance, one day when she was least expecting it.

'Two. You say goodbye to the family. Then go into your study and write a note, updating your will to cut out Queenie and Mum. You then swallow a few painkillers and slice open your veins and slip away peacefully.'

He smiled and nodded in approval. It was the sort of choice he'd have come up with for an old man. She'd certainly learned more than he previously appreciated all the years of her upbringing.

'Three. No note, no messages or goodbyes. A trench has been dug on the inland side, by the old cowsheds. We used that new fancy digger you bought to impress everyone. A bullet in the back of the head. The three guys who dug it will follow you in. Such loyalty! Then the earth will be closed over you. I'll do that so nobody else knows. Quick, simple, efficient. You'll disappear. A big mystery for a few weeks. I'll wear black!'

He kept his eyes on his daughter. 'Not all my people have gone over to you. Makes no sense. Some must still be loyal.'

'Oh, some are. One or two die-hards seem reluctant to accept that a woman will be the new Boss. No room for them in my organisation, of course.'

He shook his head, mentally going through his people, to think who that applied to. 'I gave everyone a choice between two punishments. Sign a loyalty contract to me in blood and accept terrible consequences for failure.'

She paused for dramatic effect. 'Or go their own ways never knowing when a car would run their kids over, when their child would drown in the pool or be snatched or when a fire would break out at home after doors and windows were sealed.'

As Princess looked at the wall clock, a grossly over-priced imitation ormolu piece, noise outside indicated a new arrival. To his shock and some horror, it was Billy, walking in swinging a cricket bat and looking very much alive.

Statton stared at the apparition. His mouth was dry. What the fuck? Billy grinned – he was enjoying this. If Statton had a weak heart, this would have seen him off.

His mind went back to the moment Billy had made his choice. Of course, untrue to form, Statton hadn't stayed in the room to watch the suicide.

Lily smiled, watching the old man thinking it through. She filled in the missing details for him. Billy joined her and they performed a kind of twisted double act in front of him while he kept glancing at the window and door, hoping for some loyal person to appear.

Ellen was still upstairs changing. Not, he suspected, that she'd lift a finger to help him. She was as soft on Lily as he'd been.

He was told Billy didn't shoot himself in that room but fired out the window before climbing through and making good his escape. Princess's car picked him up and facilitated his arrival at the port where he was smuggled onto a fishing vessel she owned.

He went to Holland where he started working her new Dutch subsidiary, but she alone knew that. The clever thing she did was to have Billy's 'body' removed from the room by two of Statton's closest that she'd recruited with lucrative offers and threats to their loved ones.

When Billy's sexy wife made a constant nuisance of herself begging Statton to have him searched for, he quite genuinely thought Billy was six feet under somewhere, so his denial of information was sincere and certainly fooled the poor woman.

Lily stood directly in front of him. 'One more thing, your kind offer to look after Billy's wife, late wife I should say, after she thought she was a widow, was not a complete secret. Mum knew. We all knew. Your betrayal was common knowledge. And those junkie prostitutes. Oh, and the private STI clinic you paid for tests.'

He brushed that aside, smiling as if she had now lapsed into the surreal.

'Right, that's enough of the story to satisfy your curiosity, Pa. It's time to choose your punishment. One, two or three.'

She stared at him to help concentrate his mind. Billy moved round behind him, so he couldn't watch and keep Lily in sight. The sidekicks had already spread out around the room. Even if he was armed, Statton knew he couldn't take more than one of the bastards before he was a gonner.

Billy placed the heavy bat on the desk just out of reach of Statton's fingers. So, he wasn't going to be clubbed to death. Would have ruined the carpet, of course.

'Well, Pa? Decide or I'll choose for you.'

'Does it have to be this, Lily? What if I make a new deal, three different choices that are not punishments at all?' If he had a gun, he knew in that second that he'd take Lily out first.

'I'm afraid it does. Blood is thicker and all that shit. But you see, Mum hinted to me when I was at high school, that you aren't actually my biological father, so I can do what I want. What I must do, if I'm to take control of this whole operation.'

Statton hadn't seen that coming. It shocked him even more than Billy's miraculous resurrection. 'What about your mother? She's upstairs.'

'She'll stay up there till I tell her to come down. Good old mum, hey?'

Hearing nothing, he was swept with instant panic as a cord was slipped round his neck from behind. Wiry old Billy had the strength of the demented bent on revenge.

Legs kicking out, he tried to get up while reaching round for the face of his attacker and simultaneously getting a hand between the cord and his neck. She continued to speak.

'Looks like it's choice 4, or a version of choice 3. No bullet, but that trench will come in handy.'

Within nine minutes of her arrival, the Boss was told everything, offed and buried in the trench.

The Boss is dead; long live the Princess.

24. Your Speech Shall Whisper

For a few years in the late 1960s and early 70s, *The Lowestoft Journal* ran a readers' monthly short story competition with a prize of 5 guineas (five pounds and five shillings).

For December 1970 they chose the theme of 'ghosts'. Not necessarily Christmas, but mindful of Dickens and other great ghoulish tales, Christmas was a natural hook for the event.

Having applied for a journalism apprenticeship with the *Journal's* parent company, Ray Boon knew he should enter. What else would a young man with aspirations to amount to something in life do?

In October while he waited for a response, he'd created a little story about time changes and clocks; in November he'd joined in the fun for gunpowder and explosions.

However, they were certainly taking a long time to decide on his application. He wondered if his mother had posted the letter as she promised. But he wasn't going to show dependence on her by asking.

Ray knew the youngster who'd created the vacancy, who'd abandoned his prestigious apprenticeship after just eighteen months, sick of sitting three days a week in the magistrates' court reporting on minor misdemeanours and two days a week at the cemetery, reporting on dull, predictable funerals.

Boon was sure he'd cope. Once his talents were recognised, he'd be put onto interesting investigative journalism. He'd heard something dodgy about a couple of freemasons and there was a clerk at the Town Hall with very deep pockets.

However, he was not blessed with great patience. The ghost story would be his last. Perhaps he should write about a phantom room of newspaper seniors who were invisible but pretended they weren't.

If they turned him down, they could rot in hell. If he was accepted, he'd be ineligible for the competition anyhow. The face of his mother smiled encouragingly, so proud of her little boy.

Turning away, peevishly, he refused to smile back. Why did she keep doing that, smiling in such a sickening, cloying manner?

He knew trains were frequently the setting for ghost stories, especially steam trains. Apparitions on lines. Unexplained presences in carriages. Wraiths on luggage racks. Headless spectres on deserted station platforms and howling down old coal stoves in damp, dingy and drafty waiting rooms.

The former 3ft gauge Southwold railway that ran through the Blyth Valley to Halesworth from 1879 to 1929 came to mind. Notoriously slow, gangs of youths would frequently outrun it on certain stretches, it was much loved locally. That affection was insufficient for it to survive into the 1930s.

He could write about the ghost of the only man ever run down by one of their engines, a soldier home on leave from the war in 1916. His poor wraith was condemned to forever try to get home to Southwold for a weekend, but never did. His body hung limply across the front of the engine.

Boon envisaged that train running on rails that glistened in the moonlight of a frosty winter night, unseen by anybody but a little girl in the present who 'saw' things.

And she saw some terrible things, that little girl. Murders, desertion in love and military, robberies and a band of rough-neck criminals crashing the train. He wondered if he hadn't read about her years ago. So that was a no.

His mother's face looked concerned. Was the little girl her? How many of the terrible things she saw had she shared with her little lad? She couldn't remember. Was she older than a little girl, a housemaid going home on compassionate Christmas leave who'd conceived her son on the train with a soldier she had known from their village?

All she knew for certain was that she'd birthed the boy, breast fed him for two years as was customary and guided him every step of the way into his schooling and hovered like a guardian angel as he blossomed into a sickly, strange but living young man.

And her own old, Victorian mother had been convinced she'd never do it, never bring little Raymond to term much less be around as he grew up. She smiled at him again as he sat pondering the story challenge. He'd come up with something, of course he would, cold as it was in the dingy, squalid rooms they rented.

Without looking at her directly, he just knew she was smiling that adoring grin at him. Oh why? If he locked his hands round her throat and squeezed, would she stop rambling? He wouldn't have to feel the hangman's noose strangling him, as they'd abolished the penalty.

Moving from Southwold in his mind, Ray came nearer to home. The Lowestoft to Great Yarmouth line, opened in July 1903, had served the two rival towns, gradually failing to compete with road transport and a declining fish and passenger trade. It had closed in the summer, May 1970.

It was easy to imagine trains still running, because only recently he'd sat trackside watching them. Twice, he'd travelled to Yarmouth and back for a day out. Once with his mother who kept holding her belly and smiling inanely around the carriage as if anyone cared. The second journey had been alone, a small act of rebellion that sent her into deafening hysterics of worry.

But at night, all sorts of ghostly happenings were possible, when good citizens were abed and only those hell-bent on evil stalked the gaslit streets. The macabre just waited to be called to service.

His mother used to petrify him, making the hairs on his arms rise and his neck feel strange, with her tales of the horrors lurking in the very air after dark. She planted in him a passion to taste it for himself.

Determined to see the closed line up close, he waited till dusk. He'd use her fifth-hand mini in which he was conceived to start at each point up the line and either sleep in it or come home. When he thought of his mother's incessant probing of his whereabouts and motives, he planned to sleep in the old car.

Starting at Lowestoft central station that still served Ipswich and Norwich with functioning lines made sense. He could pass Coke Oven Corner as the former line swung northwards out of the station. The walk to Lowestoft North opposite the Grammar School was not far, and he'd do it and be back in his car well before dark.

His second evening would start at the Grammar School and head out of Lowestoft, parallel with Corton Road across Dip Farm, through Corton Woods to Corton station. The station itself was about to be sold off and the stationmaster's house was already a private dwelling.

The next night, he'd press on northwards close to Corton Church, past the little rail worker cottage on the clifftop and across open fields to sleepy Hopton. Holiday camps galore, but too few visitors to keep the line going.

On his fourth evening, through fields, woods and scrubland he'd reach Gorleston-on-Sea and Gorleston North. They were talking about building a major general hospital that would have brought passengers, but they'd be too late. Already the track at this point was earmarked for a road bypass of Gorleston.

In 1914 they'd added Gorleston Links, an on-demand halt to serve the golf course. Now there remained only a couple of sleepers to help golfers alight and a signpost without a board.

On his fifth night he'd reach Yarmouth South Town and end his journey. The original line continued across the five-span Breydon Viaduct and the Bure Railway Bridge to Great Yarmouth Beach Station. It was after the 1953 east coast floods that the powers thought it too costly to repair the viaduct so all services from Lowestoft terminated at Yarmouth South Town.

He was less interested in the Yarmouth end, recalling how his mother often laughed that the only good thing to come out of Yarmouth was the road to Lowestoft, after all. So, Yarmouth South Town station, soon to be lost under a road, was his destination.

Along the way, he'd have found many points from which he could watch old supernatural trains rattle past with passengers on board squirming under his ghostly presences. His mother could sit back and relax, he'd survive with a plan for a winning story. It might even be picked up by entrepreneurs who wanted to reinstate it for holidaymakers and visitors partial to the bizarre and quirky.

He didn't look to see if her face was showing pleasure at his plan. She was on her bed, sheets twisted and wet, legs curled under her, nursing her stomach and shrieking in agony, showing no pleasure at him or anything else.

The simple mention of station names in the story would conjure images of several of the good old boys, real characters, who worked the line and served in the repair shop. Memories of passengers would be stirred as the steam smoke cleared or the grind and smell as the diesel units slowly gathered speed. It would appeal to all local people, surely? They'd be there, back then, reliving it.

Hard-hearted would be the reader who wouldn't sense his or her blood curdling while a ghost that only he or she could see reached out a misshapen hand to touch him or her on the neck, to peel the skin from his or her back or slide an arm down his or her throat in order to pull him or her inside out.

Better still, what if it was a child? As the ghost, of course? A child from someone's loving womb turned bad. He looked for his mother, but she was being treated by medical experts in bloody white coats. A man from Yarmouth stared through the window, spoke no words, but his face looked distraught.

And just as he was getting as excited as he ever did and breaking through the flimsy fence to start his walk of the line with most of its rusting rails and sleepers still on their granite chip bed, Ray heard his mother croaking in his grandfather's voice, quoting from *Isaiah 29* in a sermon he'd sat through at Christ Church, the most easterly church in Britain.

'And you will be brought low; from the earth you shall speak, and from the dust your speech will be bowed down; and your voice shall come from the ground like the voice of a ghost. And from the dust your speech shall whisper.'

And there was his title. *Your Speech Shall Whisper*. Though he was struck by *Like the Voice of a Ghost*, *From the Dust* and *From the Earth You Shall Speak* almost as much. The whispering voice, the sound of the dead and the scarcely living, it just sounded right.

Knowing the title, helped him travel with a sense of purpose. Not only would the five guineas be useful – he had a funeral to pay for – but it would bestow local importance on him in his town.

His mother's hand reached out to stroke her son's face and tousle his hair in a little show of affection. But he moved away, not deliberately, but just as if he hadn't seen her. In fact, as if she wasn't there.

His imagination then focused on the image of the last corpse he'd seen being lifted into a wooden box at the undertaker's where he'd been a Saturday boy, helping for a half a crown a long day. That dead body had spoken to him, revealing horrors from her life, cut cruelly short by the disease that racked her lungs and brought blood from her mouth.

She whispered. Her speech shall whisper. And it did. His mother? When had he last seen her? She must have been there, at least for his birth and early years, but he couldn't swear to it, hand on the Bible.

His pilgrimage done, all he had was a twisted ankle from a split sleeper, a blister on his left big toe and a handful of ideas that went nowhere. There was no hint of thrill or forbidden ecstasy. No sense of direction. The ghost train was as pointless and fleeting as his dreams to be somebody of value.

With time running out and attending yet another funeral as practice for his apprenticeship in a chilly graveyard, watching a former town Alderman laid to rest, he fancied he could see his ghost train hurtling across the graves, mowing mourners down. But it was miles from the line. It was a silly image.

He'd have done better to have dreamed up a hellish, God-forsaken creature arising from a long-forgotten grave in the corner stuffed with plague victims. But by then, he'd had enough of thinking. He was tired. Wearier than he thought a man of his age should be.

If he was the trainee journalist, what on earth would he write about this worthy stuffed shirt being lowered into his own hell pit by eight strapping men? Why was his coffin so heavy?

Checking the newspaper archives in the press offices for a phrase or two he could lift to praise the departed, he happened upon the obituary of a man who seemed familiar, though he'd never known him. A young man of immense promise taken too young. A man with a connection to Raymond Boon.

Did everyone have not only a double in life, but also a look-alike who went ahead of him while identical children followed? Would that make a story?

Ray felt decidedly queasy. His stomach wasn't helped by the train jolting on lines submerged in the rising sea.

There were voices without mouths, jabbering in a language no humans knew. He was sinking fast or derailing or being sidelined into a dead end or running out of coal or diesel, or …

His unsmiling mother was being delivered of a baby. Not her first, but this time she was terrified. Hot and cold. Scared to open her eyes as the midwife and doctor worked over her. Afraid to see the accusing eyes from the walls.

This baby had been conceived in her little mini car to replace his brother who died of a terrible disease nobody would talk about and had been buried in a lead-lined coffin, like royalty.

A man, the father, paced outside the ward, given a little extra time to try to make things right.

But the man had failed miserably.

The son saw his mother through a membrane and called out feebly, 'Mummy, Mummy.' She wanted to smile at him but was too far gone.

She saw the father through the darkness under the train wheels, she gurgled gibberish.

She saw her baby through the membrane and yelled, 'Raymond, Raymond.'

She saw her sons through the wooden boxes and said nothing.

Not even a whisper.

25. Last Man Standing Can't Bury Himself

Doctor Naismith smiled at his patient. Jack Talbot was an ordinary, run of the mill guy who'd gone down with this new disease, Russian virus. But Doctor Naismith was going to keep him alive.

'Listen, Mr Talbot. Hundreds are saved from this now. It's not the killer it was. We have better treatments.' They'd indeed come far from the early days of mass deaths, an overwhelmed health service and global terror.

And all because a bunch of old, drunken steelworkers in some hell hole in deepest Russia had slaughtered a cross-bred dog and roasted it on a brazier.

That dog had been swimming in a turgid lake and picked up a new virus.

A week later, the workers were dead along with all they came near, though officially the men did not exist and had never existed.

'How long have I got? Weeks? Days? Hours?'

'Don't be so gloomy. I guarantee you'll live at least a full year.'

After a pause, Talbot stuck his chin out, nodded and replied, 'And how will you guarantee it, Doc?'

Well,' he smiled confidently. 'I'm so sure that you'll live at least a year that I'm willing to pay for your funeral if you die in under a year.'

'That's quite an offer.'

'I'm that confident.'

'My family would appreciate it if I topped myself just on the year and you'll pay for my funeral.'

'No, you must die from this disease and no other cause.' While Jack pondered the offer, Naismith stood from his desk and made for the door.

'You're a grave-digger, aren't you? Well, the world is not dying off from this. Last man standing can't bury himself, can he?'

'He could have a bloody good try, if you're paying for his funeral.'

Laughing, Naismith opened the door. 'See you in a month, Mr Talbot, when you'll feel so much better. In fact, why don't you keep a daily diary to prove to yourself you're progressing and that the year is rushing past?'

And that's what Talbot decided. Keep a diary. He shuffled from the new high-focus Russian virus ward to the shop that took up most of the hospital foyer and bought a fat, hard-cover notebook with more than 365 pages.

3rd March

Dear Diary. How are you today? How do you do? Have you travelled far?
Shall I address you in the first person? Must you be addressed? Or can I just write thoughts of how I feel?

4th March
The day my neighbour, Joe Braithwaite, convinced he had the virus, pushed away the stool and kicked the air for a few moments, was memorable because Mrs Smith, my other neighbour, lost her cat to a killer with a hatred of felines who waited patiently at night to catch them one by one and knock their brains out with a lump hammer.

5th March
I've decided to have a Word of the Week, which I will drop into any and every conversation, email, message or business that I can. Today's is *fetid*. I like it. Fetid expresses enough disgust to cause pain.

6th March
How do I feel today? Well, aches in most joints, slow walking about, a little harder of hearing and not seeing as well as I did. In other words, I feel my age and then some. What did you expect?

7th March
Routine tasks. Yes, I wash up once a day, usually after my evening meal. I vacuum a bit and dust here and there when I can face it. People seem to think I'll need a cleaner one day. I shop when I must, and still use the supermarket delivery service, though their deliverers are scared shitless of catching the virus from me.

8th March
It's pointless nursing regrets and grudges. I caught the virus. End of story. I know I could die from heart, liver, brain, stomach, mishap, falling, choking, a stroke, by my own hand or at the hand of an assassin. But I've a feeling it'll be the virus on my death certificate, whatever pushes me over the edge.

9th March
One of my grandchildren called me on the computer and we talked for half an hour. I now know more than I did about her school, dancing lessons, best friends, hated enemies and what she wants next birthday. I love them so much. They'll be the hardest to let go, those children of my children.

10th March
The world is a big, yet ever smaller, place and I still take an interest in geo-political issues, conflicts and agendas. Daily, I check the price of wheat, rare metals and power. One thing affects so many others. Now they're saying a hungry Russian soldier, lost from his company during a violent annexation of another slice of Europe, killed and ate a dog. The dog was sick. It gave him a virus which has now come to me.

11th March
My legacy will be the recording of my thoughts for my children, my grandchildren, the children and grandchildren they will have and my beloved country. The one that exists and always has done.

12th March

Word of the Week is *hieroglyph*. It's a character in the ancient Egyptian writing system. Hard to bring up in everyday social intercourse. But I'll give it a go.

13th March
How do I feel? Well, a lot better than I was, thanks. But not as well as I used to when I was 20 or 30 or 40. I'm on enough pills to seem important and worth keeping alive. But I must keep the right pills in the right order and I'm not very good at swallowing. Psychological, they told me once.

14th March
Went to work digging graves, and because I've been off sick for a time, the bodies had stacked up. What the hell have my team been doing? Bugger all, by the look of it. And nobody had updated the charts, so nobody really knew where the bodies were buried. If I had a pound for every time somebody told me that joke.

15th March – The Ides of March
Went shopping for a few groceries, unable to recall why I should beware the Ides of March. I tried listing things I'm likely to forget. One of the side effects of this bloody virus is that memory collapses along with the nervous system, the bowels, the heart, liver and kidneys, the blood, the eyes and ears, the smell and the muscles. Everything else is fine.

16th March
Some of my family are planning to see me this weekend. Not sure if they'll be allowed to talk face to face, within touching distance. Or if they'll have to clown around outside my window while I nod and

grin. Better than nothing, I suppose. But it really is nothing.

17th March
More people are locked down. It's like Covid was back in 2020-22. But this is worse because incubation is longer; recovery time is endless. And those who recover are more likely to catch it again. And again.

18th March
Sometimes at work, I wander down the straight aisles that I've created and wonder if I'd get away with carving my initials on every headstone, just to tell those I leave behind that I achieved something. Straight lines and gleaming headstones.

19th March
Word of the Week is *temerity*. How dare doctors have the temerity to tell me I have the disease that will kill me? I'm far too young to die, despite evidence to the contrary.

20th March
Dropped one of my little pills in the kitchen; it vanished under the cooker. My knees won't let me kneel to retrieve it. So, do I pretend I took it, or do I grovel for an extra allocation?

21st March
Went to work again. Not much of a job but someone must do it. Trouble is if Naismith is right, I'll have to do it for almost a year. If I'm right, I could hand in my notice today. Last man standing can't bury himself. But his body will just rot. I don't want to be that man.

22nd March
Asked to write notes for a talk to be given to future gravediggers. I should have been asked to deliver it. I like speaking. But somebody thought I wouldn't be up to it, so I just do the donkey work for someone else.

23rd March
Had messages or calls from all my grandchildren now. The message has circulated. I've not long left hovering about this world. I was relieved that none of them asked to be remembered in my will.

24th March
Strange that recently we were bowing in homage to renewable energy while cursing old but reliable fossil gas and oil, coal and internal combustion engines. Since the last pandemic with values up-ended, we now accept the old pollution in exchange for living within some sort of functioning economy.

25th March
This is the anniversary of my wedding, aeons ago. My legacy, well, our legacy, is the 4 children we produced and raised, the 9 children they have produced and raised and the 17 children they in turn are raising.

26th March
Word of the Week is *incongruous*. It would be incongruous if I led a ballroom dance in the hospital foyer after one of my regular check-ups while wearing my gravedigger's uniform.

27th March

Another bout of eye treatment. They seem to be causing more suffering than the testicle pain, stomach ache, cramps, heart twinges, toe rot, belly button oozing and arthritis. Mustn't grumble. Always find others worse off.

28th March
Couldn't climb from the cab of the little mechanical digger. Legs refused to respond to brain instructions. And I felt weary. I'd asked to use the digger which is for straightforward plots in even ground. It's normally less hard work than breaking my back using a shovel. Had to be helped down. I hate that. Resented Claude who supported my weight.

29th March
Forms to complete. Leave of absence from work when the time comes. Ridiculous. Once I stop work, that'll means I'm counting down my hours. But obviously forms are necessary. They insist.

30th March
To eke out the remaining burial spaces, somebody suggested upright burials, heads up or down, according to taste. Perhaps leave the embalmed heads sticking out as a reminder of what they looked like?

31st March
Friends, I had a few. Seem to have lost them on the way here. I did bump into one today, coming through the doors of the little all-purpose general store which now houses the last postal service. Had a job to hide my certainty that he'd died a decade ago. When he said we should get together, I pretended to have gone deaf.

1st April – All Fools Day
World affairs always seem to be worst on this day of the year. As if wars, sieges, military obstacles and crime aren't enough, today of all days they put up taxes including car fuel, clothing, shoes, utilities, basic food, health levies and dental charges.

2nd April
Legacy, I often think of it. The more as this final year goes on. Will I be remembered as a superb, dedicated, assiduous local Member of Parliament, one of the best teachers to enter a classroom, the finest performer, debater and writer of my generation? Or the man who helped that old woman over the road after she'd made it clear she didn't want to go?

3rd April
Word of the Week is *inelegant*. Speaks of clumsiness, stumbling about and losing balance. It describes those failing to fight off the dreaded virus, which doesn't include me, but I do walk in an inelegant fashion.

4th April
Headaches, one piled on another. Side effects of the pills? My head pain relief tablets warn, 'you may experience headaches on this medication.'

5th April
I never got a dishwasher after the first four broke down. I was the washing machine. Today I just let it all pile up, like a poor sad, on-his-own man, dying

gradually. When I can't find a clean plate, I know I'm a poor sad, on-my-own man, dying gradually.

6th April
Snows in early April means climate change (the universal scapegoat these days). Or it's often snowed in April, and I've been allowed to forget.

7th April
Family is planning a variety of gatherings over Easter. I said I'd come if I was up to it. Egg hunt for the little grandkids, compulsory attendance for the teens. They don't all know that it'll be my last Easter. Shall I announce it as everyone sits to a bucket of chocolate?

8th April
Russia has announced arrest and interrogation for any of their benighted citizens who call the virus 'Russian.' Amputation for the second offence; execution for the third. I'm told that some of their security guards can't count.

9th April
At a funeral only one mourner wailed out loud. He was the best friend of the bereaved husband who remained quite calm. The crying man had had a long affair with the deceased. The husband patted him on the arm and said, never mind, there, there, don't worry, I'll be marrying again.

10th April
Word of the Week is *lurgy*. It always has 'dreaded' attached to it. The dreaded lurgy. It's already had a week of use, replacing inelegant totally.

11th April
A bit of a set-back. A blight of rashes across my chest, back and down my legs that hadn't been there previously. Some sort of medicinal reaction, they told me. All very well, but when I feel like shit, I don't want to be told everything is progressing to plan. What bloody plan is that?

12th April
A good day for working, weather wise. And I got up feeling refreshed, ate a decent amount of approved breakfast and bounced into work. Managed to keep the vomit out of sight and flushed before anybody saw or smelt it.

13th April
Short of time to dig deep, we made a shallow grave and stood by, shovels out of sight while the ceremony was completed. Once everyone had gone, we pulled the coffin up and transferred it to a nice deep one nearby. You must improvise in my line of work.

14th April
I was born not long after German bombs had rained down on Britain and they tried to wipe us off the face of the earth. I do just wonder if some residual anti-British feeling in a handful of manic Germans isn't behind this virus. Russians are good for blame taking.

15th April
Still wondering about the real cause of this killer virus, I made the mistake of asking a search engine on my computer. It triggered a written warning to search the internet more responsibly and not to seek

someone or something to blame for everything. How far we've sunk.

16th April
Dr Naismith invited me to participate in a clinical experiment, trialling a new drug to build resistance to the virus. I declined. He pushed me on giving something back, helping the next generation and handing down a worthwhile legacy. I said I'd rather be known for my poetry. And I write lousy poems.

17th April
Word of the Week is *capacious*. Lovely word to describe big, luscious space. The space that so many people have in their heads. The lucky ones.

18th April
Made a little device from cardboard boxes, a structure of little labelled boxes in which to sort my tablets. Monday, three yellows; Tuesday one yellow with six red and so on. I heard the pills are all the same, regardless of colour. They're just trying to keep us alert and caring.

19th April
Shopping is a pain. Even worse than other pains, to have to decide what I want, order it, go and collect it, put it away and then cook and eat it. I just long for a different routine. Well, it won't be long now.

20th April
I'd love to have slept with all those girls I fancied but were out of reach, not interested, belonged to others. That's a typical regret, I believe. What man on his deathbed ever wishes he'd had less sex?

21st April
I talk to one or two fellow sufferers when I see them at therapy or check-ups. Of course I do. But it's always the same stilted, pointless conversation. How are you? How the fuck do you think I am? Lovely weather. What fucking difference does that make?

22nd April
The world shrinks with every technological advance. Every war in every corner of the diminishing globe makes it smaller still. At least, that's what I picture when I imagine the rest of the planet beyond my tiny horizon.

23rd April
Sorting out my loft while I still can, I came across the manuscript of my autobiography. It was for my grandchildren and their offspring yet to come who might want to know about me one day. At least one of them might.

24th April
Word of the Week is *time*. Timely, timeless, time running out, time out of mind, time to kill. If only I could. I'd soon end all the trouble. Kill it. In time. On time. Time after time. With time to spare. I read once that Queen Elizabeth I wouldn't allow a clock in any building she was in to chime the hour. She'd defeated time, she'd live forever. Of course, she didn't.

25th April
Didn't feel great today.

29th April
Most of last few days I lay in bed. Slowly rotting.

30th April
Dr Naismith had another go at me about the trial of the new drug. He spouted the death rates and how the hospitals are over-run by sick people as if they shouldn't have to treat the ill at all. One jab a day for a week and then monitoring at home with some device they've invented and a nurse would come to take blood every other day. I was shamed into agreeing.

1st May – May Day
Word of the Week is *maypole.* Dance round it, happy boys and girls celebrating the festival of May Day which they have no clue about. Mayday, the distress signal for ships and planes, travellers and Armageddon worshippers. Maypole, stick it somewhere, as I told a medic who was really hurting me looking for the virus which was unlikely to be in that place.

2nd May
After the last week or so, feeling much better. Or less bad. Some interesting drug therapies being trialled in South Africa and India. Not sure that they'll arrive here in time to save me.

3rd May
I've given up shaving except for special days. Even for my hospital visits, it doesn't matter if I look like a tramp. They treat everybody the same. Good old health service, we love you. Or at least the front-line staff.

4th May

I think today is the birthday of a grandchild, but I've lost my list. Usually, one of my own children sticks a card in front of me in good time, I sign it and authorise whatever the agreed present money is.

5th May
Sat at my old trusty desktop computer. Read local paper online. Better than trying to buy a copy. Two men from my class at school were mentioned. One celebrated his 75th birthday with a party and hired a kiss-o-gram girl. It was newsworthy because she was arrested halfway through for animal cruelty. The funeral of the other was reported on.

6th May
Thought I'd try national papers online today. Well, only the front pages; stories inside are charged for. There're wars, insurgencies, rebellions, conflicts, old hatreds flaring up in 105 of the independent nations of the world. And the death toll from this Russian virus is 14 million and counting. Felt better to have caught up on world news.

7th May
I can't see my legacy being built on the back of this bloody trial. The pills are not making me feel great (mind or body) and the giving of blood in my own home is a nuisance. But I signed up, so I must finish it, even if it kills me.

8th May
Word of the Week is *Caerphilly*. Don't like too much cheese and I went to Wales once as a child. I remember it rained endlessly and there were a lot of steep roads. I recall a man everyone called The Pervert being led away by police officers.

9th May
Headaches are a side effect of both the virus and the trial. So, what do I expect with this thumping head of mine, flashing before the eyes and a desire to shut them and sleep?

10th May
The fridge stinks, so my daughter arrived with a trolley of fluids and wipes and an energetic application of elbow grease. Over half of the contents were binned and the cabinet was left open for a couple of hours to air. And I received a good lecture wrapped up in a tongue bashing on expiry dates.

11th May
Finished listening to my Bob Dylan and Leonard Cohen songs. I soared. Not only because they produced so many great songs, but they spoke of my now lost years, when we were younger, teenagers, then raising our family.

12th May
Heard from work, where I'm expected back soon. It was about my former school mate buried last week. His family are creating a fuss because he'd gone into the wrong plot. What did they expect me to do? Dig him up in the night and put him where they wanted?

13th May
Some hallucinations from the trial drugs; my first. I was made the Emperor of some tin-pot country that was an amalgamation of Russia and the newly independent California. I hated it.

14th May
Completed the trial. Had to rest. Dr Naismith interrogated me and brought in twenty medical students to pore over my records, analyse the test results and ask me fatuous questions like what could I still keep down by way of food and how did I think my grandkids would view me in the future? As dead, I imagine.

15th May
Word of the Week is *towering*. Towering inferno, towering bulk, towering rage or just towering over the pygmies. A useful sort of apparently inoffensive word that can be as kind as anyone needs it to be. Or not.

16th May
Finally, well into what Dr Naismith called my final year, I told my family the true prognosis. Tears, anger, fingers pointed at me, walking out with doors slammed. Not because I have months left, but because I didn't tell them months ago.

17th May
I'm handed a timetable telling me which of my family is doing what and when. Shopping, cooking, cleaning, changing sheets, laundry, ironing, bins out, how much supervised exercising I'm to do, what to watch on television and when to go to the toilet. Well, OK, not that last one. But it will come before long.

18th May
When I started on my grave-digging career years ago, I used to be interested in where people passed away. Driving cars, in their beds, in gardens, in front of their TVs and on their toilets. A hell of a lot leave

this earth while on the crapper. It's certainly speeded up my time in there.

19th May
Somebody I vaguely recall asked my daughter if he could come over to my house, leave his coat dripping in my hall, sit in my armchair, drink my coffee, scoff my biscuits, bore me on his family, work and political views. I had to prolong a fit of coughing which the family took for a no. Lucky escape.

20th May
The price of food, drink, wheat, rice, hops, fruit, oil, gas, asphalt, anything manufactured, transport, storage and care has gone 'through the roof' as they keep banging on about. Someone spouted that the world is too full of people. Well, there'll be one less soon.

21st May
Asked the family over in small groups – too many at once tire me out – to see if they want to keep anything of mine or of their mother/grandmother/great-grandmother. They ruffled through my old photos, including those of my childhood, parents, grandparents and grandparents. But colour, size and videos with no adverts didn't hold their interest.

22nd May
Word of the Week is *turbulence*. It swirls around, rocking and bending, breaking and unsettling. It's the wind, or the mind. I stood on the sea edge in a storm. I was blown over. They've advised me to stay clear in my condition.

23rd May
Can't cut the fingernails on my right hand anymore. Now I must use a nail file, which has made my blood run cold and goosebumps stand up on my arms and neck since I was a child. It's the file, cold blood and goosebumps or long, broken nails.

24th May
They tell me I've run out of ginger preservative to spread on my toast, despite having at least ten in stock. They say it's too sugary, too unhealthy. What they mean is it's too enjoyable. Or else they like it for themselves.

25th May
Sometimes I long to dance like an angel. Dance free of mobility limitations, stumbling, dizzy non-balance and the stupidity of actually dancing now. But then, I never really danced when I was physically able to. So, what am I grumbling about?

27th May
Two pages were stuck together and I missed one out. Suppose it doesn't matter. Dr Naismith can be as critical as he likes when he reads them.

28th May
Returned to old photos, sorted by facial resemblances. One of my daughters looks like my maternal grandmother; one grandson is a spit for my wife's father at the same age. I can't bear to throw them out, but they don't sell shrouds with pockets.

29th May

Word of the Week is *Nebuchadnezzar* ruler of the Babylonian Empire from 605BC to his death in 562BC. Why do I remember that? He was a hugely successful commander with a few misses which caused uprisings. These he crushed ruthlessly. I like that. Crushing ruthlessly. He's linked to Daniel in the Lion's Den. I like that, too.

30th May
Fell. Not badly. I think it's the medication and lack of proper exercise.

31st May
Saw the GP. Sprained my ankle and left wrist. Good job I'm right-handed.

1st June
Lying on the sofa, watching old movies. Feeling sorry. For myself.

2nd June
Trying to generate enthusiasm for life. Got up. Hobbled around.

3rd June
The walking stick arrived. Useful for support. And hitting people.

4th June
Ditched my music and film cassettes years ago. One of my kids nicked all my 33rpm records when they became cool again. I spent thousands on CDs, creating my own favourites from the 1960s and 70s with a few odds from later years. Nobody will want them, and, really, why should they?

5th June
Word of the Week is *misery,* that abject kind that rots the soul from within. Some days I experience it; other days I watch others suffering. Not much I can do about it, except use it once an hour every hour.

6th June
This is the feast day of St Norbert of Xanten on the Rhineland who started his life in pleasure and self-centred frivolity but became a powerful preacher and guide. I must stop reading unusual news stories.

7th June
Apparently, they raised a glass to me at the pub, coupled with absent friends. I only went once to that meeting of losers and escapees and now I'm among their absent friends? Bizarre.

8th June
Thinking I should get out more, some of the family are planning a drive to a mystery venue, some food and a drive back. If I'm up to it.

9th June
An unexpected cloud burst followed by endless drizzle rather spoilt the outing. The surprise was a ride on a little motor launch up the Broads, peering at endless grey skies. Half an hour out; half an hour back. It's the thought that counts, I imagine.

10th June
When rain finally gave way to sun, I enjoyed being helped to my garden chair in a sunny corner watching kids playing, adults laughing and joking. Fun begins at home. Now we know.

11th June
Since my wife passed away, I've slipped into a typical old man. Clothes last decades; so long that they return to fashion and slip out again. I have trousers from the 1990s with another decade of life in them. I almost wish I did, too.

12th June
Word of the Week is *Scotch*. I don't like the alcohol, prefer not to be among too many Scotch people but do like Scotch pancakes and Gaelic music. I also like to scotch rumours that I'm allergic to high hills, mists, rain and midges. I went to Scotland several times in my youth. I remember seeing a man who said he was the Archbishop of Edinburgh being led away.

13th June
It seems to be my birthday, judging by the family fuss. All cards wish me happy returns. I suppose they can't find any that say, sorry old pal, this looks like your final celebration. Of course, the little kiddies could have made some to say that.

14th June
Once upon a time I'd have rejoiced in books off my wish list (which I had selected), some milk chocolates, perhaps something to wear like a shirt ... in fact, always a shirt. Now it's all been made pointless by life itself.

15th June
Itches on my back. Difficult to scratch, but I scrape against corners and doorposts. The chorus of disapproval is unhelpful, especially when they talk

about a shirt full of skin flakes waiting to drop onto the floor.

16th June
I'll mention back rashes and itches when I next see the good Doctor, but he'll dismiss them as nothing to worry about and suggest I take more assisted baths. Blah, blah.

17th June
Had to listen to a woman who rang my doorbell like there was a fire in the house. Turned out she wanted to talk to my wife. My late wife. I pointed her in the direction of the civic graveyard. She can talk to the headstone that I installed myself.

18th June
Turning next to the paintings, photos and pictures on my walls. The kids have agreed who gets what, but I suspect it's to keep me happy. One volunteered to home my own works of art, those I haven't yet given away. It's a nice thought, but none will survive into the future.

19th June
Word of the Week is *pandemic*. It became common currency during Covid 19 and even more so during Russian Virus. History had pandemics for flu, malaria, zika, ebola and even bubonic plague. Stronger than an epidemic, it's become all too easy to include it in conversations along with drought, tsunamis, floods, landslides, opioids, bacteria-resistant and climate change.

20th June

I often sit lost in past memories. But when asked what I had for dinner yesterday, I'm stuck. They say that's natural in old age. Or advanced virus.

21st June
My toothbrush looks like somebody cleaned a toilet with it. I've asked for a new one several times. Perhaps I'll start spreading toothpaste on an actual toilet brush?

22nd June
The Grim Reaper rang last night to see how I'm doing. He told me that almost every single person he approaches begs for more time. An hour, a day, a week. Ten years.

23rd June
Walking round the block for exercise, I'd often talk to someone of my own age called Melvyn. We put the world to rights – he from a political viewpoint, me from a let's-machine-gun-them-all perspective. He's dead now.

24th June
The street is closed to vehicles to allow several do-good neighbours hold a market in aid of some worthy cause. They're selling cakes, charity shop material, cakes, garden produce and cakes. I won't be going. I donated a fiver. I'll be watching for the ambulances that can't squeeze through.

25th June
Found a box of old school reports, leaflets, pamphlets, press-cuttings and the detritus of my lifetime. Faces with names I recall in patchy bursts. Some are long dead. I'm not even going to ask the

kids who wants any of that stuff. Hell, some belongs to my sister. How did I get landed storing that?

26th June
Word of the Week is *hybrid*, a sort of in-between, neither one thing nor the other. I'm a functioning human being up to a point. Drugs and painkillers keep me going. Am I half-man and half robot?

27th June
Tried without painkillers. Just didn't swallow them. I feel so much better. Like a man stretched on the rack, finger and toenails torn off, his intestines making an appearance on this belly where they'd cut me open.

28th June
Family decided to open every window, blitz vacuum, polish furniture to within an inch of its life and make things as uncomfortable as possible. I kept a low profile in case they turned their attentions to my body.

29th June
Have decided I will definitely *not* ask the Grim Reaper for a little extra time to do something off my agenda. Definitely not.

30th June
Spilt a glass of flat cola on the lounge carpet. I was caught on my knees trying to mop it up and hide the stain. I got away with a(nother) lecture.

1st July
Australia has reported more shark attacks on humans than for twenty years. Media publishes

details of the victims but not if they sat Sanity Tests before going swimming.

2ⁿᵈ July

Photos from my wedding. Our wedding. Us, grinning madly, clutching each other. Older family long gone. Little pictures, at least they were in colour. Most are blurred. You never knew what you'd taken till the developed films came back. A metaphor for life.

3ʳᵈ July

Word of the Week is *serendipity*, meaning how great it was to hook up with Dr Naismith just at the time I caught the virus. But then, if I hadn't caught it in the first place, that would have been even more serendipitous.

4ᵗʰ July

My problem before the iron tablets fixed it, was that my bowels opened at least four times a day and always have done. Often with little notice, I had to hobble-run to the toilet. Nowadays I can't move at speed, but my bowels seem to have missed the memo. Oh but the iron tablets have solved that, too.

5ᵗʰ July

If I leave my breakfast and lunchtime stuff till after my evening meal before washing up, one of the family will sigh and wash up whatever's there waiting. If I wash after every single meal, I get frowns and bad looks from the grandson who's besotted with saving the planet.

6ᵗʰ July

Watched one of our newer, younger neighbours across the street cleaning the pigeon shit off his front door and hall window. As he stepped back to admire his handiwork, a pigeon dive-bombed, splattering his head with a fresh coating of white filth.

7th July
Inspecting my overgrown hedge and wonky garden gate, a man passed me being walked by a huge dog looking to drop enough poo to fill a wheelbarrow. He asked, 'how are you?' When I answered, 'well, how long have you got?' he pretended the dog was pulling him away.

8th July
The world is such a small place that they read news and forecast weather in accents different from the accent-less norm. We're not fooled.

9th July
Sometimes I amaze myself how well organised I was. I'm looking at a box of photos, programs, tickets and a couple of maps of our holidays. Car journeys, ferry, ship, plane and a few train trips. When they talk about their upbringing now, one child will talk about holidays and day outings, opening the memory floodgates for the rest to join in.

10th July
Word of the Week is *hypothetical,* meaning suggested or imagined but not really true. My hypothetical future is all of that. I just feel that sometimes my past is hypothetical, too. Did I do all that? See all those things?

11th July

Did too much pottering about. Feel like shit waiting for the shovel.

12th July
Thought I should try to get in for some work. They all seem to know about my situation but are urging against me going in on the grounds of infecting them.

13th July
They raised the problem of me with the boss and my extended medical leave kicks in from today, despite my desire to be useful. This leave is likely to be permanent, but at least my fellow gravediggers won't catch it from me.

14th July
Asked if someone could drive me to the office so I can make faces at them through the window and pretend I'm about to step out and embrace them. But I was talked out of it, as I am from most things I want to do.

15th July
I heard that two of my colleagues have gone down with the virus. Oh dear. As long as some are left to bury them, no matter.

16th July
A man my grandparents knew was sacked from the factory where he'd worked, man and boy, for 55 years. He came home, handed his wife his last pay packet, went to bed and turned his face to the wall. Never rose again. He'd literally lost the will to live.

17th July

Word of the Week is *amalgamation*. A distinct entity caused by merging two or more other things together. Is a baby an amalgamation of mother's egg and father's sperm? And what the hell is combined to make that metal dentists use to fill my teeth cavities, amalgam?

18th July
I've run out of that special high-fluoride toothpaste only available from a dentist on prescription. I'll use salt till I get more and try to avoid puking.

19th July
I've run out of that black stuff in a little tin for cleaning my shoes. I'll just have to wait for new supplies. It's sometimes like the third world here.

20th July
I've run out of that stuff they use on babies' bums when they get nappy rash. I need it around my privates to stop the fungus expanding.

21st July
Watched a film last night, cuddling on the settee with my lovely wife. We chatted as it progressed. Just before the end I realised she hadn't said anything for a time. She wasn't there. Of course, she's been dead for four years now.

22nd July
I've run out of films to watch on my settee. Watched all I want to see. Soon I'll watch foreign films and get dizzy reading the English subtitles.

23rd July
I think it was Mark Twain who said, 'the two most important days of your life are the day you were born and the day you find out why.' Not sure I've discovered why yet, despite my family as my legacy. And not long left.

24th July
Word of the Week is *dry rot*. Perhaps that's two words. It spreads over and through everything, the entire house. This virus is like that. And even early identification won't necessarily save a victim.

25th July
A man from our church came round to drink my coffee and tell me I should return to church as people who loved me were praying for me. I told him I fell out of joy at the place when it emerged the senior people loathed each other and had been covering it up for a decade while telling us how to live. He pretended not to know what I was talking about.

26th July
Still seething about the hypocrite who called yesterday. Cancelled donations.

27th July
Still feeling put out about the business at the church.

28th July
Trying to focus on other things. Can't shake image of people praying for me.

29th July

Actually prayed today. With gratitude to the praying people and to God for the life I've had. He giveth; He taketh away.

30th July
Reading a book on successfully pitching my film idea. The 'MacGuffin' is throwing an unimportant person, object or event into the mix because it will eventually prove useful in plot or character motivation. My working title is, *The MacGuffin.*'

31st July
Word of the Week is *inscrutable*, unfathomable. It's what doctors work at being when they examine you but don't say anything. You hold your breath, you wait. You won't have to wait long; breath is strictly rationed.

1st August
They tell me to get more exercise, yet express concern about my heart rate.
They tell me to eat less, yet say I should not fall below a certain level.

2nd August
Thinking of giving up undressing, washing and going to bed. Such a palaver. I could stay on the settee in front of the telly and see if it makes any difference.

3rd August
Thinking of giving up preparing any food, other than putting something into the microwave. See if it makes any difference.

4th August

Thinking of giving up breathing of my own volition before it happens naturally. See if it makes any difference.

5th August
Thinking of one last trip somewhere and not coming back. Save the family all their trouble. See if it makes any difference.

6th August
I was never tall. Always had to try to keep a straight back and seeing past some tall bugger in front was sheer hell. But with my present standing posture, it's probably for the best I'm not seeing many people.

7th August
Word of the Week is *cast*. Cast down, cast iron, cast of this pantomime we are playing and cast in the mould of a patient who now faces increase in the dosage of one medication as it's not apparently as effective as 'we'd expect it to be.' They mean it's not killed me off yet.

8th August
When I used to buy a daily paper, I followed my modest investments in stock market reports. Then I switched online. After selling all my shares, I still look occasionally. It's like keeping up with a friend who's passed on.

9th August
In my earlier years, I suffered migraines once every three months unless I was particularly stressed. Now they come once or twice a week and

from the virus, not stress. The virus is a stress driver, as everybody knows.

10th August
A former NHS worker has been sent down for selling copies of X rays of damaged lungs and impaired brains to people defrauding insurance companies and their employers.

11th August
It turns out that I knew one of the buyers of fake medical evidence who is now facing trial and put out an appeal for funds to pay his defence lawyers.

12th August
And it turns out even more that people all around the world have been trading in fake health records. It's a thriving business, almost as lucrative as the sale of actual organs.

13th August
I wonder if I should leave my body to medical science.

14th August
Word of the Week is *tourists*. Holiday-makers, tourists, visitors and grockles. All those wealthy enough to afford a break away and healthy enough to make something of the change of scene, change of air, attractions and activities. I can't get travel insurance even I felt like going anywhere.

15th August
Preparing for an appearance at a health symposium. Ordinarily this would be exciting stuff.

But in ten minutes, how can I describe this countdown?

16th August
Decided to handwrite my speech. Two grandkids volunteered to type it out and print it off. But they couldn't read my writing; my jokes weren't funny.

17th August
Forced to do it off the cuff. But my scribbled notes on my shirt sleeves were too far away to see and too vague to make any sense.

18th August
Spent most of the day in the garden, hoping a change of scene would help me. I was there nine hours before they found me and picked me up.

19th August
When given the opportunity to do future talks online at home, I readily agreed.

20th August
Once I longed to appear on the stage, my name in lights. Now my claim to fame is addressing a symposium on *Living With Russian Virus*. Next year's follow-up is called *Dying with Russian Virus*.

21st August
Word of the Week is *philosophical,* calm and stoical in the face of difficulties. Like being able to walk less, to pee all over the place and lose my grip. Yes, philosophical as I can be, once I've finished raging against the world. Where did I put that axe?

22nd August

Several praising messages and thanks for my talk. The stroke people and the palsy charities asked to use it with a title for their particular afflictions.

23rd August
Too hot to sit in the garden. The lawn is now a brown-yellow patch of dirt, a set for an apocalypse movie. I'm the Wilting Horror Indoors.

24th August
Too hot to stay in the house. The rooms are suntraps and ovens, indoor sets for that apocalypse movie. I'm the Shadow Ghost in the Bathroom.

25th August
Day of St Genesius, patron saint of clowns, performers, comedians, dancers, lawyers and barristers. If I was a Catholic or paid attention to saints or their days, I'd dance. Why are lawyers included with clowns and dancers?

26th August
Sweating hot, no air, no clear water to drink.

27th August
Sweating hot, no air, no clear water to drink.

28th August
Word of the Week is *proportionate*. That's what some moron in the hospital waiting area told me I should be. Respond in a proportionate manner. Just to make everyone feel better and others have it worse? I know that. But what would be proportionate? Breathe on you so we both go together?

29th August
I used to go watch City play football when my lads were young. We loved it, especially if they won. One day a bloke kept pushing past us to go and buy burgers. Then to buy beer cans. Then sweets and cakes. He took offence when I called him 'pondlife.' Don't know why. He was.

30th August
They've stopped syringing people's ears, so they're filling up with wax and waiting for it to harden enough to be picked out. More satisfying than picking a nose. And they wonder why the world is growing progressively deaf.

31st August
Some snotty kid kept asking me questions while I sat in my garden. I said nothing. His dad came and told him to leave me alone and did I mind him asking questions. 'Oh, no,' I said, 'won't learn if he don't ask.'

1st September
Chilly, too windy, too much rain to drink.

2nd September
Chilly, too windy, too much rain to drink.

3rd September
Terrible nightmare. I was asleep, dreaming I was having a nightmare but there were others laughing at me. Some people's sense of humour!

4th September

Word of the Week is *small*. Small fry, small-minded, small beer, small circles and small print? Small talk. I'll small talk about the weather and the price of bread so not to upset anybody when I talk about having my legs off to ease the pain, shall I?

5th September
One of the little ones was upset because she thought I was having a leg off. One of the teenagers asked if he could keep the leg in a glass case.

6th September
The window cleaner comes every 8 weeks. But he doesn't do inside, so I've done my best with spray and a duster for years. Now my daughter does it on the grounds that I am too slapdash and too short sighted to see the smears.

7th September
Despite not being allowed to work, I received a booklet on new grave-digging protocols, presumably for my entertainment. The trade is no longer to be called 'grave-digging'; now it's 'burial ground custodian', 'cemetery operatives' or 'location transferers of the deceased.'

8th September
My family have been using our black wheelie bin for their surplus rubbish, ignoring my suggestion of dumping their waste in the neighbour's bin.

9th September
Funnily enough, I saw the neighbour outside stuffing a black bag in his bin. Looked like a cat, dog or human head inside. I didn't acknowledge his

friendly wave. I hope they ignore my warning to steer clear of his black bin.

10th September
The refuse operative found the neighbour's bin heavy to push. Those people who empty our rubbish are heroes and deserve to be praised. Unlike gravediggers who bury the dead with rarely a word of thanks.

11th September
Word of the Week is *cemetery*. I work in several. There's a travelling team of us. I'm lead digger on a thousand a year more for supervising others. Sometimes I feel spooked if I'm working in a quiet area alone. Other times, I feel at peace and relaxed. Soon I'll literally be at home.

12th September
Lazy autumn heat, summer clinging on. Gives me headaches and shortens my breath, so I'm not a fan. But hey, what's not to like about clinging on to life, even in this condition?

13th September
I must cut my toenails once a week or they grow into the curled toes. Hell of a job. I sit in a chair and rest my foot on a stool. Hack away while trying to bend the toes straight and avoid drawing blood by breaking skin. Hard to get right.

14th September
It's a fancy dress party. Disguises and masks, wigs and tat. Oh no, it's my mind reliving some of my more successful off the wall commentaries.

15th September
When I could still cope with it, the whole of my family would gather, some to sleep, all to eat and the kids to play wild games over every inch of house and garden. Of course, I loved it as I loved them. But I did find it wore out the old body. And sometimes the old patience.

16th September
On my 100-yard exercise shuffle to the end of the road, I talked to an old woman who has lived alone for four decades. She was in a state because she'd been asked to plan ahead to spend Christmas with her daughter who lives in a village just 4 miles away. Such is a shrinking world.

17th September
Thoughts strayed to all those novels and short stories I wrote and self-published. In the post digital age they'll be inaccessible. So perhaps it's an unintended kindness to me that they should be largely forgotten already.

18th September
Word of the Week is *academic*. New school year started, kids in uniforms a size too big are into their routines. I never enjoyed school. I told a kid once I yearned to be an undertaker; he laughed out loud. He was a clever, academic bugger. Well, he's not laughing now. I dug his grave last year.

19th September
One of the kids has secured me some exercise equipment on loan. They've fitted out my spare room as a gym, of sorts. I'm expected to jump for joy about weight lifting, some frame with a pull thing and a wrist

gadget to log and reprimand me when I don't walk, jump, squat, sit or stand.

20th September
One day was more than enough for this nonsense, but no, I had to go back in the room for supervised torture. Should be a law against it. Not for it.

21st September
Now they've installed a screen showing some woman who gets off on barking orders, faint praise and humiliating observations. I say it's as if she can see what I'm doing. I'm told she can.

22nd September
I think I've done my back a nasty injury. And my wrists, my upper legs, my shoulders and my knees. They say pain is gain to be worked through.

23rd September
As luck would have it, I physically chucked up, rolled about with a stomach pain and was allowed to lie in my bed.

24th September
There's talk of making a program about me adjusting to exercise to encourage other poor old buggers with the virus. No chance of that.

25th September
Word of the Week is *autumnal*, after a stretch of decent weather it's windy, leaves off trees, warm coats and staying indoors time. I've become indifferent to seasons as days shorten, along with my prospects.

26th September
Some hot news, juicy gossip would be nice.

27th September
Juicy news, hot gossip. Old man Smedley, two streets away, (I once had to talk to him in the interval of a play), has been found with his hands cuffed behind his back and a plastic bag tied over his head. He's dead.

28th September
Police, TV news and journalists started door to door. I've nothing to say.

29th September
Turns out they've arrested his daughter for dispatching old Smedley.

30th September
Everyone calming down. The Smedley case is not top of the list just now.

1st October
I'm offered ready money to be the subject of an encouragement film of me using the hellish equipment. But I've already posted it online, almost free to a good home.

2nd October
Word of the Week is *wasted.* A drunk is wasted; but a drunk sobers up. Wasted nerves never improve. This virus is like a nerve wasting condition. Wasting resources, wasting my energies, hopes and dreams.

3rd October

Medics are surprised I haven't surrendered my driving licence. I've no business driving, apparently. If I don't hand it in, they'll snitch on me and I'll lose it anyway.

4th October

Emptied my junk from the car, the historically styled glove compartment and the door pockets. Wondered whether to have it cleaned. But what's the point? I won't be enjoying a clean car.

5th October

In an Oscar Wilde play there was an invented character, Mr Bunbury, who allegedly enjoyed such poor health that his friend was frequently called to see him. It was the perfect cover. My Bunbury has died now my car is going.

6th October

I discover that two of my grandchildren had hoped to be given my old car. When they found out it was manual not automatic, one changed his mind. When it was revealed to run on petrol, not electricity, the other stepped away. I'm hoping a museum will buy it.

7th October

Electric charged cars were hailed as a great environmental benefit. The praise ignored the fact that it's not technically possible in half the world, electricity must be generated by something costly and non-green and it's too easy to run out of energy and grind to a stop in a dangerous spot.

8th October

Somewhere I have a small box with photos of cars I've owned, including my first mini when I was 18. One grandchild suggested I donate them to the same museum that is supposedly buying my car.

9th October
Word of the Week is *perpendicular*. This church is perpendicular, built by the Vikings before the railways came. That's from an old local joke, a monologue I used to perform at charitable events. Funny what fills the mind. I read somewhere the same phenomenon is noted in people awaiting execution.

10th October
Curiosity abounds. Turns out that Smedley's daughter couldn't take any more. He had dementia, Parkinsons and depressive paranoia. She lost it when her father demanded better food. I want to know where she got the cuffs.

11th October
I follow the news avidly. Speculation now mixed with what facts are known is a heady mix. My son remembers I once talked to Smedley. What, am I now a suspect? Evidently, she owned the cuffs because she'd been a police officer.

12th October
For just a moment, I seriously wonder if paying someone to cuff me and put a bag over my head would be worth it. My family could cash in, dine out on their connection to the man suffering slow Virus.

13th October
That bloke from the church must have read my mind from a distance. He's round again accepting

more coffee with biscuits this time and hopes I'm not thinking of doing anything stupid. Other than letting him in, no.

14th October
A new stranger in a sharp suit comes to sell me a funeral plan. I tell the family he's here about the cuffs and plastic bag I'd ordered. They're not amused.

15th October
They've banned me from answering the door-bell, as I'm 'a danger to myself and others.' I don't follow it, but orders is orders, mein Fuehrer.

16th October
Word of the Week is *hurdy-gurdy*, a lovely old mechanical instrument that I owned for years and passed to my son who gave it to his son. I hear it's for sale in an online charity auction. Well, charity begins at home, my loves, it really does.

17th October
Little Anglican church near, with congregation of 14, average age 79, asked if I'd come out of retirement and supervise their young sexton (62) digging a grave for their latest departure. I said yes, subject to feeling up to it.

18th October
Family none too pleased I'd agreed, but I stuck to my guns and said the change would do me good.

19th October
Having checked what tools they have, I realise they'll need more than one man with a shovel. I ring round, call in a few favours. Waiting for answers.

22nd October
Three pages stuck together after a heavy bout of sneezing.

23rd October
Word of the Week is *infrendiate,* to gnash the teeth. Before my dental plates went in, I used to infrendiate from time to time. As old age advances, they remove teeth you used to express anger, leaving you more angry, but silent.

24th October
It dawns a decent day, late autumn delight. Early to churchyard where the sexton and a couple of blokes from the pub are digging a war trench. None of my mates replied. I direct them till it looks good, if too deep.

25th October
Another glorious day emerges from the haze. Perfect for the funeral which lasts 11 minutes. I stop the sexton filling in while mourners are still standing around looking lost. Job finally done and I sit on a bench, drawing my breath, watching the sheep grazing the older end, fenced in by wire.

26th October
Return to churchyard to check everything OK. Youthful disturbances have been known. Couple with a toddler enter, she saying the child wants to look at the sheep. He replies, 'well, in 20 years' time, when her therapist asks why she remembers sheep in a graveyard...'

27th October

My pro-bono work really took it out of me. It's last forecast day of good weather. I sit on old chair outside the front of the house, finish my coffee and watch the world and its dogs walk by. When I wake, I see someone has dropped loose change into my cup, thinking I was begging.

28th October
I got two separate messages from my former mates to say that they'd be happy to help bury that poor old women, could I tell them the date?

29th October
Is it too late to write an actual memoir of my gravedigging days? Probably.

30th October
Word of the Week is *funestation*. The old boy who taught me grave digging used it freely. It's pollution from touching a dead body. It's where 'funeral' comes from. It's useful; nobody understands it.

31st October
Something got in my left eye; it's all swollen and sore. Something got up my nose; I'm sneezing it out. Something got in my mind; I'm thinking.

1st November
Didn't need a doctor, so went to the pharmacist about my eye. He said I should see the doctor, it was serious.

2nd November
Secured a precious doctor appointment as I'm on the short virus list. She said it's nothing. I should have gone to the pharmacist.

3rd November
Traipsed back to the pharmacist on daughter's arm to report doctor's view. He said, 'we have a zero aggression policy in this pharmacy,' so I thumped him.

4th November
Waited for police to arrive in squad cars and arrest me for assaulting the pharmacist. My daughter asked if I wanted to tell the pharmacist what the doctor had said.

5th November
Family discussing digital legacies. What happens to your digital lives when you pop your clogs? I never used social media, so when I'm gone, I'm gone. Checked my Amazon Wish List. Deleted the *Long Time Dying* box set of crime dramas nobody ever bought me.

6th November
Word of the Week is *peenge*, a complaint in a whining voice. I always condemned it in others, a mix of whinge and peevish. Never complain, never explain – a useful adage.

7th November
I thought it was New Year, the end of the war or I was dreaming. Fireworks all around. Pointless waste of money. And on the wrong day. Or is that me?

8th November
They told to be more sociable, not shut myself in my study. But my daughter's self-help group was in the lounge, the partners and friends of the teenagers

were upstairs, on the stairs, somebody was vomiting in the bathroom, the kitchen heaved with my son's biker friends taking one to bits and the drug dealers in the back garden didn't see me, let alone talk with me.

9th November
Hogged the settee in the lounge, tuned to long documentary about Music and Culture 1967-70 and tried not to hear the kids asking their parents how much longer, why was I there and not in my study?

10th November
This evening took an old duvet, a pillow and supply of fizzy drinks, cakes, crisps and porno videos I found in my eldest son's room out to the garage. Then they complained they couldn't do their own things in there.

11th November
That bloody man from the church returned. I said we were out of coffee, but he took tea. Said I should prepare myself, apologise for bad choices, harsh words and sinful thoughts. Before it's too late. I suspect it's already too late.

12th November
Word of the Week is *paltry*. That is what my life has become. When I think back to what I could do, dream and create. Now, I struggle walking a few steps unaided. It's a paltry life. But it's life. That's what they keep telling me.

13th November

Dr Naismith's assistant reckoned routines are like rituals; I should follow them to give my life structure and meaning. Apparently, this is helpful to the dying.

14th November
Having considered it, I might be healthier if I broke my routines. I got up mid evening, ate breakfast at midnight whereupon they gave me a painkiller and told me to grow up, stop being silly.

15th November
One of my regrets is not running naked through the college grounds when I was a student. Another is sleeping naked with that woman at my first job.

16th November
Found myself thinking about my parents. How they met. How hard it was with no money in those early days. It made me want to cry. I couldn't.

17th November
By the time I finished being a student I'd visited almost every European country. The joys of thumbing lifts, scrounging and chilling.

18th November
Is it worth trying again to get busy kids interested in the life that their grandfather led, his achievements, his failings and his dreams? Doubtful.

19th November
Word of the Week is *heroic*. Everybody is a hero nowadays, especially those over-paid jerks who play sports. Heroic defence in a game is not the same as heroic defence against an invading army. And I

should know. My defence against this virus is magnificently heroic.

20th November
Twice got heroic into conversation. None sees my life as heroic, though.

21st November
I usually wait for somebody to tell me my trousers need changing before I do it. I changed of my own volition, but nobody noticed to pass any comment.

22nd November
Life has become so mundane, that an empty goldfish bowl looks interesting.

23rd November
Family planning their holidays next year, all over the world. I listen and smile agreement at their choices. I won't be joining them, anyhow.

24th November
My son is taking his wife to Venice, romantic weekend. My wife and I enjoyed several visits, off cruises. Only way to sit is to buy exorbitant food and drink. We found a bench near a gondola starting point to rest a moment. One of them shouted at us to fuck off, it was for them only. As I walked away, my wife's arm in one hand, my walking stick in other, he shouted it was OK. Too late, mate, I shouted back.

25th November
Sudden panic that I haven't left all my financial affairs in order to leave legacy to family not the taxman. My son reminds me I did that last year.

26th November
Word of the Week is *havoc*. The chaos, the disorder, the anarchy of the house after young children have played; the bedlam in my mind when separating and making sense of conflicting voices offering advice, directing this or declining that.

27th November
One of my irregular check-ups with Dr Naismith. He had a student with him; did I mind? Of course not. How could I mind, wired up to three machines?

28th November
I must sit for longer and more frequently between tasks. Even making coffee or cleaning my teeth are surprisingly challenging events.

29th November
Grandkids had a good laugh on finding in the garage roof an old student painting of mine, a backside framed in a toilet seat. It had curled at the edges.

30th November
Grandkids spent hours searching nooks and crannies in the house for other examples of my student artwork. I hid my 'Roadkill' sculpture.

1st December
Idiots from a local campaign to make us rejoin the European Union asked people with spare bedrooms to accommodate some French people on a 'goodwill' visit. I told them the European Union was toxic and no way would I accommodate a Frenchman. I'd rather host a Scotchman!

2nd December
Some thought I should give the toilet picture to the EU campaigners. I will.

3rd December
Word of the Week is *elephantine*. The elephant in the room is me gradually sliding into an alternative reality, the politically correct way to refer to dying.

4th December
Just couldn't swallow my tablets. My throat closed. Had to grind some up, split others. It was a mess. Had to do it quickly, before I was caught.

5th December
No trouble swallowing a packet of chocolate biscuits. Funny, that.

6th December
Postal workers, train drivers, delivery drivers, cleaners, bin-emptiers. grave-diggers and psychiatrists are going on strike. Shoot the lot, I say.

7th December
Courtesy visit from the local Public Health and Safety Committee in full black combat gear to warn me against joking about shooting people.

8th December
Idiots from a local campaign to make English people support Scottish Independence asked people with spare bedrooms to accommodate some Scotch people on a 'goodwill' visit. I told them Independence was toxic and no way would I accommodate a Scotchman. I'd rather host a Frenchman!

9th December
Of my own will, decided to present the 'Roadkill' sculpture to the Scotch.

10th December
Word of the Week is *apex*. I like it for its reaching-a-summit feel. It inspires me. Makes me wish I'd actually reached at least one apex while I could.

11th December
Too weary to shout at the television tonight. I did my best.

12th December
The television shouted back. I think.

13th December
Family clubbed together to buy me a mega TV screen that fills the lounge wall and ceiling. Well, they'll enjoy it.

14th December
Most houses in the street are decorated outside with lights and sleighs, Santas, bells, angels, all without a care to the power bill. Mine isn't.

15th December
When I go out to shout at a boy delivering junk, I see that my house is also covered in seasonal rubbish. They hadn't told me.

16th December
Wasted a good twenty minutes of life I'll never get back signing Christmas cards that I should have done a month ago. They hadn't told me.

17th December
Word of the Week is *marley*, after Jacob Marley in *A Christmas Carol*. I coined it. To 'marley' is to behave like Ebenezer Scrooge, without the redemption.

18th December
I've received notes from the youngest of the grandchildren telling me what they want. Do I look like Father Christmas? They'll get what I can afford.

19th December
Against my better judgement, I fork out for all the kids to go to either the pantomime in our theatre or the circus in Yarmouth. Their parents opt for the circus, as if they haven't seen enough clowning here.

20th December
Dipped my tongue tip in a glass of sherry. Everybody kept saying it would make my toes curl. Not funny. Heaved it up at once.

21st December
Kept hallucinating it was five days before my last Christmas. When I woke up I found it was five days before my last Christmas. Goody, goody.

22nd December
Kids singing at the door, making a few quid. I listened to half an out of tune carol before someone opened the door and paid them off. All I wanted was a full carol in tune.

23rd December
If I hear people wishing me 'Merry Christmas' again, I'll scream. What's merry about it?

24th December
Word of the Week is *season*. In some places you can't wish anyone a happy Christmas in case it offends. Happy Festival. Happy Season. Not the same. And humbug to Christmas.

25th December
First day of Christmas. Undoubtedly this is my last. Dinner mid-afternoon with my family. I couldn't hear half of what was said above the noise, but it was good of them to accommodate me in the corner of their massive settee, facing away from the TV screen.

26th December
Second day of Christmas. I asked to be spared yet more celebrating. And got my wish. Listened to loads of my old music – teenage joys, pop classics and country, folk, bubble gum and Tamla Motown.

27th December
Felt under the weather. Spared another trip out to a meal with family and being brought back mid evening when the ice is forming on cars and roads. I don't wish to sound ungrateful, though.

28th December
Christmas lumbers on, people still off work, businesses closed when you want to contact them. Perhaps not the biggest complaint in the world when people around are starving, flooded out, dying of drought and this Russian disease.

29th December

Day mainly in bed. They brought me a bowl of soup made from turkey stock and leftover meat. I ate some. Enjoyed the fruit salad and cream.

30th December
My old grandfather used to tell us if we walked down the street today we'd see a man with as many noses as there are days in the year. We protested a man couldn't have 365 noses. Of course, he meant New Year's Eve, one day left so one nose. I just heard someone say New Years' Eve is actually tomorrow.

31st December
Word of the Week: *New Year's Eve*. Euphoria and hysteria that the old year is dying. The new one comes in and makes everything alright, solves all problems, reconciles all difficulties and heals all hurt. Except of course, it doesn't.

1st January
New Year's Day. I'd set this aside to watch some of my old favourite films on disks. All parts of *The Godfather* still thrill me. Then I had to re-read the original novel. Fell asleep.

2nd January
Businesses going back, shops reopening after the long break. Then I discover that some are still not because they 'treat your safety seriously.' Not sure how that works. If you're out of food and drink, but 'safe', so what?

3rd January
One of my little kids showed me the noise effects box Father Christmas brought her. She pressed

buttons to produce cackles, screams, belching, pukes, snotty sneezes, rounds of machine gun fire, sirens, falling body sounds, gallows trapdoor, being force-fed or singing off key while choking. I'd have liked one of them to take to work, back in the day.

4th January
Another child showed me what he called a selfie stick for taking silly photos at greater than arm's length. He got a new, all singing and dancing one. He promised me a phone to go on the end of it for my birthday. He doesn't understand.

5th January
The cleaner asked if I minded the Christmas decorations coming down one day early. We always used to take that rubbish down on Boxing Day. When I said I couldn't care less about decorations, she took it personally and reported me to my eldest for re-education and empathy training.

6th January
Half the day on the commode, half with a bucket between my knees and the other half fending off food.

7th January
Word of the Week is *testament*. Last will and testament. I made sure mine is up to date, properly signed and witnessed. Taking care of my family. I could name at least four families who decided to ignore the wishes of their loved ones, even as handfuls of earth fell on their boxes.

8th January

The kitchen floor sometimes seems slippery, though it's not. When I feel it with my hand as I lie on it waiting rescue after another fall, I note that it really is not slippery. Must be my head.

9th January
Whole family crowded into my room for some reason. I reached to get a swig of the flat cola on the cabinet and because they thought I was about to either fall out or throw myself out, I'm to be given a hospital bed with sides that lock up, as if I was a toddler in a cot.

10th January
The stench was pungent and pervasive. A mix of ammonia, sulphur, Marmite and vomit passed through a dog's innards. Somebody farted and while the little ones laughed, the oldies retched and heaved. Somebody opened a window, looking ashamed.

11th January
What was my new year's resolution, some idiot neighbour asked as he brought in shopping from my daughter's car? No point, I told him. Give up smoking, chocolate, walking where I want or having sex? I never smoked, chocolate magnifies my headaches, I never walked where I wanted and I was obliged to give up sex a decade ago.

12th January
From my bed I see a sheet on a line two houses down. It's driven me mad for weeks, flapping, rained and bird-shat on and forgotten. I mentioned it; they reported it. Police found the old bugger had kicked the bucket last year. After they'd cleared him and his

stuff out, the sheet remained. It'll outlive me, that bloody sheet.

13th January
A bank statement arrived. I was allowed to open the envelope but my daughter had to read me the figures. My eyes couldn't focus. I thought she said I had millions in the account. But what she really said was that everyone would be very pleased and would remember me fondly.

14th January
Word of the Week is *passion*. The passion of Christ really means the suffering of Christ. A far better word, passion. Are you suffering enough, you sick man? Or shall we pile on a little more? There, how do you like that? Are you passionate now?

20th January
Out of it. Breathing not so natural now. Am I ready? Does it matter either way?

21st January
Word of the Week is, er, I can't pull one from my mind. Too tired.

22nd January
Still feeling queasy. I thought it was the rest of the double cream left from Christmas that I scoffed, but it may just be the virus.

23rd January
Didn't see any family. They left two days of casserole with some of those desserts I like. I'm no longer to do anything more in the kitchen than make coffee. Not even washing up. I'm forbidden.

24th January
Sat watching grass grow on the lawn from my window till dark.

25th January
My daughter thinks I want my bedroom freshened up with a coat of paint. I suppose watching paint dry will make a change.

26th January
They've decided to go ahead with the painting in my bedroom, so I must be moved into the spare one. Joy of joys.

27th January
They tell me there is an auction of old landed titles in London. And included is one for the stewardship of an old part of my town. I've always wanted to be Lord Somebody, though my wife would've had no truck with being Lady Something. Family talked me out of it.

28th January
Word of the Week is *tablet*. Tablets of stone from God to man via old Moses. Tablets I must swallow. Why, when my throat is so narrow? Why can't they crush them and stick them up my backside?

29th January
After all hands on deck, they've finished the painting. I can smell the old gloss paint they found in my shed wherever I am; hope I don't get moved back too soon.

30th January

My grandchildren are all excited about some new treatment for the Russian virus. It's all over the news and people in their 20s, 30s and 40s are being saved. My explanation that a) I'm too old and b) I'm too far gone fails to dent their certainty.

31st January
A lecture from my children about not upsetting their children. I should have jumped about all excited at the prospect of younger people getting over the virus, they think. I'm pleased for them, naturally. Ecstatic.

1st February
Making an effort to read up on the latest treatments. Younger bodies are more likely to cope with the new drugs and all the trials were on people under 45. Better if I just keep that to myself and let them put me forward for the next round of experiments.

2nd February
I do appreciate how much my family care. It's certainly more than most of the world. I long ago became invisible to all but close family. All my experiences of the rich pageant of life lie wasted, a lost asset.

3rd February
I'm back in my room, fresh and neat. Lovely. I'm grateful, I really am. But I know that when they sell my house the buyer will rip out the wall to make a proper kitchen-diner area.

4th February

Word of the Week is *seven*. Seven circles of Hell, increasing layers of torture. And I should know, though I'm not alone.

5th February
I'm ready to beg the Grim Reaper for another hour. Even a minute or two.

6th February
They've brought some books through from the lounge. They've borrowed a trolley on wheels to make it easier to bring me food. A new commode has arrived. Clearly, I'm expected to leave this room on a gurney.

7th February
The commode is too narrow, so when I'm on it, the damned thing wobbles. So fearful for the relatively new carpet, they've bought a huge plastic sheet to spread under the commode and as far as the bed.

10th February
Oh, seem to have missed a couple of days. Nothing happened. I thought of little else but nothing.

11th February
Word of the Week is *death*. Third most searched word online, after love and sex.

12th February
Didn't make the clinic appointment. Felt a bit rough. But they sent a nurse, one of those ludicrously bouncy types who told me I was doing so well. Where do they get these people?

13th February

Are staff shortages such that people like this nurse must be inflicted on the weak and vulnerable? It seems they do.

14th February
She came with an assistant who'd have been at home in a concentration camp to bed-bath me and rub something smelly on my bedsores. Neither explained the point. They chirped away about the weather and what was on TV. Of course I feigned interest, even as I tipped the bowl of water all over myself, the bedsheets and plastic protector.

15th February
Two completely different nurses appeared, in the company of my son. These were men, or perhaps one actually identified as something in between. Could have been a rat or a gas cloud for all I was told. Or cared.

16th February
One of the men exudes body odour that makes me retch. It lingers in the room all day.

17th February
The men come on alternate days when I'm timetabled for a wash. The women return on the other days, one reeking of perfume that makes me sneeze. It lingers in the room all day.

18th February
Word of the Week is *rictus,* usually attached to a grin. An open-mouthed, frozen, fake smile expressing neither joy nor pleasure. My face aches with pulling such grins every time I'm asked how I'm doing or feeling.

19th February
Seem to have slept most of the day. Nightmares galore, the sort that are remembered. Looking across my lounge stuffed with family I want to tell them they're too early for the wake. I'm not gone yet.

20th February
They took the hint. I saw nobody for 8 straight hours, though my granddaughter told me I'd been asleep so of course didn't see them. Oh, the joyful life views of 6-year-olds.

21st February
Sick again. Sleep again. But it did occur to me that I wasn't sleeping. I was lying in bed, but I wasn't really present.

22nd February
Word of the Week – *shortness*, as in shortness of breath. What an effort everything is.

23rd February
Cold again, outside. I'm warm in here, with no fresh air to clear the head.

24th February
My own children seem to have said goodbye already. I think a couple of them called today. I'm not sure.

25th February
I hope my family will think well of me. I've left everything to be divided fairly. Whatever that means.

26th February
Word of the Week, in case I don't have any more. Weeks. Words.

27th February
Word of the Week, what can I say? Hard to think now.

28th February
Word of the Week – slow sand runs though the hourglass. My fingers, sand through my fingers.

1st March
Word of the Week. Can't ...

2nd March – This final entry is written by me, Dr Naismith. Jack Talbot passed away ten minutes ago. He put up a good fight. I know he'll be delighted to understand that last man standing can't bury himself. Those left behind will bury him. I did warn him he was pushing it to bank on living a full year from my final diagnosis. But, that was Jack, wouldn't hear a word he didn't want to. I'm not sorry I won't be paying for his funeral – it was a silly bet we made to keep our spirits up. My new rule is last man standing has his funeral paid for from the estate of the first man down.